Between
Two Worlds
Shelter Somerset

Dreamspinner Press

Published by
Dreamspinner Press
4760 Preston Road
Suite 244-149
Frisco, TX 75034
http://www.dreamspinnerpress.com/

Between Two Worlds
Copyright © 2011 by Shelter Somerset

Cover Art by Catt Ford

ISBN: 978-1-61581-884-6

Printed in the United States of America
First Edition
May 2011

eBook edition available
eBook ISBN: 978-1-61581-885-3

To Guido

Chapter ONE

AIDEN CERMAK navigated the central Illinois country lanes in his 1994 Chevy Cavalier, hoping he'd find the Interstate. He'd been in such a hurry to do more research for his Amish article before heading back to Chicago, he'd left the directions in his room at the bed and breakfast. He'd forgotten even his Oakley knock-offs. Not that he needed them. Drizzle had begun falling that Sunday morning the moment he'd pulled out of the inn's parking lot. He knew I-57 lay somewhere east, but each time he turned down one of those slick, buggy-battered lanes, that cross-stitch of blacktop and compacted gravel weaving through mile after mile of corn, soybean, and grain fields, he'd hit a dead end.

Heading along one such impasse he spotted, through the intermittent sweep of his windshield wipers, a black family buggy ambling ahead. He figured they were stragglers on their way to church. Once alongside, he slowed to a snail's pace and lowered the passenger window. The dark-bearded driver reined the horse to a near stop and craned his neck at Aiden over the heads of the woman and two children sitting to his left, his face screwed up with suspicion. Aiden noticed a few more children and adults crammed into the backseat. He was about to ask for directions when, out of the corner of his left eye, he saw something which struck him as odd. About fifty yards away, a pickup truck was careening toward them. The driver swerved left, then right, then left again—bearing straight at the buggy.

Aiden floored his Chevy, tires screeching and loose gravel spitting up, and veered into the pickup's path. The pickup was deflected off of Aiden's front left bumper, sending the bumper flying like a maple seed into the nearby soybean field. Aiden's coupe slammed into the legs of the horse, causing the horse to slam down onto the pickup's hood. He heard a horrible sound of crushing metal and shattering glass and felt a dizziness that seemed unearthly.

Coming out of the spin, he sat, shaking, and gazed through his shattered windshield. On the opposite side of the lane in a deep ravine, the pickup truck lay upside down. A small fire had ignited on the undercarriage. The tires, facing the dreary June sky, spun freakishly.

He looked toward the buggy, about twenty yards from where his coupe had stopped. It was upright but askew. The passengers, dressed in black church clothes, had already alighted and appeared uninjured. By the look of the shaft, twisted and snapped in half and lying in the middle of the lane, he marveled that the buggy had not been hurled onto its side, tossing out all of its passengers. The driver with the short dark beard sprinted to Aiden's side.

"Are you okay?" he asked in a husky voice.

"Yeah, I think so." Aiden scanned his body, still strapped in by the seatbelt. He swept the shards of glass from his lap. "I seem okay."

The man, his eyes so dark they reminded Aiden of deep pond water, waved over the two boys who were examining the horse that lay quivering on the side of the lane. "Take care of things here," he told the boys, one a teenager, the other about twelve years old. "Make sure he's okay. There's nothing you can do for Dexter now." He hurried to the pickup where the eldest-looking man with a long grizzled beard was pulling the driver from the truck's cab. Aiden watched the dark-eyed man help lay out the driver, then smother the undercarriage flames with his black coat.

Overcome with a sudden urge to get out of his car, Aiden unhooked his seatbelt and, with the aid of the two boys, floundered out of the coupe. Brushing flecks of glass from his jeans and hair, he suppressed an impulse to roll in the wet soybean field, as if to rub out the entire episode. He remained calm, not wishing to look like a faint-hearted Englisher in front of the Amish.

"Everything all right?" The gray-bearded man jogged over.

"Yeah. What about you?"

"Ya, we are goot." He raked a shaky hand through his beard. "By the will of God, my wife and all my children are fine, but not so much that boy."

Aiden followed the man's doleful gaze. Along the side of the lane lay the pickup driver's limp body. He looked about Aiden's age, in his mid-twenties. His eyes were closed, almost serenely. The dark-eyed man, apparently the gray-bearded man's eldest son, knelt beside him. Near the buggy, the wife and her two young daughters huddled together. Their calf-length black dresses and white capes hung heavy from the drizzle. The smallest girl trembled in the arms of her big sister.

"Do you have a cell phone?" the teenage boy asked.

"Yes, of course!"

Chastising himself for failing to have thought of it before, Aiden reached into his front jeans pocket for his Motorola and dialed 911. The father gave him their location, and the operator said she would dispatch help right away.

Snapping his phone shut and stuffing it back into his pocket, Aiden noticed his Chevy. All the windows had shattered from the impact. The left headlight was smashed in like a watermelon and the bumper was gone. The left side of the hood was concaved, the front right quarter deeply dented, and his two front tires had blown out. Aiden shook his head in disbelief and realized just how lucky he was to be standing.

He noticed the two boys staring helplessly at their chocolate-brown gelding. More had been lost in that accident than his sixteen-year-old secondhand coupe. So much more. He looked at the pickup driver lying on the side of the lane. "I'm sorry about all this," he said.

"You have nothing to be sorry for." The father stared at the injured man along with Aiden. "We saw what you did. You steered your car in front of that pickup on purpose to spare us. My whole family would be dead if not for you."

"It was all very automatic." Aiden flushed. "I guess anyone would've done it."

"Nay." The father shook his head. "Da Hah led you to save us."

A few minutes later, screaming emergency vehicles raced down what seemed the endless ribbon of gravel lane, followed by flashing red lights reflecting off the sides of the family's wet buggy and the crack of static and voices transmitted through police radios. Emergency medical technicians scrambled to the pickup driver's motionless form and rushed him off to the hospital. Firefighters doused his truck. Only the calmness of the police officer, as Aiden tried to keep his voice from quaking while giving his account of the accident, matched the serenity of the surrounding farmland.

The father stepped in and related what he knew, highlighting how Aiden had been so quick in cutting off the pickup driver from careening into their buggy and how the pickup truck had just missed striking them. Aiden shuddered, remembering the image of the pickup driver's face, twisted in horror, just before their vehicles had collided.

A second team of emergency medical technicians examined Aiden. He appeared uninjured, but based on the condition of his car, the EMTs encouraged him to ride to the hospital in Decatur for further tests. Rolling his eyes, he protested. The father insisted that he go. Embarrassed, Aiden reluctantly allowed the technicians to place him on a stretcher.

Just as the EMTs loaded him into the back of the ambulance, he heard the pop of a handgun. Poor Dexter, he thought. He closed his eyes, wishing he were back home in his studio apartment in Chicago.

THE curtain to Aiden's emergency room cubicle was pulled aside with a discordant screech, and a young, attractive doctor stepped in.

"Looks like you're good to go." She closed the curtain haphazardly so that the emergency room remained partially visible. "All your tests came back negative. No internal injuries. No contusions. Nothing broken. Barely a scratch."

"I could've told you that." Aiden sighed and rested his head back against the thin white pillow of his gurney. He turned his head away, tired of looking at the same white-tiled ceiling.

After more than six hours, he was eager to leave the hospital. Yet, with his car totaled, there was so much he needed to do before he could go anywhere. He'd already reported the accident to his insurance company. Now he needed to find transportation back to Chicago. He supposed even a small city like Decatur had car rentals.

"It was a good idea you came to the hospital to make sure," the doctor said. "You can never be too certain. You had a pretty nasty accident from what I heard. Lucky you came out unscathed."

"What about that man in the pickup? How's he doing?" Aiden knew the doctor had bad news the moment she averted her eyes toward the white granite floor.

She looked at Aiden and said through stiff, plum-red lips, "I'm afraid he didn't make it."

Aiden flinched. Even though he did "save" a nine-member Amish family from a head-on, he was unable to dispel the shock that he had caused another man's death—someone near his own age.

When he'd left for the town of Henry in the heart of Illinois's Amish Country Friday afternoon for what he'd hoped would be a productive research trip, he had never imagined he'd be involved in a fatal car wreck. He wished he'd never accepted that writing assignment from *Midwestern Life* magazine.

Initially, he had been excited about learning more about the Amish. He remembered the small Amish community where he grew up in southern Maryland and always wished he'd gotten to know them better. Being agnostic, he knew he could never share their religious zeal, but their old-fashioned lifestyle had always captivated him.

"Do you have someone to give you a lift home?" the doctor asked with a soft voice.

Aiden's mind still hovered over the dead man. "I need to pick up a rental car."

"I wouldn't recommend you drive home tonight. Do you have a place to stay locally?"

"He'll stay with us."

Both Aiden and the doctor looked in the direction of the coarse, yet warm, voice. The Amish father from the accident stood in the opening of Aiden's curtain. In one hand he held Aiden's duffel bag and in the other a black, wide-brimmed hat. His grizzled beard fell nearly to his belly and his gray eyes sparkled under the fluorescent lighting.

"I'll be taking him back home with me," he said.

"Just in time," the doctor said. "I just gave him the green light. He's looking fine. I'll go get his release papers." She smiled and eased past the Amish man with a nod.

"We got this from your car." The man took one step into the cubicle and set down Aiden's duffel bag. "I was going to leave it for you earlier but wasn't sure you'd get it. You were getting tests."

"Thank you for thinking of it." Aiden sat up on the gurney, his eyes riveted on the middle-aged man. "I'm glad it was in good hands."

"I'm Samuel Schrock." He offered his large hand. "We never got a chance to formally introduce ourselves."

"I'm Aiden Cermak." The two men shook hands. Aiden noticed the rough calluses on Samuel's farm-worked hand, and he was embarrassed Samuel might think his computer-using hand was too soft. He feared two years of city life was rendering him squishy. He had always wished he could live a more subsistence lifestyle like the Amish. Modern life, with urban-centered jobs, made that dream near impossible.

"Ach." Samuel dropped himself into a chair in the corner of the cubicle. His chubby belly pushed passed his suspenders. "Getting your release papers might take another two hours. You know hospitals. They do their job, but sluggish machines."

Aiden pondered how an Amish man would be such an expert on the running of hospitals, but he smiled in agreement. Still gazing at the man in wonder, he said, "You really don't have to put me up."

"Where else would you go? Hotels are costly. It's the least we can do."

"I don't want to be a burden. It's asking too much."

"It's no burden. My wife and me discussed it, and we both agree you should come. Nimmand hott graysahri leevi vi dess, es en mann sei layva gebt fa sei freind." Samuel interpreted for Aiden, although Aiden understood enough textbook German to figure out what he'd meant: "No greater man of God than he who lays down his life for another."

"Oh, but really." Aiden flushed.

"I heard you telling the police officer you're here from Chicago doing research on the Amish, ya?"

Aiden lowered his eyes and nodded. "I'm writing a magazine article."

"It'll work fine for you then. You can see firsthand how we live, for your article. My family's a large brood, but we have room for you. You can stay with us until someone comes and gets you or until you rent a car. Your car, like my horse, didn't survive the accident."

The legendary Amish generosity left Aiden near speechless. But he worried whether such devout Christians would be so quick to welcome him into their home if they knew the truth about him. And on top of that, he was a non-believer.

"I really don't know what to say." He pushed aside his concerns for the moment. "I'm very grateful, beyond words."

"It's us who are grateful to you."

Samuel gazed toward his lap, slowly shaking his head. His beard swept across his belly like a furry pendulum. "If only we had been a trifle earlier leaving for church, maybe things would've turned out otherwise. With nine of us going off to the same place in one buggy, we can sometimes be sluggish. Ach, but when God wills things, there's nothing to be done."

God's will—something Aiden failed to understand in Amish culture, in any culture. He knew the Amish placed everything in the hands of God, no matter what, good or bad. Aiden could not reduce everything so simply to a matter of mystical forces, not when people ultimately caused most of life's heartaches.

A specter of the pickup driver's horrified face just before their vehicles had collided flashed through Aiden's mind. He gathered his hands into a tight ball and swallowed. "Do you know anything about the man in the pickup?"

"Bobby Jonesboro? He's a local English boy. Twenty-three, I think. The sheriff said it was pretty clear by the accident he was at least double the legal limit. I was sorry to hear he died, but the Jonesboro boy was known for his weekend binge drinking. In a way, you saved him, too."

"How's that?"

"You saved him from killing nine people."

A nurse broke their contemplative silence when she brought in Aiden's release papers. After she left with the signed forms, Samuel gave him privacy to dress. Before stepping outside his cubicle, he tore off the hospital bracelet, tossed it into a receptacle, and washed his hands of the whole place.

He expected to see a horse-drawn buggy idling in the hospital's main entrance drive-thru, but when Samuel slid open the door to a passenger van, he flushed from his assumption. A half hour away by even a fast-moving ambulance, Henry was, of course, much too far from Decatur for a buggy ride.

"Hi there," the driver said. Samuel introduced him as Joe Karpin. Samuel explained that Joe shuttled the Amish, or anyone else needing a ride, for a small fee in his fifteen-seat Ford Club.

"You folks buckled in?" Joe asked, grinning through the rearview mirror.

"Ya," Samuel said. "We're all settled. Off for home, Joe."

Chapter TWO

DANIEL SCHROCK was measuring an oak plank for his mother's corner kitchen cabinet in the quiet of his woodshop when he heard the crunch of gravel from an English vehicle pulling into the driveway. Peering out the window, he saw that it was Joe Karpin dropping off his father and that Englishman from the crash scene. He was unsure what to think of his parents inviting a stranger to stay with them. He understood the man had risked his life to save his family; still, they knew nothing about him, other than he was writing some article about the Amish.

Few people stayed with the Schrocks, particularly anyone English, and Daniel preferred it that way. Strangers, from his experience, caused too much trouble. Especially those from the big city who made their living by prying into other people's lives. Not that he disregarded all that the man had done; he was impressed with his fast thinking. He simply did not wish to deal with a pesky guest.

With just five bedrooms, it was hard enough to squeeze in the nine of them. His parents had made him give up his bedroom for the Englishman and temporarily move in with his two younger brothers. They didn't seem to care. Young David was excited to get to sleep in Daniel's sleeping bag. But Daniel cared. He'd felt bad enough when he had moved back home three months ago and had forced his teenage brother back in with David. And now with an extra body, things were really going to be tight. He hoped the Englisher would have enough modesty to keep his visit short.

Whether he had saved them or not, the whole idea of his staying there seemed ridiculous. What would an Englisher know about life on an Amish farm, Daniel thought, as he watched his father place a bill in Joe Karpin's hand. He seemed sturdy enough. At least he had the gumption to swerve his car in front of that crazy Bobby Jonesboro. But he was obviously too city-soft to be of any practical use on their labor-intensive farm.

Daniel watched his father and the Englishman wave to Joe as he pulled out the driveway, then head up to the house. What was it about the stranger's eyes? He remembered being struck by them when he'd first craned his neck to look at him when he had pulled them over, most likely to ask for directions. He'd never seen eyes so pale brown, like the color of honey. And that raven-black hair of his. Shiny and curly like a lamb's. Tugging at his beard, he turned back to finish up his work before heading in for supper. He figured he had no choice but to officially meet the Englisher.

DUFFEL bag in hand, Aiden followed Samuel up the gravel driveway and gazed wide-eyed about the midsized farm. The two-story white house stood on a manicured lawn surrounded by a weathered white picket fence. Across the driveway sat a metal-framed shed and large brown barn, both a bit worn but functional-looking. A thin windmill leaned toward the barn. Next to what he assumed must be the henhouse stood a smaller wood-framed building; a moment ago he had thought he'd seen a man with a beard peeking out the window.

An oat field stretched across the flat land to what seemed the horizon. Oat bundles lay in the field in tidy rows like strange, furry creatures. The unharvested oats swayed in the light breeze and sparkled golden as the afternoon sun broke through the gray clouds and the temperature rose.

Samuel held open the door. "Come the house in."

Aiden wiped his feet on the well-trodden welcome mat and stepped inside, inwardly chuckling at the man's interesting vernacular.

Surrounded by the smells of beeswax and wholesome cooking, he thought the house looked similar to the typical American home. The sitting room where they entered was furnished with what one would expect to find in sitting rooms across America, except perhaps less ornate, and of course they had no television. No pictures or knick-knacks hung from the ivory walls other than one red and blue patchwork quilt above the sofa. Rag rugs were strewn over the dull and worn mahogany floor. An enclosed staircase led from the hallway to presumably the upstairs bedrooms.

He saw down the hallway into the large eat-in kitchen where Samuel's wife and daughters scurried about preparing supper. There looked to be a refrigerator and oven, but he was uncertain how modern. He caught a glimpse of the wife opening the refrigerator and made a mental note to ask about the use of modern conveniences once he became more comfortable with the family. In his online research before leaving Chicago, he had been confused about how modern the Amish really were.

"The kinner are around someplace." Samuel hung his black hat on a wooden wall peg. Many other wide-brimmed hats hung from pegs, along with bonnets and shawls. Grunting, he took Aiden's duffel bag and leaned it against the wall. "Ach. Here they come."

One by one, Samuel's barefooted kinner shuffled in from all parts of the house. They undoubtedly recognized Aiden from the accident scene, but no introductions had been made. Samuel gathered his children closer and introduced each one: Elisabeth, twenty-three; Mark, eighteen; Grace, fifteen; David, eleven; Moriah, nine; and Leah, seven.

"Goot. You're here." Samuel's wife came in from the kitchen wiping her hands on her apron. Samuel introduced her as Rachel. She blushed under her white head-covering, a tad longer in front than those worn by her daughters. The kapp pushed out in the back, and Aiden knew it hid hair that hadn't seen shears in perhaps as many years as she and Samuel had been married.

"It's very good to make your acquaintance," Aiden said.

"Yours, too. I hope your stay in the hospital went okay."

"For my first time in a hospital, it wasn't too bad." It was, in fact, for Aiden so far a trip of firsts: first ambulance ride, first time in an emergency room, first visit in an Amish home. What other firsts lay ahead?

"Doctors didn't find anything wrong with him," Samuel said. "He's in goot shape."

"Fine." Rachel grinned with a blush.

"Supper ready?" Samuel arched his eyebrows high on his forehead. Rachel's unwavering smile indicated that it was. Turning to her two middle daughters, Grace and Moriah, she instructed them in Pennsylvania German to set the table. Obediently the girls set off for the kitchen, where Aiden heard them grab dinnerware from cupboards and place it around the large oak dining table.

"Where's Daniel?" Rachel glanced around.

"I'm here." Daniel had just opened the front door and was wiping his boots on the mat. He stepped inside and hung his hat next to his father's. Samuel took his dark-eyed son by the arm and introduced him to their guest.

They shook hands clumsily, like bashful schoolboys. Aiden was surprised the stalwart twenty-five-year-old didn't clasp his hand with two or three forceful pumps. Impossible that Daniel could've been as flustered as Aiden was at that moment. Easily six-four, near a man's hand-length taller than Aiden, Daniel's masculine physique forced blood into Aiden's cheeks. With all the commotion at the crash scene, he'd failed to notice his striking good looks. Now it was impossible not to. But the eyes he remembered. They were as dark as onyx. His handsome features snatched Aiden's voice.

Like his father, he sported a moustacheless beard. His was much shorter and a deep brown. Aiden knew the Old Order Amish of central Illinois permitted only married men to grow them. He figured Daniel lived on a farm of his own someplace with a wife and perhaps a few small children, yet he did not see any sign of them. Come to think of it, they hadn't been with him in the buggy that morning, either. He wondered where they were hiding.

Daniel released his awkward grip and quickly excused himself to wash up. Aiden watched the brawny Amish man march down the hallway and disappear around a corner. He mentally punched himself for what he was thinking about Samuel's eldest.

DURING the lengthy meal prayer when Samuel thanked da Hah for sending Aiden to save the family, Aiden was glad everyone's eyes were shut. He didn't want anyone to see his searing cheeks. Glancing around the sturdy dining table as he pretended to pray along with the family, he believed he was undeserving of such praise—especially since he remained unconvinced there was a god who had sent him. A spasm shot through his throat when Samuel paid tribute to the deceased Bobby Jonesboro. Difficult to believe that a mere eight hours ago he'd been involved in a car accident in which someone had actually died.

After the prayer, heavy bowls filled with baked chicken smothered in cheese sauce, mashed potatoes, succotash, homemade biscuits, applesauce, pickles, and peanut butter circled the table. Aiden asked about some of the food. The Amish peanut butter interested him the most; it was a mixture of homemade peanut butter, marshmallow cream, maple syrup, and butter. He put some on his biscuit and took a taste. Everyone giggled when he moaned with pleasure.

Everyone but Daniel. He sat stiff and austere, his dark eyes focused on his plate, as if he held the weight of the entire house on his back. Since taking his seat at the other end of the table, Daniel had not paid any attention to Aiden, who was only too aware of the handsome man's presence. Aiden thought he appeared preoccupied, perhaps even angry.

He speculated whether the day's events might've affected him worse than the others. The smaller children seemed remarkably unfazed. Still, Aiden had a deepening impression that Daniel resented him for everything that had happened. Daniel had been so quick to rush to him at the crash scene—why the sudden aloofness? Remembering the way Daniel had knelt beside Bobby Jonesboro, Aiden wondered if he and Bobby had been close friends. Did Daniel blame him for Bobby's death?

Excited in front of an English stranger, the other children lavished Aiden with attention. They smiled at him with unblinking eyes, eyes that seemed to come in all colors, from the palest gray of Grace's to the softest brown of Mark's. The youngest girls in particular peered at Aiden over their food, turning away giggling when he looked their way. Using Pennsylvania German, Samuel and Rachel admonished them for their poor table manners. Aiden waved it off, chuckling.

"What? You understand the German?" Samuel said.

Aiden explained that while in college he minored in German to get in touch with his "roots." But he understood only a fraction of their unique pronunciation of German words.

"My mother's ancestors came from the southwest German state of Baden-Wurttemberg," he told them. Samuel nodded, asserting that they could trace their roots back to that same area in Switzerland on the banks of the Rhine River where the first Anabaptists broke from the Catholic Church, giving nascence to the Amish faith.

"We'll have to be careful what we say," Samuel said. "No retsha in front of you."

"Don't listen to him," Rachel said. "We don't gossip."

Glancing at the surprisingly contemporary-looking kitchen with its numerous stained oak cupboards, full sink, two ovens, and large refrigerator, Aiden thought it an appropriate time to ask about modern conveniences for his article. "Are you allowed to use plumbing and electricity?"

"We can use plumbing," Samuel said. "We get water pumped in from the windmill by the barn. Gives us good enough pressure for our kitchen and the bathroom. But electricity? Nay."

Rachel shook her head. "All our appliances are gas-powered," she said. "We can use gas for our ovens, refrigerator, and lanterns, but never electricity. Nothing from a public service."

"With the price of gas these days," Samuel said, crinkling his bulbous nose, "it's just as costly."

"Are you not married?" eleven-year-old David asked out of the blue, his large dark gray eyes shiny like marbles. He wore a mound of bowl-cut hair atop his head like his eldest brother and father. Only the teenage Mark stood out; his hair was rebelliously cut short.

"Don't be so shussly," Samuel said, tossing a stern glance at his youngest son.

"I'm not being silly," David said. "I was just wondering. Englishmen don't grow beards when they marry, it's hard to tell."

"You can tell by their left hands," nine-year-old Moriah said from across the table, as if she and she alone possessed this knowledge.

"Hold up your hand," David said.

"Kinner, shtill!" Rachel shot her children an admonishing glare.

"That's all right." Aiden flushed. "I don't mind, really." He laid his fork aside and raised his left hand, showing the children the back and then the palm.

"See, he has no ring, he doesn't," Moriah declared. "He's not married."

"Why aren't you married?" David asked.

"That's his business," the oldest daughter Elisabeth stated, as if she, at twenty-three, had been asked the same meddling question many times before.

Moving his food with his fork, Aiden tried his best to appear unruffled. How honest could one be with the Amish? He couldn't tell them the truth—that he was gay.

Would they even know what that was?

Being gay for Aiden was never a large part of his identity, yet it was still a part. Could he tell the Schrocks that right after college he'd followed his boyfriend, Conrad, all the way to Chicago like a lovesick puppy—something he'd promised himself he'd never do again—to be dumped two months later, abandoned and alone in a strange city?

Could he tell them his desires weren't much different from theirs, only he envisioned himself "married" to another man, living a subsistence lifestyle, much like the Amish, but without religion?

Aiden knew he could not. If he dared, the fears he had while at the hospital would no doubt come true. Surely they would throw him out, slam the door behind him, wash their hands of him for good, whether he'd saved their lives or not. In their world, Aiden's "lifestyle" renounced acceptance. Such notions of sexuality must be as alien to them as milking a cow was to Aiden.

Surrounded by the Amish, he figured the best approach to answering questions such as "why aren't you married?" was to avoid particulars.

"I guess I haven't met the right person yet," he told David, the wholehearted truth.

"You should get married and buy a farm," David asserted, repeating what he'd most likely heard all around him since the day of his birth.

"He's a city folk," eighteen-year-old Mark said. "That would be like you moving to Chicago or St. Louis."

"Actually, Mark, I don't like the city much." Aiden was happy to shift the conversation away from the topic of marriage. "Chicago is great as far as cities go, but I would love to live in the country, someplace out west."

"Like a cowboy?" Moriah asked. The table vibrated with giggles.

"No, not really like that."

"You like the mountains," Mark stated, biting into a buttered biscuit.

"Yes, exactly. I would love to live in the mountains. My dream is to one day live someplace like Montana, maybe buy a small cabin with some land." With the man of my dreams, he wanted to add, but held the musing for himself.

Daniel stirred in his seat and seemed to stiffen; fifteen-year-old Grace looked as if she adhered to his every word.

"Do you know how to farm?" David asked, shoving a heaping forkful of mashed potatoes into his mouth.

"My grandfather used to own a small farm where I grew up in southern Maryland. I even helped out on it a few times when I was a kid."

"Ach." Samuel's gray eyes widened. "What did you do there?"

"He grew tobacco. I used to cut off the flowers that grew on the stalks, I think he called it topping. I only did it a few times. He sold the farm when I was thirteen. Sold it to an Amish family, actually."

"Ach, he did?"

"Most the tobacco farms in Maryland are owned by the Amish," Aiden said, recalling an article he'd written on the topic for his college newspaper his sophomore year. "There's a really interesting story about how that came to be."

The fascinated gapes of his host family prodded him on.

Taking intermittent bites of the hearty Amish meal, Aiden related his article about the Maryland government's attempt to eliminate the tobacco crop from the state by offering buyouts to farmers and how the local Amish capitalized on the move.

"The state forgot that it's against the religion of the Amish to take government subsidies," Aiden said. "The English farmers were quick to take the buyouts, but no matter how hard the government tried, the Amish wouldn't go against their customs. Before long the Amish were the only ones farming tobacco. On top of that, with all that vacant land laying all around them, the Amish realized they could buy their English neighbors' farms and expand their own crops. My grandfather was one of the first to sell. It meant he couldn't get the government subsidies anymore, but he didn't care. Like most of his English neighbors, he was just happy to take the good money the Amish offered and retire to Florida once and for all."

Samuel threw his head back and laughed. His grizzled beard, speckled with food crumbs, jiggled. "So the Englisher's government wanted to get rid of tobacco and only succeeded putting it into the hands of the Amish? Ha! That's goot!"

The rest of the family giggled also, even the younger children, although Aiden suspected they did not quite understand the story and found amusement only in their father's mirth.

"Sell is en goodi!" Samuel dabbed at his eyes with his paper napkin. "That's the best story I heard in a long time. Sweet justice. I don't remember reading about that in *The Budget*. We should all know about that."

"I got a kick out of it myself," Aiden said, beaming from Samuel's reaction to his story.

"We don't believe in government." The amusement evaporated from Samuel's eyes. "It's not the source or the center of our lives."

"Yes, well, I'm with you on that." Aiden lifted his glass of whole milk, mimicking a toast. "I wish more people thought like that "

"God is the center of our lives," Samuel said, returning to his chicken and biscuits.

Aiden reddened. Whenever people talked about God, he always grew ill at ease. Visiting among the Amish, he knew he would have to adjust to religious references being liberally expressed, no matter how uncomfortable it made him. Their denomination, after all, dictated their entire existence.

Staving off his discomfort, he looked to Daniel to gauge his reaction to his tobacco story. Just as before, he sat erect on the bench, his ebony eyes peering at the food on his plate, as if thinking deeply about the story… or some other matter on his mind.

Chapter THREE

DANIEL was grateful when supper finally ended. What a relief when the last morsels were eaten and everyone could go about their after-supper chores. He didn't think he could get through another moment listening to that Englisher…. But he liked listening to him. That was the problem. He liked it too much.

He carried his plate to the kitchen sink, grabbed for his straw hat in the utility room, and bee-lined for the barn to tend to the animals. Moriah followed him.

"Why are you going to the barn?" she asked.

"I got to care for the animals." Daniel stomped ahead.

"But you always say caring for the animals is for kinner. I was going to do it, like I always do after supper."

"I changed my mind and decided to do it tonight." He stopped at the barn's swing door and turned to his little sister. "But just for tonight. Now go back inside and help your mom with the kitchen scrubbing.'

Confusion etched all over her face, Moriah shrugged and turned back for the house. Alone in the barn, Daniel relaxed. A little. He nudged away the straw layering the floor with his booted feet, irritated. Two wayward chickens scurried from him. He was never that fond of barn work, even when he was a kinner. But he needed some excuse to get away. To occupy his mind and try to straighten his thoughts. He liked caring for the horses, especially the standardbreds. They always seemed to appreciate the attention. The rest was a thankless, dirty undertaking.

He put fresh hay in the miniature horse stall. Frieda and her new foal, Magpie, lay on their sides, sleeping. The stallion, Jake, stood in a corner, as if he were a stranger. Daniel could relate. He was feeling pushed out of his home too.

As he fed the animals, his stomach growled. With that Englishman sitting across the table, he hadn't eaten as much as he usually would have. His appetite had lacked its usual bite, even after such a trying day, and he never got around to his usual seconds. His mother always said he ate like a horse with a bottomless stomach. Tonight he had nibbled on his mother's tasty cooking like a hen pecking the ground for worms. He barely was able to enjoy Elisabeth's chocolate cream pie. His mind had been on one thing: getting away from the table and Aiden Cermak.

After feeding the mule, their two goats, and the three draft horses, he spent extra care tending to the needs of the three standardbreds. These were his animal friends. They were the horses that led him wherever he needed to go. He mourned the loss of Dexter. He was a good friend in a horse. He understood the need for euthanizing him. He did not blame the Englisher for Dexter's death. Aiden did save his family. He only wished poor Dexter could've been spared somehow. Enough death in his world already.

He supposed it was all God's will.

Peppermint stirred in her stall. She needed milking. He chuckled, thinking of little Leah's naming their one dairy cow after her favorite candy. He felt silly calling her Peppermint. Animals probably shouldn't have names. Grace usually did the milking. Of all the barn chores, hand milking was the most taxing. But the job would chisel away some time. Time he wanted to avoid spending with the Englisher inside the house.

Daniel led Peppermint from her stall, but she seemed less than willing to follow, as if she didn't trust Daniel. She balked, shook her head, and mooed. Daniel pulled on the lead, and eventually the cow, giving in to Daniel's authority, followed him. He tied her to a post and filled a trough full of oats to keep her occupied.

He pushed his straw hat higher up on his head and wiped down the udder with an old rag lying in some opaque water. Clean enough, he placed the stainless steel milk bucket under her udder. The last time he'd milked was three years ago, and that was to show some English tourists, who his mother had allowed on the farm, the art of hand milking. Lots of the local Amish let the English tour their farms for a small fee. He'd felt like a showman then, disgusted almost. He was glad to be away from the latest tourist inside their house.

Daniel took hold of the teats. Peppermint pulled her snout from the oats and shuffled back and forth, yanking on her lead.

"Steady, girl, steady."

The cow, finally relaxing with her teats in Daniel's hands, resumed eating the oats. A steady zip-zap of the warm shots hit the bucket. The air in the barn seemed to fall heavy over his head. The late afternoon sun sparkled like miniscule fireworks as it pierced through the slits in the barn. Perspiration dribbled from his armpits and trickled down his sides, but he did not mind. It felt good to be breaking a sweat doing something productive rather than wasting time with that stranger. Above on the gambrel roof, he heard the powerless ventilation system switch on, humming rhythmically.

Each time Aiden entered his thoughts, he shook his head, like a dog shaking itself after a swim in a pond. No point pondering about the man. The moment he'd grasped his hand, no matter how clumsy it had been, he'd felt a strange twinge of discomfort. Aiden's hand had been so soft, almost like dough, like so many other Englishers' hands he'd shaken.

Why did he resent his being there so much? After everything he had done for his family, he should probably be a bit more receptive. Squaring his shoulders to get a better grip on Peppermint's teats, he didn't want to dwell on the question. The Englishman would be gone in a few short days. At least Daniel had his woodwork and the farm chores and the furniture shop in town to keep himself busy until then. He was sure he could steer clear of him most of the time.

He picked up his rhythm and thick milk soon filled halfway up the bucket. The smell of the raw milk reached his nostrils. He never did like the smell. It was mildly acrid, like chicken fat.

Peppermint snorted, stomped a hind foot, and with her tail swatted a horsefly that landed on her rump, all the while keeping her snout in the feed trough. Milk flowing in thin streams from the teats shot sideways onto Daniel's broadfall pants. He jumped back from the unexpected squirting.

"Boogered cow." Daniel grabbed for a new set of teats and readjusted his pinching to slow down the heavy stream. From the corner of his eye he saw Grace strolling into the barn.

"What you doing?" she asked, waddling up to him.

"You never seen a person milk a cow?"

"I know what you're doing, just not why." She cupped her hands over her bent knees as she leaned in closer. The strings of her kapp dangled near Daniel's shoulders. "I was coming out to do it, like I always do."

"You were slacking off with that Englisher." Before Grace could protest, Daniel handed her the full bucket. "Fill the jugs and get them in the refrigerator, will you?"

"Goodness, you're in a mood tonight." Grace sighed and slumped off to the kitchen with the heavy bucket.

Grace was right. Daniel was in a mood. So much so he didn't want to go back inside the house. Too much commotion with that Englishman there. His mood would only worsen. He looked around, wondering what to do next, and decided to take refuge in his woodshop. He still had work to do on his mother's corner kitchen cabinet. Her old one was coated in grease and she had a tough time keeping it clean. He planned on giving it to her as a birthday gift. On the way, he caught sight of his little brother David and the Englishman coming out of the hen house. Averting his eyes from them, he took two large steps into the woodshop and quickly shut the door.

WATCHING Daniel scurry into his woodshop as he walked back to the house with David, Aiden again wondered if Daniel resented him. He had been avoiding him from the moment they'd sat down to supper, and afterward he'd rushed out of the kitchen faster than a man on fire. What reason would he have to loathe him?

Attracted once again to his tight beard that anchored such full lips and fierce dark eyes, he thought about Daniel's wife. He knew he had to be married. Amish moustacheless beards were not meant to be fashion statements.

He wanted to ask about the mysterious wife, but the words lodged heavy in his throat. Setting the basket of eggs on the dining table while Rachel and her girls scrubbed the kitchen, he decided it best to keep quiet. No one in the family had mentioned his wife or any children thus far. He sensed he should follow along. At least for now.

"You'll be sleeping in Daniel's bedroom," David said once they settled in the sitting room. Aiden had followed him while the others finished their after-supper chores. He watched from an armchair as David retrieved a coloring book and a twelve-pack crayon set from a pine chest and tucked his scrawny legs under the coffee table. David seemed only half-interested in his coloring. But in a home without video games, computers, or television, what other activity was an eleven-year-old boy to do?

"He's sleeping with Mark and me while you're here, so you can have your own room," David said, his upper lip curled as he colored.

"I hope I'm not putting anyone out."

David shrugged. "We're used to room hopping. Mark got the room after Daniel got married, then when Daniel moved back home a few months ago, Mark had to move back in with me. We're like toads, hopping all over. I don't mind because I get to sleep in Daniel's sleeping bag while you're here."

Aiden gazed out the window where a male cardinal fluttered past his view. Daniel had moved back home a few months ago? But why? Did his wife move with him? Impossible that Daniel had divorced and moved back home like any American male might—no divorce existed in Amish culture for any reason, he was certain. Did they allow separation?

So much he wanted to know, yet he feared by asking he would cross an unmarked Amish barrier. He knew personal information from the Amish must come voluntarily. And with Rachel within earshot just around the corner in the kitchen, he did not want to step into anything too intimate with young David.

His inquisitiveness might have made him into a good journalist, but he also knew it could break apart good friendships. He learned that the hard way when he had inadvertently outed his best friend in an article he wrote for his college newspaper about gays in fraternities. His friend never forgave him. The last thing he wanted was to alienate the Schrocks after they had been so kind as to invite him into their home.

"You had a long day, for sure, my friend," Samuel said, lumbering into the sitting room. With a sigh, he sat in a well-worn recliner and fully extended it. "Surely days like this come once in a blue moon."

Aiden flushed from across the room. "Yes, sir."

"We won't forget it for as long as we live." Samuel shook open a newspaper he carried under his arm. He put on his bifocals and peered at the front page. "I figure God throws us days like this to keep us on our toes."

He offered Aiden a section of his newspaper and Aiden gladly accepted. Sitting back on his chair, he glanced over *The Budget* and learned it was published by and for the Amish and Mennonite communities. One item made him giggle: a Mrs. Miller from New Hope, Ohio had sprained her ankle while chasing the family goat out of the house. She was unsure how it had gotten in, but was certain to make sure that it never happened again.

Rachel entered the sitting room, her clogs tapping against the hardwood floor, and sat in an armchair next to her husband. A lit Coleman gas lantern swung evenly from her fingertips. Nearing eight o'clock in the early part of June, enough natural light streamed through the curtainless windows that they did not yet need the use of lanterns, but Aiden guessed once darkness came, it would descend rapidly and she would want to be prepared.

Samuel peeked at his wife over his bifocals and scrunched his bulbous nose. "It's not yet dark out."

"It'll be dark soon," she said, setting the hissing lantern on an end table beside her. She reached into a drawer for a wooden crochet box and took her crocheting into her lap.

Samuel returned his eyes to his newspaper. "With the price of gas, I think you'd want to wait some."

"I waited long enough," Rachel said, her fingers already churning out eggshell-colored love knots.

Before long, everyone—everyone but Daniel—had gathered in the sitting room. Two more gas lanterns were lit as the daylight faded. Soon the hiss of lanterns, with patches of orange glow throwing pulsating shadows against the furniture and white walls, filled the room.

Though the house held onto the day's heat, Aiden did not mind. He was feeling rather serene now that the initial awkwardness of meeting the family had passed. No surprise he enjoyed such a setting. He always dreamed of a life like the Schrocks', with all its simplicity, devoid of the blare of televisions, video games, and air conditioners.

He noted how the family seemed unfazed by the day's events. Even the children, contentedly going about their diversions, appeared to have forgotten the grim scene of the accident. Mark stretched prone on top of a rag rug reading what looked to be a car magazine. Grace sat on the sofa hemming an apron by light thrown from her mother's lantern. Moriah held a skein of wool looped over her arms while Elisabeth wound the yarn into a ball. And little Leah, concentration etched across her crinkled little face, pink and golden from the glow of lanterns, lay prone on the bare floor by her mother's feet, lost in her drawing tablet.

Aiden's guilt over Bobby Jonesboro lessened too. Perhaps Samuel had been right when he'd said that Aiden had saved Bobby from the legacy of killing nine people. Surely Bobby would've been killed too, whether Aiden had swerved his car in front of him or not. Although he feared visions of the man's panicky face might forever haunt him, he garnered strength from the Schrock children's stoicism. Mark's mentioning his rumspringa plans to the Texas shore brought a soft smile to his face.

"Me and some cousins and friends are going to drive a car down to Mustang Island after Thanksgiving," he told Aiden. A small battery-powered Coleman sat on the bare floor by his head. As far as Aiden could tell, he was the only family member using a lantern powered by batteries. The lantern's light stroked the side of his face, highlighting the soft stubble that would be allowed to grow into a beard once he married. "It's going to be some trip. Want to see the car I went to get to drive down in?" He held up his magazine for Aiden to see a full-page photograph of a black Corvette.

"That's pretty nice," Aiden said, mindful of Samuel and Rachel's disapproving expressions.

Mark's revelation of wanting a car did not shock Aiden. He knew that during rumspringa, the infamous rite of passage for Amish teens just before they are baptized into the church, many boys and girls will buy and drive cars.

"It's a 1977, L-forty-eight, one-eighty horsepower," Mark said, "with a four inch bore, thirty-six hundred rpm, four-speed, automatic transmission, and aluminum wheels."

"Wow! Sounds like you know a lot about cars. You earned that just from magazines?"

"I talk a lot with my English friends. They even let me drive their cars."

"You have a license?" Aiden asked.

"Ya, I got it in February. Daniel has one too. He keeps his current, even though Mom and Dad don't like it. He uses it when he goes on backpacking trips so he can rent cars."

"Backpacking trips?" Aiden's eyes widened, his section of the newspaper now limp across his lap. An Amish man who liked to backpack? Backpacking was one of Aiden's most ardent pleasures. He missed the many backpacking trips he used to take when in college with his ex-boyfriend, Conrad. "Daniel likes to backpack?"

"He used to do it all the time," Samuel said. He swiped his fingertip across his tongue and turned a page of *The Budget*. "Goes off by himself most the time, as far as I know. He even went out west about a year ago. Burned off some youthful energy before settling down, I figure."

"Really? How long was he there? Did he like it?"

"About a week, wasn't it, Rachel?"

"About a week," Rachel affirmed, never missing a stitch of her crocheting. "And I think he liked it fine. He didn't talk much about it. It was just right before he got married."

"I'd like to ask him about his trips sometime," Aiden said, more to himself.

After a while, the Schrock children asked Aiden about life in Chicago. He chuckled, thinking they should find his life as intriguing as he did theirs. The conversation fell into that awkward hole when Mark, David, and Moriah pressured him on why he wasn't married. He circumvented the question the best he could, telling them he was far too busy for a relationship at the moment—not altogether untrue.

Evading such delicate topics with the Amish, Aiden was learning, was like sidestepping thorns barefoot in the scorching sand.

The children's assertive questions, although harmless, brought up painful memories for Aiden. Conrad and he had been together almost a year. He'd been Aiden's only serious relationship. Two months after moving with him to Chicago, he had come home from his new part-time job to discover a blur of brusque packing, followed by a quick hug goodbye and a curt "good luck" before another blur of body and luggage bouncing down the hallway steps.

He recovered from Conrad's abrupt leaving him for another man and soon began hunting for another relationship. But no one shared his interests. Gay men often scoffed at his dream of wanting to live monogamously in a cabin in Montana. They accused him of "trying to act straight." Many labeled him a "homophobe." He never could quite understand how wanting to subsist off the land made him a homophobe, but he did know that by asking he would only entrench them deeper into a painfully doctrinaire discussion. He'd learned to shrug and smile.

In his short visit with the Amish, Aiden already believed a stronger bridge connected him to their world than to his own. Even without any religious convictions, he saw much of himself in their simple ways. Not everything came down to his sexuality. He saw his being gay as a small part of his identity, yet others, whether for or against homosexuality, often saw it as his only part.

That was what forced a wedge between him and Conrad. His ex-boyfriend celebrated homosexuality as a lifestyle rather than a simple orientation. Despite sharing a love for the outdoors, Conrad found someone more interested in parties and parades than a domestic life. The more Aiden discovered Conrad's disposition commonplace, the more he foresaw a future alone.

He was grateful when Samuel pushed his recliner upright and announced time for bed. "We had a long and stressful day today, kinner. Best we get some sleep if we're to be any good tomorrow. Where's Daniel?"

"Out in his woodshop yet, I guess," Rachel said, packing her crocheting into her wooden crochet box with a snap and stowing it in the drawer. Standing, she lifted her lantern, illuminating her gentle face, pretty without the need for makeup. "He'll be in soon enough."

Upstairs, Rachel showed Aiden to Daniel's bedroom. Simple and comfortable. One twin bed, covered in a blue monochromatic patchwork quilt, a night table, a dresser, and a ladder-back chair, all crafted from oak. The twitter of night birds and the vacillating shrill of treehoppers flowed through an open window. Rachel lit a gas lantern on the night table. An old-fashioned windup alarm clock next to the lantern showed it was nine thirty.

"Mark left some of his old clothes in the dresser," she told him, backing up to the threshold. "They're a bit worn, but you shouldn't have trouble fitting in them. Don't forget the suspenders. You'll stand out without them."

"Aren't my clothes okay?" Aiden nodded toward the duffel bag Samuel had carried up for him earlier. "My jeans should be able to handle whatever I—"

"You can't wear English clothes while staying here," she said. "Not if you're working on the farm. It's not proper. Goot nacht." And with those words she shut the door. The hiss from her gas lantern faded as she made her way downstairs.

Aiden chuckled, looking around the dim room. Hard to believe he was spending the night in an Amish home with an Amish family. When he had set out for Henry two days ago to research his article, he'd never imagined anything so up close and personal.

He leaned against the windowsill and inhaled the country air. A young man had lost his life earlier that day, yet the accident seemed so far away, from another time. As the soft, warm breeze wafted past his shoulders, he wondered what the next few days would bring.

Still early, but the day's events made him drowsy. Crawling into bed, he blew out his lantern and allowed his thoughts to fall back onto the handsome and puzzling Daniel. Just what was it about him? He didn't dare do what he was considering, as his mind pondered over Daniel. He'd gone without for so long. But not after everything that had happened that day. Not in an Amish house. Not in Daniel's own bed.

Frustrated, he turned to his side and wished for a fast sleep.

Chapter FOUR

"GET moving!"

Daniel drove the three-horse team onto the field. His shirt sleeves were rolled to expose the sinewy muscles on his forearms that flexed with each authoritative tug on the reins. He sat on a metal seat high atop the binding machine, the cutting reel rotating like a windmill. Daniel and the horse team passed down the first row of swaying golden oats. Aiden and the boys followed behind, "shocking the sheaves" (setting the cut oats upright in tight bundles) to ensure they would dry in time for the threshing in September.

The sun nudged above the elms and hickories along the blacktop lane. The pink sky, streaked with wispy indigo clouds, slowly faded to a washed blue. Aiden hadn't been up and out that early in a while, but the filling breakfast of thickly sliced bacon, fried potatoes, "dippy eggs," and stove-top brewed black coffee gave him a light-headed sense of vim.

When the youngest boy, David, had awakened him at four thirty, Aiden had needed a few moments to reorient himself. Sitting up in bed, he winced from an image of Bobby Jonesboro's face. But by the time he dressed in Mark's clothes and came down for breakfast, the vision had dimmed to a subtle irritation and he focused on the day ahead.

He dismissed Rachel's concerns that he might not be rested enough after the accident for strenuous field work. For his first night in a simple Amish bedroom without air conditioning, Aiden had slept surprisingly well.

The younger children thought he looked like a "real Amish man" in Mark's clothes. Rachel even took an Amish straw hat from one of the wall pegs and placed it on his head before she and her daughters left for the flea market to sell their homemade pies and breads. "It's a bit small, but fine enough," Samuel said, standing next to his wife.

Aiden was a little surprised that any of them showed an interest in his appearance. Amish clothes were not meant to enhance one's appearance, although the broadfall pants were a smidgeon tight around his backside. He had a rounder butt than average from doing squats regularly at the gym. Nonetheless, he was delighted to have gained the family's approval. He hoped to impress them further with his old-fashioned work ethic.

Samuel directed much of the action from the sidelines, now and then stepping in among the hip-high oat stalks to instruct or guide Aiden and his sons. Aiden learned mostly by watching. His quick grasp of the field work and willingness to sweat earned him respect from Samuel and his younger boys.

While waiting for Daniel to drive the Belgians farther ahead on the old McCormick, Aiden and the boys scattered across the golden field, looking for rocks and tossing them into wheelbarrows.

"This is the worst part," Mark said, digging up a rock with his gloved hands.

"Where do they come from?" Aiden assumed the rocks would have been cultivated out of the earth years ago. He used a small pick Samuel had given him to loosen the rocks, careful not to disturb the unharvested oats. He did not recall needing to rock pick when helping out as a boy on his grandfather's tobacco farm.

"They keep popping up out of the ground." Mark tossed a rock into his wheelbarrow. His shirt sleeves were rolled to his biceps in typical Amish teen male fashion, showcasing farm-honed muscles. He kicked soil back into the hole with his black boots and wiped the sweat from under his straw hat. "If we don't get rid of them, they'll ruin our equipment and can harm the draft horses. No matter how many we toss, they keep coming back out of the ground; it's just the way it is. They're worse than weeds."

Daniel jostled back and forth in easy unison with the binder, calling out orders in German to the three Belgians. Their anvil-shaped heads hung low and their coats frothed with sweat. Aiden kept one eye on Daniel, mounted on the McCormick. He thought Daniel looked like the bearded Greek god Zeus charging across the sky in his chariot.

One of the outside horses hesitated with a squeal, forcing the other two out of step. Samuel whacked the mare on her hindquarters to get her moving. He grabbed onto her hind legs and squatted down. She refused to budge. Holding his straw hat on his head, he pushed into her mammoth hindquarters with his whole body.

"We gotta get these groundhog holes filled in," he hollered up at Daniel. "They're coming up and out again."

"We need some new hounds to chase those hogs out!" Daniel tugged the reins, getting the horses moving again.

"What happened to your old hounds?" Aiden asked Mark, once the commotion of the holdup had died down.

"They both bolted three months ago during a really bad storm. Haven't seen them since. We need to get new ones but haven't gotten around to it." Mark stooped down and lifted a rock. "Boogered hounds. They're fearless around the Belgians and will fight a fox, but a thunderstorm sends them scurrying like cowards."

With their wheelbarrows full of rocks, Aiden and the boys dumped them into a pile by the horse pen to be washed and dried and sold to gardeners, landscapers, or anyone else interested in rocks.

"We don't waste anything," Mark said. "Not even rocks."

On the way back to the field, David suggested they make a contest out of the rock picking. Whoever filled his wheelbarrow the quickest would be the winner. Half-heartedly, Mark and Aiden went along. Forty minutes later, standing in the midst of the tall oat stalks, David threw his thin arms into the air to celebrate his victory.

"You're a rock star," Aiden said.

The two boys stared blankly at Aiden, then, with enormous smiles creasing their young, tanned faces, they laughed. David, holding onto his brother's arm, nearly keeled over. Aiden realized his metaphor was not lost on the two young Amish boys who, in some ways, were as much a part of the twenty-first century as he.

"Dummkop!" Samuel chastised David with a stern look for his silly game-playing. Aiden understood why Samuel used extra harsh words with David in the field. David, being the youngest son, would someday inherit the family farm.

The sun lifted high over the field. At eleven they broke for the lunch Rachel had left for them in the refrigerator. Aiden had never imagined he'd have such a large appetite after such a filling breakfast, but after choring four hours under the hot sun, picking rocks and shocking sticky oats, he ate himself full as if he'd had nothing but a crumb all morning.

Daniel still did not speak to him. Aiden caught him a few times glancing at him during lunch. But when Aiden met his gaze, he'd look away and busy himself with his cold chicken and sliced trail bologna.

In some ways, Aiden supposed he exemplified the typical Amish man: austere and aloof. Yet the other Schrocks were so much different. Even Samuel, the patriarch who had chastised his youngest son for making a game out of rock picking, displayed a levity that took Aiden by surprise. None of them, not even their chatty neighbors Micah Yoder and Gunny Rupp, who had stopped by for a short visit to meet the "English hero" just before lunch, fit the Amish stereotype. None but Daniel.

Each of them—including little Leah—had expressed gratitude for his veering his car in front of the drunken Bobby Jonesboro. But Daniel had yet to utter a word of thanks. He'd been the first to rush to his side at the accident scene to make sure he was unharmed. Now, he seemed unable to bear his presence. Aiden was more certain his aloofness had to do with the man's death.

Aiden had even thanked him for letting him stay in his bedroom, but Daniel had sidestepped his gratitude with a grunt. Aiden got the message and avoided him whenever he could.

As the lunch table cleared, Samuel stepped onto the small patch of garden outside the utility room, where they grew vegetables and herbs. The garden was perfect for tucking away their oblong gas tank. One area was reserved for strawberries. Samuel picked a handful and popped them into his mouth. He called to the others to try some.

"Sour, yet," he said, his mouth puckering. "But goot! Let's not tell Mom we picked some before ripening."

Daniel did not have any of the strawberries. He was back out on the field, driving the Belgians down the rippling rows of golden oats. The team turned easily and avoided groundhog holes as the sheaves swept to the sides. The others soon joined him, spreading out in the field, their collarless shirts spotted in sweat. After a while, Samuel waved Aiden in from the back field where he was rock picking with Mark and David.

"Let's get you up there and see what you can do with those Belgians, Englishman," he said. Daniel looked down at his father with animus, and even with the Belgians snorting and neighing, Aiden heard Daniel sigh with rancor.

"Come from down there, Daniel. Let our English friend give it a try. Give him something to write about."

Sighing, Daniel climbed down from the McCormick, and Samuel boosted Aiden up to the seat. To Aiden's relief, the older Schrock climbed up after him and stood on the aft shaft.

"Don't worry," he said. "Wouldn't let you up here alone on your first time out. Those beasts know who they can take advantage of."

With Samuel's guidance, Aiden steered the draft horses forward. Mark and David took a break from their rock picking and looked on and cheered when Aiden made his first turn with the team without so much as a jolt. Folding his arms across his broad chest, Daniel watched also.

But he was clearly not so joyful. Aiden watched him turn hastily and stomp through the corrugated field toward the house as he yanked off his gloves. Just as Aiden focused his attention back on the binding, one of the horses stepped out of sync and stumbled headlong, forcing the binder to jerk. Samuel, experienced with such bumps, held steady to the seat post, but Aiden tumbled over the side. Samuel grabbed for him, but he was gone before he could reach him. Snatching the reins, Samuel wrenched the Belgians to a halt and climbed off the machine. He squatted next to Aiden.

"You get hurt?"

"No," Aiden said, standing with Samuel's aid. "I'm okay." He took off his canvas gloves and inspected the swelling on his palms. Even with the gloves, the reins had left burn streaks from when he had instinctively grabbed onto the reins tighter before sailing over the side.

Mark and David rushed over.

"What happened?" Mark asked.

"Hit a groundhog hole!" Samuel poked his boot into the offending hole. "Those holes. Need to get some hounds to chase out those rodents."

Aiden wiped the soil and straw from his Amish clothes, his palms stinging, and looked around red-faced. David handed him his straw hat, which had flown off when he fell.

"You sure do get into a lot of accidents," he said, straight-faced.

"Looks that way," Aiden said, putting on his hat, happy to hide his burning cheeks.

"Well now," Samuel said. "How you like being an Amish man, huh? You like being Amish now?" And he laughed as he climbed back up on the McCormick and, still laughing, commanded the Belgians forward.

DRINKING a bottled water in the utility room, Daniel had watched the Englishman fall from the binder, and he continued to stare out the window as Aiden brushed the straw and dirt from his clothes and examined his palms.

"Something yet not right about all this," he said under his breath. "Something bad will come from it all, I know it. It's all boogered. Des is shlecht."

Chapter FIVE

TUESDAY morning Aiden awoke to his alarm clock at four thirty. He ached to get back into the field. After his embarrassing tumble from the binding machine, he longed to redeem himself in the family's eyes. Samuel had hesitated letting him back up on the McCormick after his fall; he had relegated him to rock picking and shocking the remainder of the afternoon. Dressing in the flickering light of his gas lantern, he hoped the family did not already view him as a city-soft oaf.

The lingering burning on his palms, which Rachel had treated last night with aloe, failed to stymie his determination. But as he headed downstairs for breakfast, the sound of Rachel and Daniel's stiff voices coming from the kitchen stopped him at the top of the enclosed stairwell. His ears heating with blood, he listened in, trying to interpret their unique German words.

"It will be good if you take him," Rachel said.

"I will not do it."

"But there is nothing for him to do here today."

"Why does he not go with Mark and David?"

"Stuck all day at the shop alone with those boys and your Uncle Eldridge?"

Listening in, Aiden learned that the family owned a furniture shop in the town of Henry, with Samuel's eldest brother, Eldridge. The Schrocks and Uncle Eldridge's family took turns manning it. But today,

Daniel needed to travel to some kind of a horse auction to replace their buggy horse, Dexter, and the shaft, both destroyed in Sunday's accident. The journey entailed an hour-long buggy ride each way.

"It would be good for you, too," Rachel said. "You will want the company for such a long trip."

"I do not mind being alone," Daniel said. "I like it that way."

"Can I go too, please, Mom?" came Grace's imploring voice. She spoke in English, and her segue into the language seemed to lure the others to naturally follow.

Rachel wasted few words. "No."

"But, Mom—"

"Grace, this is no time for you to be running all over a horse auction. Besides, today's washday. I need you here. I'll be at the doctor's with Leah most of the day."

"Take Aiden, Daniel." It was Samuel's voice, gruff and commanding, yet compassionate. Speaking in English like the others, he sounded closer. He must have been standing in the hallway, perhaps on his way out the front door when the conversation had caught his attention.

"You shouldn't drive so far alone," he said. "It would be good for our friend to go. We're all busy today with me needing to do watch repair, and your brothers going to the shop, and your mom taking Leah to the doctors'. Give him something to write about."

"Why doesn't he go back to Chicago yet?"

"Shtill, eah zayl hare," Rachel reprimanded. Aiden understood that she was warning Daniel to keep his voice down.

"I'd rather take Grace," Daniel said curtly, but quieter.

"For your mom. Do it, Daniel."

The silence that followed signified Daniel had lost the battle. At breakfast, Rachel's pleasant way of telling Aiden about the horse auction failed to mask what he already knew. That Daniel did not want him to come. Daniel's absence from the table affirmed as much. Aiden wanted to refuse, to avoid the awkwardness of spending the day with someone who clearly disliked him. He almost volunteered to stay and help the girls do the washing with their gas-powered Maytags. But knowing how Rachel and Samuel had put up such a noble fight on his behalf, he forced a compliant smile.

Near eight in the morning, Daniel was hitching one of their buggy horses to the market wagon in the driveway when Aiden stepped onto the stone footpath. He expected to travel in the more common top-covered family buggy, but realized Daniel would probably want more space in the back for whatever purchases he might make at the horse auction. Flinching from an already muggy morning, he figured an open wagon ride was a blessing compared with being cooped up in one of those stuffy black buggies. Such close confines with Daniel wouldn't be too comforting either.

Like a tentative lamb, he walked down the gravel driveway and made his way along the right side of the wagon. Daniel's sharp stare stopped him.

"Are you going to drive?" he asked, his eyebrows fused.

"What?"

"The right side is the driver's side."

Hanging his head, Aiden shuffled around the back of the wagon to the passenger side—the left side. Though it would've been just as easy for him to climb up the right side and slide across the bench, he did not want to butt heads with Daniel over trivialities. With a few slips off the wagon's wooden wheel, he did a pretty good job climbing into an Amish vehicle for his first time, if he did think so himself. Daniel climbed up the driver's side and remained mute. Once settled, Daniel, his sleeves rolled exposing muscular, tanned forearms, tugged the reins and murmured, "Get, Badger," without so much as a glance at his English travel companion.

"Should be a good day for an open wagon ride," Aiden said as the sleek black gelding pulled them down the driveway with the crunch of gravel under the wagon wheels. "With the heat it'll be a lot cooler. By the look at the sky maybe we'll even get a little sprinkle."

"Doubt it'll rain this early." Daniel steered Badger left, past the Schrock's mailbox and onto the blacktop lane.

Out of the corners of his eyes, Aiden studied the stalwart Amish man to his right. He's a stern one, he thought, wondering just what compelled Daniel to dislike him so much. Last night during supper, Daniel again had spoken not a word to him, and had looked away whenever Aiden had caught him glaring. Even when the family had gathered to play Blitz in pairs at the dining table and eat Jiffy Pop, Daniel had avoided him. After five hands he'd grown restless and again had hid out in his woodshop for the remainder of the night.

Aiden thought it best to refrain from forcing a conversation until Daniel's bitter mood mellowed—if it would at all. For the time being, he settled into his seat and watched the landscape pass by.

Rich green farmland, almost dripping with humidity, stretched all around them. The muggy air held the stench of manure and the tea-like aroma of the sycamore trees that clustered by the white farmhouses. The Amish owned most of the land on this southern edge of Frederick County, and many were laboring in their fields. Aiden watched the women and girls putter in their country gardens or hang laundry on clotheslines. Small children frolicked in their yards barefoot or stood on porches eating apples or oranges and watching passers-by on the lane. One small boy balancing himself on crutches waved to them; Aiden waved back.

A black family buggy approached from behind and Daniel gave the driver a wider passing berth. Both Daniel and the driver nodded to each other, touching the rims of their straw hats. Daniel mumbled something about Badger being slower than poor Dexter and how he wished he was at the furniture shop with Mark and David instead of driving to the horse auction.

Daniel's grumbling gave Aiden an opening.

"I'm really sorry about Dexter," he said, hoping Daniel would now want to chat.

Daniel's broad shoulder's tightened. He tugged at Badger's reins. "Horse is as slow as molasses."

"I'm sorry about Bobby Jonesboro too," Aiden dared say. He squinted at him, bracing for his reaction. He had to know for sure if Daniel resented him for the man's death.

Daniel huffed. "He asked for it."

Aiden sat up, stiff. "What do you mean?"

"He was a drunk. Never did care for him, or his type."

"You two weren't close friends?"

Daniel snickered. "Me and Bobby Jonesboro, friends? What gave you that idea? He's somewhat of a different character from me. A crazy Englisher, that's what he was. God has His hands full with that one."

Shrinking in his seat, Aiden wondered why Daniel acted so irritable around him if he didn't blame him for Bobby Jonesboro's death. He wasn't like that with everyone. When his neighbors Gunny and Micah had stopped by yesterday, he had behaved as charmingly as a diplomat. Maybe he thought Aiden a sissy for falling from the binding machine? But Daniel showed contempt for him even before that, from the moment they sat down to supper that first night. Did he resent Aiden for taking his bedroom? No grown man could be that childish.

Was he angry with him for writing an article about his family, trying to profit from them in some way? Few people enjoyed being thrust under a microscope; still, outsiders were interested in how the Amish lived. Pretending otherwise would be impractical. Even the Schrocks profited from English curiosity, selling hand-crafted Amish furniture that the English took back to their modern suburban homes.

Aiden wondered if his temperament had to do with his mysterious wife. Did she run off, leaving him shattered and bitter? Aiden sympathized. He too had brooked the pain of abandonment.

He wanted to ask Daniel about his wife, and why three months ago he'd moved back home, apparently without her. But, of all the Schrocks, Daniel was the least approachable. Discussing personal matters with him would be like salmon-fishing alongside a grizzly.

A new thought bit into Aiden. Did Daniel, an ultraorthodox Christian, suspect he was gay and resent him for it? He never perceived himself so easily identifiable, but he supposed some might guess, especially since he was unmarried and never pretended to show any interest in females. Was it obvious to Daniel that Aiden was physically attracted to him? He had faced antipathy for his sexuality in the past, but nothing blatant. No one had ever denounced him for it, at least not openly. The notion that Daniel might bothered him a great deal.

They stopped before a two-lane county road. Daniel checked for traffic and steered the gelding right onto the busier thoroughfare. Two passing cars took Aiden off guard, and he instinctively clutched his straw hat and held onto his seat.

"How do you get used to that?" he asked, straightening as the cars sped off.

"Actually, you don't."

Scenes from Sunday's car accident flashed across Aiden's mind. Riding in the open wagon, he realized just how gruesome a speeding car plowing into a horse-drawn vehicle could be. Certain things about the Amish and English worlds, despite generations living rather harmoniously side by side, still made a horrible match. Nothing, he thought, made for a collision of cultures more than horse-drawn vehicles and modern automobiles.

Daniel had yet to thank him for saving his family from such a ghastly scenario. Whether one disliked a person for whatever reasons, surely such an act warranted at least a rudimentary expression of gratitude. Even if Daniel did despise him for being gay.

He could tell Daniel did not want to talk with him. Yet, despite Daniel's remoteness, Aiden yearned to build a bridge. He thought back to his first night relaxing with the family amid the glow of lanterns. Better judgment eluding him, he blurted, "So, I hear you like to backpack."

Daniel waited several seconds before responding. "Ya."

"I was surprised when your parents told me that. I didn't think the Amish did that kind of thing."

For the first time Daniel looked straight at Aiden, but he shot him a hostile, condemning look, a look so harsh Aiden would rather he had continued to peer over the horse's rump and ignore him.

"Amish do lots of things real people do," he said, and faced back to the road.

Aiden heard a loud grunt. Whether it came from the horse or Daniel, he did not know. "I meant that you're so busy with all your hard work, too busy for, well…. Your whole life is sort of like…. You live a subsistence lifestyle every day. Most people backpack so they can be more self-reliant, to get away from modern life. That's why I do it. I love to backpack." He scrutinized Daniel's unmoving face. He wondered if he could ever say anything right in front of the Amish man.

HIS expression remained hard, but inside Daniel knew he should lighten up on the poor Englisher. Aiden did save his family, he reluctantly admitted. He should probably say something to him, express a few words of appreciation. He feared becoming too friendly with him. What good could come from it? They lived in two different worlds.

Sure, he liked Aiden. He liked him more than he wanted to admit. He simply did not like spending an entire day with a stranger one who was most likely taking mental notes about all he said for some English article. He didn't trust reporter types. He didn't trust anyone outside of his own community. He still thought his parents' inviting him to stay with them a shussly idea. Nonetheless, Aiden was trying his best to be civil. Perhaps he should too.

"Ya, I figure you didn't mean no harm."

Aiden's shoulders lowered. He apparently wasn't so quick to give up trying to pull Daniel out of his shell. "What places have you gone backpacking?"

"Different places around," Daniel said, his tone stubbornly insipid. "Wisconsin, Kentucky. Downstate at Shawnee National Forest."

"Shawnee? I've heard of that place. I'd like to check it out some time. Is backpacking one of the things you did for rumspringa?"

"While most my friends lived English lives doing things I wouldn't do, I backpacked different places. I did Shawnee for an entire week alone. I hiked the River to River Trail that goes from one side of the state to the other, the Ohio River to the Mississippi."

"Wow!"

"It's only about fifty miles, but it was real nice."

"Where else have you been?"

"I backpacked Montana about a year ago."

"Montana? Really? Your parents told me you traveled out west. Where in Montana?"

"Glacier National Park. I always wanted to see it. Don't think I'll ever much forget it." Daniel spoke more to himself than to Aiden. He almost smelled the pine-scented forest, felt the cooling shade from the towering hemlocks. "I would like to go back; I miss it. I like for sure the western US and the mountains."

"Me too." Aiden stretched out his legs. "I've always thought about living out there. It's been a dream of mine."

"So you said at supper the other night."

Daniel could see Aiden relax. He had tilted his head toward the washed sky and was smiling at the warblers and robins flying from branch to branch in the trees that dotted along the road. He was glad that he no longer caused him as much anguish, but he was unsure how long it would last. He still believed Aiden's being there was just not right. He made everything all boogered.

"I'd love to buy some land near Glacier, build a cabin," Aiden said. "If I ever get out there."

"There's a small Amish community near Glacier," Daniel said, his worries scratching at him like an old worn-out straw hat. "A town called Rose Crossing."

"There is? Really?"

"I visited while I was out there. They even asked me to stay, since the community is only a few years old and they would like new members. Not a lot of marriageable men my age there. But I couldn't do it."

"Why not?"

"You know how it is. A man can't just up and leave. I got family here. There's the shop. Besides, I was to get married in a few weeks."

"It would be nice to live there, though."

"Ya." Daniel sighed. "It would be nice."

An unexpected slope in the road caused Aiden to press against Daniel. Unable to resist the centrifugal force, Aiden pressed against him for what seemed several minutes; in reality a few seconds lapsed. Daniel felt Aiden's surprisingly taut muscles. He tensed, but held steady to the reins and focused on the road.

"Sorry." Aiden slid farther to his side of the bench once the wagon came out of the slope. "I can be a klutz sometimes, I guess."

"Don't worry about it." Daniel tugged on the reins and squirmed in his seat. "Not your fault you don't know how to ride in a wagon."

AS THEY neared the I-57 underpass, Aiden saw something that furthered his embarrassment. Larger than some of the region's barns loomed an adult "superstore." A sign jutting high above the vast parking lot, tall enough for drivers on the Interstate to see, proclaimed everything inside: adult books, erotica, DVDs, sex toys. Several semi-trailers, commercial pickups, even a few RVs, filled a quarter of the lot.

Aiden slumped in his seat and lowered his hat to conceal his eyes. The morning sun burning through the haze added to the heat on his searing cheeks. Glimpsing under the brim, he gauged Daniel's reaction. Surely he'd traveled this road many times. But Daniel fixed his eyes as if he saw only Badger's collar.

Along the northbound lanes of I-57, Aiden saw something else that made his cheeks burn: a huge billboard with a picture of Jesus Christ gazing down disapprovingly over the adult store. Large block lettering underneath read: "Jesus Is Watching You."

Trapped in a horse-drawn wagon with an Amish man he knew distrusted him and seeing such a radical display of sexual solicitation and religious iconoclasm, both frowned upon by the Amish, demonstrated within one small parcel of Midwestern land, Aiden's mind whirled. He wanted to ask about the adult establishment and the billboard, but Aiden knew better than that. Talking with Daniel about the weather stirred up enough trouble, much less sex and religion.

Daniel paid no attention to any of it; he held Badger farther to the right of the road to avoid being sideswiped by the occasional car using the on and off ramps to the Interstate.

Badger led them farther along and Aiden, pondering what he'd just seen, settled back in his seat. Perhaps the adult establishment explained why the Amish had prospered in the United States for so long. Sex shops and religion may seem as incongruous as skunks and hawks, but Aiden reckoned that in their own way, one could not exist in America without the other.

Just another square sewn into the great American patchwork quilt, he figured, the wagon jostling rhythmically down the road.

AT THE horse auction Daniel became even more distant. His body language told Aiden he had no time for playing tour guide to an Englisher. For Aiden, he had no idea where to begin. He had never been to a horse auction before; he had gone to tobacco auctions as a boy in southern Maryland with his grandfather, but nothing on such a large scale with so many different attractions.

He left Daniel to his essential farm business and wandered about the grounds on his own. Aiden respected the Schrocks' ways by keeping his cell phone shut off and stowed in his duffel bag while at their farm, but before leaving the house, he had concealed his old Motorola RAZR in his pants pocket. Hidden behind a signpost, he took the opportunity to call his insurance company regarding a rental car. The company was still processing his accident claim, but he could pick up a rental anytime—he only needed to fax the receipt for reimbursement. He called information and the operator connected him with the nearest rental agency that guaranteed him a car for tomorrow.

Aiden snapped his phone shut and kicked at the dirt. In his short stay with the Schrocks, he had already grown attached to them. Somehow he imagined he would even miss the aloof and handsome Daniel. His heart a little heavier, he gazed around the expansive auction grounds, tucked between fields of soybeans, corn, and grains. His first time in public dressed as an Amish man, Aiden was unsure how to react when some of the tourists ogled him. One elderly woman snapped his picture. He scowled outwardly; inwardly he grinned.

But Aiden, being the astute journalist, intended to snap a few photos of his own to accompany his article. Taking furtive snapshots of the grounds with his Motorola, he discovered not everything up for auction was a standardbred horse. There were many other livestock— cows, pigs, goats, sheep, and farming merchandise too. Patchwork quilts were on auction in a large barn. Vendors sold everything from potted plants and chicken feed to cream-filled whoopie pies and faceless Amish dolls.

In the auction arena near the sale ring, he found Daniel huddled with a large group of Amish men. He tucked his phone into his pants and, standing in the background, watched the groundsmen haul out the different tack supplies and farming equipment up for bids. The auctioneer cried out rambling sentences that, although spoken in English, Aiden hardly comprehended. Only Daniel bid on the eighteen-inch buggy shaft.

Aiden noticed Daniel tense with anticipation when the groundsmen brought the standardbreds into the sale ring. Three others bid against him, but they did not stay in long and Daniel won a twelve-year-old muscular black mare named Gertrude for just under nineteen hundred dollars. He paid for the horse along with the buggy shaft and a few other vendor items he needed for the farm at the cashier trailer. An agent would deliver the horse and shaft by Thursday, the cashier said. Aiden was surprised when Daniel pulled out a credit card for the payment.

"You can use credit?" Aiden stared transfixed at the Visa card in Daniel's large, calloused hand.

"We pay it off," Daniel grunted. "Besides, Bobby Jonesboro's insurance will likely reimburse us for the horse and shaft."

Aiden did not mean to insinuate the Amish were unable to make payments. He decided against clarifying himself, leaving well enough alone. Regardless of reason, Aiden figured nothing would change Daniel's determination to dislike him.

On the return home they spoke even less than on the trip out. To Aiden, the clip-clop of Badger's hooves on the buggy-battered blacktop proved as good a distraction from the silence as a radio.

Passing the adult superstore, Aiden noticed that Daniel and the Amish woman driving the buggy on the opposite side of the road refrained from even glancing at it. The "Jesus Is Watching You" billboard receded into the distance. A few miles down the road, Daniel steered Badger into a country store with a gas station.

"Are we getting gas?" Aiden joked. But Daniel acted as though he didn't hear. He brusquely set the brake and, alighting without comment, tied the gelding to a hitching post.

"I'm getting a root beer," he said, and marched inside.

Aiden jumped off the wagon and stretched. He decided he could use a cold drink, too, and trailed after Daniel.

Five minutes later, Aiden walked out of the store. Daniel was already back in the driver's seat of the wagon, a scowl on his face as he took sips of his root beer. Aiden paid his sullenness no mind. He unwrapped the two impulse items he'd bought by the checkout counter and handed them to Badger.

Daniel stood and looked over the horse's head, his brow braided. "What's that?"

Badger's thick tongue lapped over Aiden's palm. "Filling her up," Aiden said, grinning. "Peanut butter granola bars."

Daniel, tightening his lips, sat back down. Aiden finished feeding Badger and climbed into the wagon with a wide grin. Tugging the reins, Daniel barked "Get!" and Badger, happier, trotted out of the parking lot toward home.

THE horse auction had hay and water for all the stabled horses, but Daniel knew the sweet-salty granola would make a good spur to get Badger to trotting speed, especially with halfway still to go. Yet he hadn't expressed his approval to Aiden. He did not want to be too friendly with him. What was the point? If he was too kind to him, it might give him the wrong impression. Aiden, in some ways, was like a puppy. Feed him with compliments and he might never leave.

They were turning onto the blacktop lane where the Schrocks lived when Aiden commented that the gray clouds had formed into long, corrugated rows and the south sky was darkening.

"Just in time. Storm coming."

"How do you know?" Daniel said, although he too knew a storm was fast approaching.

"Years of backpacking and camping, I guess. I figured out what the different cloud formations mean. Kind of comes second nature to me now."

When the gelding pulled into the Schrock's driveway, the first heavy drops of rain fell from the darkening sky. By the side of the house, Daniel spied Grace and Elisabeth yank the last of the clothes off the line and dash inside with their large bundles. He said, "Make wet."

Aiden giggled. "What does that mean?"

"Means it's raining."

Once he climbed down from the wagon, Daniel looked toward the encroaching storm and tugged on his beard. He loathed thunderstorms. Hated them deeply.

With a quiet, almost sympathetic, manner, Daniel and Aiden unhitched Badger and led him to the horse stall in the barn. Taut lips stretching across their faces, they unloaded the wagon of the wild bird seed and peat moss Rachel had asked Daniel to buy and pulled the emptied wagon to the metal buggy shed. Daniel secured the swing door extra tight in anticipation of the storm.

"Nix sunsht?" Aiden asked Daniel in Pennsylvania German.

Daniel gawked at him. It was the first time he had heard him use the "correct" way of speaking instead of his aggravating textbook German. "Where did you learn that?"

"I picked it up listening to the vendors at the horse auction. After a while, I could tell what they were saying."

Daniel was impressed that Aiden learned things so quickly. "Nay, I don't need anything else."

"Better get inside then." Aiden scurried for the house. Just as he reached the stone path, he stopped and looked to Daniel. "Thanks for taking me with you to the horse auction."

Double checking the latch on the shed, Daniel murmured, "Du wilcom."

Daniel did not follow Aiden inside the house. Instead, he took refuge in his woodshop, where he worked on his mother's corner kitchen cabinet. Wood shavings curled from the plane as he pushed it smoothly over the oak plank. His bare forearms moved back and forth, smooth and steady. A gas Coleman hung from overhead and spotlighted him in a circle of soft golden light; the smell of hot sawdust surrounded him. Hens rustled agitated in their coop just a few steps away. He only half noticed, since he'd become used to their prattling through the years. Even if the hens' chatter was unusual, his head was too full of heavy thoughts for him to have cared.

He watched the first sharp flash of lightning through the woodshop's window. Squeezing his eyes tight, he waited for the inevitable boom. Thunder plowed over the landscape and into his woodshop; the loud rumble seeped into his soul. His arms froze in mid-motion, his eyes gaping. A slight tremble filled his muscled forearms as he clutched onto the motionless plane.

Shuddering, he let go of the plane and dropped to his knees on the chip-covered floor. He pressed his palms together and brought his fingertips to his beard. Frantic prayers fluttered from between his quivering lips. Weakening, he fell to his haunches and dropped his wet face into his palms. His body convulsed with sobs.

Chapter SIX

EARLY Wednesday morning Aiden strolled to the phone shack just down the lane from the Schrock farm. During breakfast, Samuel had told him Joe Karpin's number was tacked to the wall. Aiden needed Joe to drive him to the city of Mattoon to pick up the rental car he had reserved while at the horse auction. Daniel and the boys were manning the family's furniture shop in Henry, and Samuel was going to be busy with watch repair, which he did on the side for extra money while Rachel and the girls baked bread all day. He figured today was as good as any to pick up the car. He was in no mood to go, or to leave the Amish and the Schrocks, but he knew his time with them had neared its end.

Thirty minutes after Aiden called, Joe pulled his Ford Club into the Schrock's gravel driveway. There were no other passengers for the fifteen-mile trip, so Joe had Aiden, dressed in his jeans and Oxford shirt, hop up front. The icy blast from the air conditioner caught Aiden off guard. Already used to being in a non-air conditioned environment, he instinctively closed his vent.

"Off to Mattoon, huh?" Joe craned his neck from side to side and backed out of the driveway.

"Yeah," Aiden said, fastening his seatbelt. "They have the closest car rental office."

His liver-spotted hands clasped onto the steering wheel, Joe made his way down the Schrock's lane. At the end of the lane he made a left where smaller farmhouses almost abutted the side of the grave lane. A quick right took them down another gravel lane that opened up so that larger farmhouses sat farther off down long tree-lined driveways. Oat shocks sat atop green fields where dairy cattle grazed. Aiden watched, amused, as a white-tailed yearling nibbled on fallen sheaves Farther down, they passed a small Amish cemetery. The nondescript stone markers jutted out of the lawn like crooked teeth.

"I been making a lot of long trips lately." Joe grinned. His tanned face stretched with deep corrugated lines. "Not that I mind. Since I retired, it gives me something to do. I just took Rachel and Leah over to Decatur yesterday."

"Yes, I know. You took them to the hospital, right?"

"Yep, been there three times this week." Joe chuckled. "Each time driving the Schrocks. Samuel twice in one day, then Rachel."

He was glad Joe had brought up the subject of the Schrocks; he'd planned all along to ask about some of the nagging mysteries that surrounded them. He had feared offending the family by asking them directly, but with Joe, English like he, none of those uncomfortable cultural potholes lurked between them.

"Hope nothing is serious," he said, raising an eyebrow.

Joe slowed as he approached a wagon and waited a respectful time before passing. Aiden and he nodded at the cheerful-looking red-bearded driver as they went by. "You don't know about Leah?"

"No." Aiden shook his head. "The Amish are pretty tight-mouthed."

"You notice anything strange? I mean, for her age?" Joe glanced in the rearview mirror before pulling back onto the right side of the lane.

"Well… I guess. She doesn't talk much. She's adorable though."

"They found out last month she's got something called… Hard to pronounce. I think it's Muscular… Meta… Micha… Well, the short name for it is MLD. Ever heard of it?"

"No, I haven't."

"Causes some kind of deterioration of the brain or nervous system, or something like that. Used to drive another Amish boy to Decatur a few years back for the same treatments. Then one day he just never woke up. Rachel says Leah's got a milder form, but it'll all have the same results. She looked pretty good yesterday. Once the symptoms become worse though, well.... That's how it was with that poor boy."

"That's terrible." The words seemed trite, but Aiden meant them with all their force. "I never imagined."

"The Amish have ways of coping." Joe shrugged. "They talk a lot about God's will."

"How do they pay for their hospital bills?" Aiden asked. "I know they don't have insurance."

"They have a community fund to pay for medical expenses. Usually get the money from proceeds at flea markets and auctions and things like that."

"That's good."

"Nice to have a community like that, isn't it?"

Joe stopped at a junction and checked for traffic before turning left, then headed south on the paved two-lane county road toward Mattoon. For five miles the road continued straight without a single bend. The farms here were larger. Aiden noticed farmers using modern machinery as the Amish center of the region was left mostly behind.

"Yep, the Schrocks sure have been through a lot lately, lucky you saved them like you did." Joe shook his head, his thick silver hair barely moving. "Can't imagine what might've happened if you weren't there last Sunday. You were a Godsend to them. The more I think about it, the more I'm convinced God was working through you. My wife says that's how miracles happen, when you're open to God."

Aiden did not wish to crush his family's faith by telling him he wasn't so open to God. How could he be when he doubted one existed? "What all have the Schrocks been through?" he asked.

"You don't know about Esther and Zachariah, either?"

Aiden shook his head, wide-eyed. "Esther and Zachariah?"

"Daniel's wife and son."

Finally. He was to learn about Daniel's elusive wife. And he had a son too. Happy to have the most pressing of the Schrock mysteries about to be solved, he sat back in his seat and beamed.

"Did his wife run off with their son without his permission? With another man, maybe?" Yesterday, during the drive to the horse auction, Daniel had mentioned traveling to Glacier National Park just before his wedding. Daniel's mentioning his marriage had stoked Aiden's curiosity. But he had kept his throbbing interest in Daniel's personal life to himself. Now, safe with Joe, his reporter's instincts clawed to the surface uninhibited.

"Run off? Oh, no." A deep pinch formed between Joe's bushy white eyebrows. "Esther would've never done that."

"They're not separated?"

"Separated? No, the Amish can't do that, not even for infidelity or being married to a good-for-nothing drunk."

"Then what happened?"

"Esther and Zachariah, they were both killed."

Aiden's smile vanished in an instant. Stung by Joe's words, he slumped in his seat. The chest strap of the seat belt pressed into the right side of his neck, but he hardly noticed the irritation.

"Daniel's wife and son were killed?" He mouthed the words, trying to comprehend the awfulness of it. He knew something hung heavy over the tall, good-looking Amish man; he had never imagined anything so awful. He mentally kicked himself for assuming Daniel's bitter mood had come from a broken marriage, and how he had taken a certain pleasure in the thought.

Joe shook his head, his pale blue eyes on the blacktop. "His son was only a month old too."

"A baby?" Aiden gaped.

"Yep." Joe nodded. Deep canyons framed the sides of his frown. "Sad, isn't it?"

"How did they die?"

"Killed by a tornado. Just this past March. Hit their house. Destroyed the whole thing. Most of his farm gone. Lost almost all his livestock. Three more people died up in Champaign County from the same storm. Oh, but whenever a child dies, it's.... Well... at least the mother and baby are together in Heaven."

Overwhelmed by all Joe was telling him, Aiden stared transfixed at the passing corn and soybean fields. He thought back to yesterday when he and Daniel had returned from the horse auction, and how afterward Daniel had climbed down from the wagon and had stood looking toward the coming storm so introspectively. Aiden had scoffed at his somber mood then. Now he realized that Daniel would of course look at dark skies differently than most. A dark sky had devastated his entire world, producing a tornado that had taken from him his wife and baby son.

Not only had he suffered emotional losses—the deaths of his wife and son, and then learning of little Leah's illness—but also economic losses: his farm, most of his livestock, and just Sunday, another horse was taken from him. Aiden wanted to insist that Joe turn back and take him to Daniel so he could somehow comfort him.

"The Amish community wanted to rebuild for him," Joe went on, unaware of the impact his words were having on his passenger, "but he refused. He moved back home with his mom and dad right after it happened. Rents his land to an English farmer now."

Exhausted with emotion from all the things Joe had revealed, Aiden leaned his head against the headrest. "So that's why Daniel has a beard." He never considered it before that moment. "Amish men keep their beards even after they're widowed...."

"Yep, that's right," Joe said. "You didn't actually think he was divorced, did you?"

"Well ..." Aiden flushed. "I guess there's a lot about the Amish I still don't know. I just feel so bad for Daniel. What a horrible thing to have to live through."

"Sure is. Like I said, lucky you saved them from more tragedy."

"Yeah," Aiden said, mostly to himself, as the farmland whizzed past his window. "I guess it was kinda lucky."

Chapter SEVEN

"YOU don't like Aiden Cermak, do you," David said to Daniel at the family's furniture shop.

"That's a hasty assumption." Daniel was checking inventory tags on several of the shop's items, trying to ignore his little brother's bothersome accusations. He wanted to ready the shop for the "early weekenders" tomorrow. After the lackluster winter and spring months, he was hopeful shoppers would want to add more digits to their credit card bills.

No doubt competition was rife, even in the best of times. Amish woodworkers in the county were as common as fireflies in summer. Although a handful owned shops in town, hundreds more operated woodworking businesses from their farms, some displaying rather prominent signs alongside the busier thoroughfares to bait tourists. Each had his own skill level, as well as business acumen. Daniel's reputation honored him for his attention to detail—in both artistry and commerce.

Checking and rechecking, he needed everything organized and properly marked. Almost a week had passed since his last stint working at the shop, and he did not trust his uncle's family, or his own for that matter, to run things as efficiently as he. Uncle Eldridge's family would be manning the shop during the weekend, and the extra effort to arrange things would make it easier for them all.

He always suspected his father wanting to own the shop with his eldest sibling was nothing more than an act of charity. A few times Daniel had caught the sixty-three-year-old sitting at the desk in the back with his feet up and his hands cupped behind his head, snoozing. His children, Daniel believed, had inherited their father's faulheit. Bad enough most of what they sold derived from Daniel's own hands.

He wished he could focus more on the shop, but the oats permitted little time away from the farm. On several occasions, Samuel insisted he did not need to work the farm so hard, but Daniel knew that until David got older, his father could use the extra hands. Besides, the farm work allowed Daniel to take his mind off things. The slow and quiet shop sometimes made his thoughts wander.

He'd hoped to rid his mind of some of those irksome thoughts while immersed in inventory work, but his pesky little brothers would not let him.

"You don't like him, admit it," David persisted.

"Stop being so shussly," Daniel said.

"I think he's nice," Mark said from the shop window where he was wiping off smear marks with a chamois cloth dampened with vinegar and water. "Even if he is a bit clumsy."

"He's a nuisance if you ask me," Daniel said, annoyed with the topic already.

"We're learning him things," David proclaimed. "He's doing better."

"Ya, and at least he's not lazy," Mark said. "A lot of those Englishers are for sure lazy."

"He chores real hard," David said. "You have to say."

"He chores like an old woman." But Daniel regretted having uttered the caustic words the moment they had slipped past his lips. He didn't want to ridicule the Englisher in front of his brothers. He liked him. He liked him a lot. He simply did not want his brothers, or anyone else, to know.

He shook his head. Whether he did this to organize his thoughts or jumble them further, he was unsure.

"You should try be nicer," David said. "You can't forget he saved us from that crazy Bobby Jonesboro."

"Ya," Mark said, "we'd all might be dead for not him."

"Shtill!" Daniel swept an abrasive look from one brother to the other. "Are you going to needle me all day or do me some work?"

"Don't get all upset," David said.

Daniel softened his tone. "Look. You boys keep an eye on things out here. I got some work to do in the back." He set down his inventory pad and trudged past David for the storeroom in the back.

The smell of mildew and dust surrounded Daniel the moment he shut the storeroom's door. He inhaled deeply, appreciating the momentary quiet away from his brothers. He almost resisted switching on the light, for he welcomed the darkness. It stilled his thoughts. But he knew there were too many loose items and boxes lying about for his safety.

He switched on the flickering fluorescent light and nudged a path to a wood crate. He wished his thoughts could be so easily pushed aside. Seated, his elbow pressing into his thick thigh and his fist pushing into his beard, he peered at the dusty concrete floor.

For too long now, his thoughts were a whirlwind of distractions slipping through his fingers. Guilt, remorse, anger, illicit desires, all rambling through his mind like debris in a whirlpool. Which notions would surface from one moment to the next he could only speculate.

Thoughts as tangled as the shredded remains of his farm after that fatal tornado had rampaged through it.

He didn't like dwelling on Esther and Zachariah's deaths. What good came from it? Whether God's will or a random act of nature, it was done. Life continued in the same way as when the Belgians found their pan-sized hooves stuck in a groundhog hole. Jolting and irritating. One still needed to shake free and move forward.

Since that horrible day, he had spent countless hours wondering what he might have done to prevent their deaths. So engrossed at the furniture shop the day of the storm, he hadn't bothered to heed the tornado sirens. It was March in the Heartland, after all. It seemed the Englishers' sirens were blaring every other day. Why should he have taken them seriously then, when all the other times they had been false alarms, merely green skies and high winds?

Just when he began to tune out those crazy spring storms and the never-ending warnings that came with them, an F-3 twister tore apart his world. Maybe he could have done something, raced back to his farm on his bicycle, to have saved his family?

The twister hit so early that Esther's mother and some of the other women helping her care for the newborn had yet to arrive at the farm. He cringed when he learned Esther and the baby were alone when they died.

The emergency technicians found her crouched in the corner of the basement, her body shielding Zach's, what used to be the house piled on top of them.

Even if he had been able to reach them in time, what difference could he have made? Wouldn't he have been killed too? For sure he would have chosen the same safety zone as Esther. They always headed for the basement whenever they decided to heed the English sirens. Maybe he would have done something different, made one tiny decision that might have altered the deadly course of events? Maybe he would've insisted they seek shelter at the high school the community used as its official storm shelter?

He and Esther weren't even married a year when the tornado ended her life. Sweet for each other since the eighth grade, an eight-year span had passed before he asked her to be his wife. The afternoon after their baptismal before Bishop Hershberger, he popped the question in typical Amish understatement while standing under a tulip tree: "You want to get married?"

Her simple reply: "Okay."

He knew by his late teens there was no loving her the way she deserved. No matter how pigheaded he sometimes treated her—to chase her off, perhaps?—her love for him was as enduring as wisteria. Ultimately he did what she, and the community and God, expected of him. She would still be alive today if she hadn't accepted his sham of a proposal.

His Amtrak trip to Glacier National Park a few weeks before their wedding, with the thorns of guilt pricking him, was to give him some solace, some understanding of his life. No one understood why he wanted to go. His running-around years were behind him now that he was baptized and about to be married. But Daniel made himself clear. He needed to get away for a short while. His "bachelor party with God," he had chuckled to himself at the time.

Surrounded by the towering hemlocks, the peaks of the Livingston and Lewis Ranges glistening with a freshly fallen June snow, gooey-looking like marshmallow cream, he concluded he'd made the right choice in asking Esther to be his wife. Men and women were supposed to marry and have families. That was God's will. No one was to question it.

Kneeling before the Bishop at their long-awaited wedding a week after returning, he knew he was an imposter. But what else could he have done?

Nine months later, Esther's giving birth to a boy, his son, astonished him. He dropped to his knees and thanked God when the midwife came downstairs to tell him of Zach's entry into the world. At that moment, everything seemed in its rightful place. God beamed above. The love for his newborn echoed throughout the community. Although the love he bore for Esther never went further than the love a brother would have for a sister, he believed he was doing what the community expected of a man.

He exemplified the Old Order Amish more than anyone in the community, he was certain. His beliefs stood as stalwart as his ancestors' who migrated from Lancaster, Pennsylvania by wagon train. He never transgressed against the Ordnung, the church rules... not really. During his rumspringa, he spent most his time alone, avoiding those "barn parties" and English hot spots most of his friends scurried off to each weekend. He preferred to spend his time with nature, listening to the wind rattle the leaves of the elms, or watching the Canada geese cut through the crisp blue sky.

Daniel was as plain and simple as one could be.

Sure, he wore English clothes during his running-around years. Jeans, flannel shirts with buttons, his favorite hiking clothes from the Sierra Tracing Post. But that was more out of practicality than some youthful rebellion.

No, he never really transgressed. He always deferred to the ministers. Once baptized, he took the route expected of all men in the community—marry, start a family, work hard, and be a good provider. Nevertheless, God smote him.

Was it all part of His plan? Did God send that fatal tornado as a punishment for his wrongful thoughts? Would he be forced to forever suffer, though he tried to fight against it and do right?

He lumbered to a small wooden vessel sitting on a crate. He had carved it the winter he turned twenty, but never knew for what purpose. Others felt the same, for he had difficulty selling it. He had stowed it away with a few other items several months ago as "unsellable inventory." Lifting the vessel, he blew off the dust. The buffed pine felt smooth to his touch. His broad thumb caressed the grain, his eyes far away.

Should he have stayed leddich? Is that how God wanted it, for him to remain single the rest of his life? Did God make him that way so that he would refrain from marriage? Had God been listening to his prayers all along, and Daniel had failed to heed His clues in the same way he'd failed to heed the tornado sirens?

He knew of a few people in the community who never married. All but one were women. His sister was one. At twenty-three, Elisabeth was at an age when every Amish woman was at least courting, if not married. As far as he remembered, Elisabeth hadn't courted since she was nineteen. Did she intend to never marry? Perhaps her charm and intelligence frightened the men off? There was talk of her becoming a schoolteacher. She would be good at that, he always thought. Many times he wanted to ask her why she refrained from marriage and courting, but faltered whenever he tried. It was her life; he shouldn't want to pry.

As uncommon as it was for Amish women not to marry, it was even more so for men. There was only one man he knew of who had never married, still into his thirties. He spied the man from the eastern district a few times at the flea market. Good-looking, a pleasant man who, each time he saw him, wore a smile. So strange to see an Amish man his age with a smooth, clean-shaven face. Surely there were many maydels in the community who would have been interested in the man. Why did he shun them all?

Did he feel the same way as Daniel?

He had hoped that marrying Esther would put such notions behind him. For a while it worked. Even after Esther and Zach's deaths, he stowed those pestering thoughts in the far reaches of his mind, hidden away, like the items in the storeroom. Like the silly wooden vessel he now turned over in his calloused and nicked hands.

Then Church Sunday came, and that Englishman with curly raven-black hair and eyes the color of honey literally crashed into his life.

Mark and David had it wrong, of course. Daniel did not dislike Aiden Cermak. His feelings for him were anything but dislike. He had the coordination of a one-legged chicken, but his gumption and the warm smile that curled his upper lip like a blooming rose petal brought out desires in Daniel he wanted buried for good.

Plain and simple? Plain and simple, he fancied the plucky Englishman. He could no longer hide the fact from himself. Just looking at him made him catch his breath. He knew from the start. The way he'd looked, like a wayward cherub standing by the front door, the day his father had brought him home from the hospital. He bore the weight of his longing like a horse collar strapped to his neck, invisible hands yanking hard on the reins, jerking his emotions.

How long had it been since Daniel had felt the intimate touch of a lover? A week after Esther had given birth, in February? Although Daniel held no strong physical attraction for Esther, not the way he knew he was supposed to, they still had carried on marital relations, as outlined by Scripture. The Bible was very clear on that point: a husband and wife belonged to each other, in body as well as in spirit. Being with Esther was pleasant. He liked the touching. He enjoyed the feeling that he was loved and cared for by someone whom he trusted. But never did he have the physical urge for her, or any woman, not the way he occasionally had for men. Not the way he had for Aiden Cermak.

Was the Englishman just another one of da Hah's tests?

He thought that maybe, maybe, Aiden was "one of those." What did the English call it? Gay? He never understood why they used such a term. Nothing happy about such feelings.

Aiden said he never married. The English, he knew, often waited until their thirties to marry. What with so much premarital sex in the English world, he supposed there was no need to hurry. Such a strange, selfish existence the English led. Readying for bed a few nights before in the room he temporarily shared with his brothers, Mark and David said something about Aiden mentioning he was not even courting. They all thought it peculiar, a good-looking man in his twenties without at least a girlfriend. Yet none of his brothers suspected he was "one of those," at least not openly.

Daniel understood that an entire community of people like that existed. Though mildly curious in his teen years, he had no real desire to explore that world, well-known to be found in inner cities across the United States. Only once did he ever dare venture inside a gay bar. That was in Paducah, Kentucky, after hiking the River to River Trail in downstate Illinois. He had left almost as soon as he had stepped inside. The men, much older than he, had ogled him like hungry hounds before feeding.

Men from that distant alien world occasionally visited Henry, their sexuality uncomfortably clear. Sometimes even the Amish chuckled at an English kemmahrah, a man with noticeable homosexual traits.

Through the years, he knew of a few Amish men he considered kemmahrah. They all married, so Daniel never thought anything of them. Aiden wasn't effeminate, not by any means. Still, there was something—something about his expression. A compassion, a keen insight that extruded through those eyes of his, golden like the sunset.

As Daniel himself proved, most times no one could tell. No one ever guessed about his second cousin, Kyle Yoder, either. At least he hadn't thought anyone had. Had Kyle been "one of those"? He regularly prayed to God to forgive him for that one little transgression with Kyle so many years ago. He was the only man he'd ever come close to… close to sharing his body with. No one had ever found out about Kyle, found out about "them." Except for Kyle's father.

He could scarcely think of that now….

He shivered from such dreadful thoughts.

"What are you doing back here?" David poked his head into the storeroom.

Daniel jerked. At first irritated by his little brother's invading his space, he grew grateful for the distraction. His bearded face softened. "Just thinking about having you and Mark clean out the storeroom. It's for sure a mess."

"Well, there's a customer out here." David scrunched his small nose. "Some English woman. She wants to talk to you about ordering a chest of drawers. She looks rich."

Nodding, Daniel told David to tell the woman he'd be right out. Happy to have his thoughts chased away, if temporarily, Daniel set the wooden vessel back atop the crate, switched off the light, and went to greet the English customer.

Chapter EIGHT

AIDEN drove back to the Schrock's in his Ford Focus rental, along the same route Joe Karpin had taken, barely noticing the passing farmland or the rush of wind on his face through the half-opened window. His thoughts were still stuck on Daniel and his losses.

Widowed and losing a baby at twenty-five. The picture disturbed him.

Aiden recalled telling Mark, after breakfast, that he'd stop by the furniture shop and let him give his rental car a drive. He detoured left just before the Schrock's lane and headed back toward town, five miles north. He told himself it was to keep a promise to Mark; in reality, it was all for Daniel. Speaking intimately with him about his personal losses he knew was impossible, yet he simply could not resist seeing him.

He craned his neck to read the different shop signs along Ivy Street, the town's main business district: "Yoder's Amish Bakery and Pretzel Shoppe," "Stoltzfus Woodworking," "Hostetler's Candle Company." At last he saw what he was searching for: "Schrock Furniture." The sign was written in old-fashioned white script on the green awning of a shop. Underneath in smaller lettering: "Authentic Amish Woodwork." He parked his rental car in a small lot next to the shop.

Brass chimes on the door handle jingled when Aiden stepped inside. Instantly he was surrounded by the soothing smells of pine and oak, with a spicy hint of cinnamon-apple potpourri. The shop was empty of people except for the Schrock brothers, who he heard in the back. Daniel's voice traveled to him as he spoke in a flurry of Pennsylvania German. Aiden assumed he was barking orders at the boys.

David strode up to him. By the surprised look on the boy's face, Aiden suspected he was expecting to greet an English tourist.

"Hi." He grinned. "I almost didn't recognize you in your English clothes."

Aiden glanced down at his Oxford shirt and jeans. "Oh," he said, flushing. "I forgot I was in them."

"I didn't know you were coming by."

"I kinda promised Mark. I was on my way back from getting my rental car."

"We're all in the back. Come on."

Aiden gazed at some of the woodwork in the good-sized shop as he followed David. Throughout was furniture and objects clearly built with a love for the craft, made of oak and pine, a few of mahogany and maple. Tables, chairs, beds, desks, wine racks, even toys. One piece made him pause: an oak shelf carved from one solid tree trunk. Adorned with faceless Amish dolls and a few other country knick-knacks, the shelf undeniably demonstrated skill and ingenuity.

"It's Aiden," David announced as they reached the back.

"Hey," Mark said, looking up from his desk work.

Aiden gaped at Mark sitting before a large older model computer, and Daniel standing behind him, talking into a cordless phone.

"We're allowed to use computers and phones for business," Mark explained, as if he'd read Aiden's thoughts. "Just not for personal use."

"Ya," David said. "We wouldn't be able to make any money if we didn't have computers or phones."

"Even the old-fashioned ministers know that," Mark said, turning back to the moderate-sized monitor where a spreadsheet of the shop's monthly wood purchases was displayed.

Daniel glared at them down his nose as he talked on the phone. He turned his back to them as if seeking more privacy, his Pennsylvania German words rolling off his tongue in quick succession. Aiden understood enough to know that Daniel was bargaining down the price of wood from a local Amish distributor. After everything Joe Karpin had told him, he now saw Daniel in a different light. No longer did he fear his chilly demeanor. Compassion filled his throat as he stared at Daniel's back. He had to swallow his sympathies to keep them from gushing out.

With Daniel's intimate secrets now scattered all about his feet, Aiden wanted to respect his privacy and avoid the subject of his wife and son, no matter how difficult it was to keep from reaching out to him. He understood how horrible it was for him. His entire demeanor—silent, austere, harsh—was no doubt due to having suffered so many losses. If only Daniel trusted him more, opened up to him, perhaps he could ameliorate some of his pain.

Dissatisfied with the results of his bargaining, Daniel told the distributor he'd call back and he clicked off the phone. Laying it in its cradle on the desk, he glanced at Aiden before nudging Mark out of the chair.

"You have a great shop," Aiden said to Daniel. "Did you make all of this stuff?"

"Most of it." Daniel focused on the computer screen and scrolled down the list of purchases with an effortless use of the mouse.

"Ya, but he doesn't make the quilts or dolls." David chuckled. "Mom and the girls make those. Some come from other ladies in the community."

"We sell them on consignment," Mark said.

"It's really impressive," Aiden said. "Especially that shelf up front, the one carved out of a tree trunk."

"He just finished that up a couple weeks ago." Mark grinned. "He made it from a tree that got knocked down by a storm. He's teaching me all he knows. I hope I get half as good."

"I try to use the gifts da Hah has given me," Daniel said.

"Hey." Mark widened his brown eyes. "What kind of rental car you get?"

Aiden chuckled. "Sorry, just a Ford Focus. No shiny black Corvette this time."

"Ach, well, that's okay. You still going to let me drive?"

"I'll tell you what, I'll help you out at the shop until you close up, and then you can give me a lift back home. Not much going on back at the farm anyway."

"But we rode our bikes to the shop today, what am I to do with mine?"

"You can shove it in the back, there's room." He looked to Daniel. "Is that okay I let him drive?"

"Sure." Daniel shrugged. "It's his bike, your car."

"Great," Mark said.

"Do you mind if I take a look around the shop a bit?" Aiden asked, still looking to Daniel.

"Sure," Daniel said, with another unceremonious shrug and downturn of his mouth. As Aiden wandered the shop, he felt the Amish man's solemn eyes peer holes into his back.

HOPING the computer monitor would conceal him, Daniel eyed Aiden as he pretended to do desk work. His cheeks burned. It bothered him that his little brothers noticed how uncivilly he'd been treating Aiden. Undoubtedly, the sharp Englishman had noticed too.

David and Mark were right to praise Aiden for how he'd saved the family. With everything the family had endured the past few months, another tragedy would have been too great to bear—that's if any of them had even survived the accident. Aiden's being there Church Sunday was true Divine providence, even if his presence did force to the forefront of Daniel's mind all those unattractive thoughts. God must have known what He was doing when He directed Aiden to cross their path. How many other people would have risked their own lives like Aiden had, steering in front of a drunk driver to save a family of strangers?

He'd been so considerate the past few days, always thanking everyone for their hospitality and asking how to be more helpful. How had Daniel responded? With sneers and grunts. He didn't mind that Aiden was staying in his bedroom. Only a child would gripe about that. On some level he liked giving up his room for him. He shuddered, remembering how he had treated him during the trip to the horse auction.

Daniel, realizing why Aiden had assumed he was friends with Bobby Jonesboro, winced. He must have mistaken Daniel's harsh behavior as blaming him for Bobby's death. The poor Englisher probably thought he'd done something awful, when he had committed a wonderful and unselfish act.

Daniel's behavior from their first meeting had been nothing less than coarse and disrespectful. His eyes burned as he retraced in his mind just how horrible he had been to him. One thing was clear. The more he realized how much Aiden attracted him, the more he mistreated him.

He knew that Aiden would be returning to Chicago any day. Though the knowledge both bothered and relieved him, there could be no harm in being hospitable during the remainder of his stay. He should at least show him some courtesy for his saving his family from another tragedy.

Time he made up for his surliness.

Aiden was admiring a child's mahogany rocking horse when he sidled next to him. He was not surprised when Aiden flinched. Other than the drive to the horse auction, they had spent very little time in each other's company alone. And Daniel hadn't exactly gone out of his way to show him any hospitality.

"I made that about eight years ago," he said, hoping to be a bit more cordial.

"It s beautiful," Aiden said. "You have a lot of talent."

"I made it for Leah. But Dad wouldn't let me give it to her; he was afraid she'd fall off. So I stowed it away. A few months ago I decided to bring it out to the shop and sell it."

"It really is amazing," Aiden said. "Look at the detail in the face; his mane looks real." He touched it as if stroking a real mane.

Daniel noticed the thin gold chain around Aiden's neck. Jewelry was forbidden in his order, but on Aiden it looked fitting. The sparkling chain seemed to accentuate Aiden's amber eyes. The clasp had wound its way to the front where the first three buttons of his shirt were undone. Daniel badly wanted to straighten it for him, any reason for a chance to touch his neck.

With his arms stiff by his sides, Daniel led Aiden through the rest of the shop. Silent contentment flowed around him. He elaborated on the pieces Aiden admired most. They stopped before a queen-sized bed he had crafted from oak logs, covered with a multicolored patchwork quilt Grace and Elisabeth had made last spring.

"What a beautiful bed." Aiden caressed the stained wood of the footboard. "It would go perfect in my dream cabin. If I had money, I'd buy it in a heartbeat. I'd buy everything in here, actually. You really are more than just a woodworker; you're an artist."

Daniel felt his face heat above his beard. So not right to feel hochmut. Pride was a sin. But then so were many other things, he mused. He liked being complimented by the Englisher. He liked the sensation a great deal. Standing so close to him, as Aiden stroked him with compliments, he felt his lungs fill as if with oat heads.

"I'm humbled by the talent da Hah has given me," he said, stifling his erratic breathing as best he could. "I only wish I could put more time into it."

"Why can't you?"

"Dad needs help with the farm, at least through the fall harvest."

"Look on the bright side," Aiden said, "working around the farm lets you spend more time with your family. That's a good thing, isn't it?"

Daniel tugged on his beard. He had never thought of it that way. He did love his family. As undemonstrative as they sometimes could be, they were there for him when it counted. After the tornado, he'd chosen to live with them rather than have the community rebuild his farmhouse. The idea of living alone seemed unbearable. He realized now how he had been hurting himself, hiding away from them… brooding. He'd already lost his wife and son, and was on the verge of losing little Leah; he did not need to lose any more.

The Englisher had a way of seeing things, he was discovering. He liked that.

They smiled at each other, their eyes twinkling under the recessed lighting of the shop. It was the first smile the two had shared. Regrettably, Daniel could not help but scowl and turn away.

OUTSIDE on the street, loud hip-hop music blasted from a yellow Mustang convertible stopped alongside an Amish carriage at a red light. For some reason the scene aggravated Aiden. He and David were on their way to the IGA to get pops to go with the ample lunch Rachel had packed her boys—enough that Aiden did not have to go without—and he thought maybe the blaring music might be an affront to the Amish driver and others on the street. The Mustang turned right down a residential street, but the loud hip-hop remained in its intensity, not fading with the Mustang as Aiden had expected. Aiden realized the music had been coming from the Amish carriage all along, driven by a rumspringa youth cruising Ivy Street with his portable boom box. Flushing from his gaffe, Aiden supposed not everything was always as it seemed.

Old-fashioned candy sticks in jars displayed along the IGA's front counter grabbed Aiden's attention when he and David walked in. A few candy sticks would make a pleasant goodbye gift for the younger Schrocks, he thought. Poor little Leah, a special and brave girl, would especially appreciate the sweet treats.

He browsed the aisles while David got the drinks, longing to buy something for Daniel too. He chose a baseball magazine that he guessed Daniel might like. A small gesture of friendship couldn't hurt anyone, he figured. As an afterthought he grabbed up a Corvette magazine for Mark so that he wouldn't feel left out.

He was amused to find a small group of Amish youths gathered around an arcade game by the refrigerated drink cases. They were a few years before their rumspringa years, but he figured the electronic game, obscured by a tall store shelf, was too tempting for them to pass up. They were cheering and poking fun at each other like any American boys would. His amusement turned to shock when one of the boys called another a "faggot," and the insult was followed by steady laughter.

Aiden held no mawkish views of the Amish; still, such crude behavior surprised him. He supposed there were differing degrees of good and bad, even among the Amish. Just like Daniel had told him so sharply during their drive to the horse auction yesterday: *Amish do lots of things real people do.* Including use derogatory language and cruise main streets with blaring boom boxes, he concluded. He was glad that David, who was reaching into the case for bottled pops next to him, seemed oblivious to the foul-mouthed youths.

"Mark likes Mountain Dew and Daniel likes Dad's Root Beer," he said, handing Aiden the pops. "I like Orange Nehi. What do you like?"

"Diet Sprite." Aiden smiled at David. A rush of big brother affection for the eleven-year-old warmed his heart. "You're a good kid," he said, patting the top of his straw hat.

"Thanks," David said, raising an eyebrow as he handed Aiden a bottle of Diet Sprite.

The cashier's teenaged pimples turned two shades darker red when David introduced Aiden. News of "the Jonesboro incident" had reached throughout Frederick County, she said, with a healthy grin. She acted as if she were meeting a true celebrity. Aiden was embarrassed, but charmed by her kindliness. He was grateful when David tugged on his shirt and insisted they had better head back to the shop.

With his brown bag filled with his purchases in hand, something from across the sun-soaked street caught Aiden's eye. He stopped in his tracks and stared. Puzzlement marked David's tanned face.

"What's wrong?" the boy asked, squinting into the sun.

Still peering across the street, Aiden handed David his bag with the candy sticks, magazines, and his pop, along with the two pretty pen sets he'd bought on impulse by the checkout station for Elisabeth and Grace. "Here, take this for me. I'll be along in a minute."

"Where you going?"

"Don't worry, I won't be long."

Leaving behind a perplexed David, Aiden crossed the street and bee-lined for what had captured his attention. He stood before the town's sole newspaper office, *The Henry Blade*, and tilted his head in contemplation. A small sign hanging in the window read: "Reporter Wanted." Tentatively, he walked inside.

Forty-five minutes later, Aiden stepped outside the *Blade* office, happy to watch his new boss, Kevin Hassler, strip the "Reporter Wanted" sign from the window. Unable to curb his enthusiasm, he picked up his pace and jogged to the Schrock's shop. He barely noticed the increased number of midweek tourists strolling the sidewalks, licking ice cream cones or window shopping, as he sidestepped them.

Mark was back at the computer desk when Aiden bounced into the shop. The brass chimes clanked from his swinging open the door with so much enthusiasm. Mark looked up from the monitor and ogled him. David, sucking on a candy stick that smelled like sour apples, also eyed him, his forehead full of inquisitive wrinkles.

"Meet the newest Henry resident." Aiden grinned, his arms raised in an embellished display of showmanship.

Daniel, cleaning up their lunch wrappers, froze in mid-motion. The balled-up aluminum foil he was about to toss into a receptacle by the desk dropped from his still hand and rolled by his feet. As if completely stupefied, he gaped at the beaming Englishman.

Chapter NINE

THURSDAY afternoon at the Schrock farm, Daniel and Samuel helped the horse auction agent unload the buggy shaft and the mare Daniel had won on Tuesday. Hesitant to leave the trailer at first, the glossy black mare named Gertrude seemed happy once she was in her stall, almost spotless from the rigorous scrubbing Aiden, David, and Grace had given it earlier that morning. Fresh hay and water awaited the horse, along with two crisp McIntosh apples handfed by Moriah and Leah to make her feel more welcome.

Surrounded by her new environs, Gertrude flicked her ears and nuzzled the hay around her as if to make things more customized. The other buggy horses sniffed and snorted at the new arrival from their stalls. Gertrude seemed little interested in whether her new roommates approved of her or not. As usual, the Belgians paid no mind to the diminutive standardbreds. They stood in their nearby stalls, as placid as statues.

Daniel, gazing at the bright-eyed mare, was certain he had picked a fine one. Her legs were sturdy and tight, her shoulders and quarters rippled with muscles, her ears flexed alert. Her muzzle was dark so Daniel wouldn't have to worry about her getting sunburned. Dexter often needed sunblock spread over his pink nose before long trips. No doubt Gertrude would make a healthy horse, capable of pulling heavy loads and going long distances without any difficulty. Samuel agreed. Nodding as he circled the mare, he told Daniel he was pleased with his purchase.

"Da gaul is goot," he said.

Yes, Daniel had picked a good horse, a fine replacement for Dexter. Gertrude would make for a nice addition to their small parcel of earth in Frederick County, Illinois.

But would Aiden Cermak? How would he fit into their tiny rural community?

As Daniel and his father piled more hay near Gertrude, Daniel worried that Aiden's moving to Henry was a disaster in search of victims, much like that March tornado that took his wife and son and three others. What had he been thinking when he'd walked into Kevin Hassler's newspaper office and applied for that job? Did a city boy like him really think he belonged in Henry?

Aiden was currently at the *Blade* office to prove himself to Kevin. Daniel was not surprised. Aiden had a fortitude even some Amish lacked. He'd helped David and Grace all morning with getting the stalls cleaned and ready for Gertrude, a not so pleasant job. And while Grace and David had complained as usual about the grimy, stinky work, Aiden had seemed to savor it. He'd even done something that Daniel had never seen an Englishman do before—he had hand-washed the largest of their three family buggies, all without anyone suggesting it. Smiling in that adorable way of his, he'd said a new horse must have a spotless buggy to lead.

After washing up from his chores, he had let Mark drive him to the *Blade* in his rental car. In a little over an hour, his rumspringa brother would pick him up. Aiden's silver Ford Focus rental looked peculiar parked in their gravel driveway, surrounded by their simple Amish farm. Much the same way Aiden would stand out in Henry, Daniel mulled.

By now he was probably more familiar with how the *Blade* operated than Kevin. Always giving his best. He was sure he'd make a better reporter than a farmhand, though. It didn't take much coordination to ask questions and take notes.

A jostling ride of emotions flustered Daniel. Thrills, then dread, filled his head thinking about Aiden's moving. Worse, Aiden would be working almost right across the street from the furniture shop, where Daniel would be spending his summer, at least twice a week. Daniel would have to find some way to avoid running into him if he were to have any peace of mind.

The others were delighted with news of Aiden's moving to Henry. Last night during supper, the large oak table had pulsated with vigor and excitement as Aiden told them about his new job. The sturdy bowls of food were passed around as if floating on air. Mark and David had been quick to volunteer to help unload Aiden's moving truck once he returned from Chicago, although Aiden had assured them he didn't have much to move. Rachel had offered to let Aiden stay with them until he found a place of his own. Samuel had said he would keep his ears and eyes open for any houses up for rent in town.

How strange the turn of events.

God had placed the Englisher in their path Church Sunday, and now, apparently, He wanted him to remain in their lives a great deal longer. But what for? How many more tests from da Hah did Daniel need to pass before proving his worthiness?

The stench of livestock was thick in the warm barn. Daniel did not mind. The farm was one of the few constants in his life that seemed right. Everything else in his world was nothing but confusion and heartache.

Samuel looked to his son. Worry lines pinched between his nose. He let go the mare's back left leg after inspecting her fetlocks and cleats and said, "You okay, Daniel? You seem burdened with something."

"Ach." Daniel shook his head with a slight smile. "I'm goot. Just want to make sure the new horse is to be okay here, that's all."

"Don't worry about that." Samuel chuckled, patting Gertrude's powerful hindquarters. "She has a new home fit for a queen, for sure. She'll be right happy here, no worries about that."

Daniel nodded. Keeping himself busy, he retrieved a curry brush from a bin outside the stall and slipped the strap over his hand. He returned to Gertrude and brushed her fine black hair. No worries? Maybe no worries for Gertrude, but there were plenty of worries jarring Daniel's life. At the moment he supposed it was all out of his hands. What was there to do?

FOR Aiden, there was no question what there was to do. After he telephoned Mark from his new desk at the *Blade* to tell him he didn't need a lift home after all (he'd also loaned Mark his Motorola, with Rachel and Samuel's permission), he went through a mental list of all that he needed to accomplish in the next few weeks. Indeed, the list was long.

Most importantly, he needed to find a place to live. Henry had no plethora of apartments, and he wasn't interested in renting a bedroom from a homeowner, as Kevin had suggested. That would not do. He'd prowled around town after Mark had dropped him off, scouting for "for rent" signs in front of houses. He saw two "for sale" signs, but nothing else.

There was hardly anything suitable on the Internet search engines either. Frustrated, he had perused the latest edition of *The Henry Blade*'s classifieds section and found two apartments for rent in Unity, a larger town off I-57 about fifteen miles east. The idea of apartment living in a rural community revolted Aiden.

He wanted to stay as close to work as possible. As close to Daniel? Besides, who needed to deal with a commute in a small rural community? He was leaving Chicago and all that nonsense behind.

Rachel had been kind to let him stay on. But Aiden worried about keeping Daniel from his own room. He would try his hardest to find a place of his own before returning from Chicago, so he would no longer be a burden on the family. With luck, Samuel or Kevin would come up with something before he returned.

And he must finish that article for *Midwestern Life*, the sole purpose for his being in Amish Country. If not for that, all of this newness and excitement would never have happened. He could use the money earned from it, as scant as that was. A couple thousand dollars might mitigate his first several months' rent for one of those amiable Henry bungalows he'd already fallen in love with, especially now that his salary was nearly cut in half.

He would be as busy as a nesting bird the next few weeks, but he rode on adrenaline.

"You ready, young man?" Aiden's new boss stood on the other side of Aiden's spiffy desk, cleaned from all the clutter. Keys in hand and a grin on his round face, Kevin Hassler had offered to drive Aiden home—but Aiden knew Kevin's motives derived from more than selfless generosity.

"Mark didn't sound too happy when I told him you were giving me a lift," Aiden said, putting on his Amish straw hat outside as Kevin locked up the office. Before heading out to the *Blade* that afternoon, Aiden had decided to wear Mark's old Amish clothes to please Rachel. Yesterday he'd gotten the impression, from the way she'd scanned him in his English clothes, that she had disapproved. Kevin had laughed when he saw his new ace reporter saunter into the office looking like one of his Amish neighbors. Aiden did not mind. He liked being mistaken for Amish.

"Probably not such a good idea to let him drive a rental car without you being with him," Kevin said, leading the way to his Buick, parked along Ivy Street. "Besides, giving you a ride home gives me a good excuse to get out to the Schrock farm and get some interviews for the *Blade*."

Aiden had conceded that the community would appreciate reading more about "the Jonesboro incident;" he just wished he was not part of it. But to refuse his boss, even before he officially started his job, had seemed unwise. While talking with Mark on the phone earlier, he'd made sure to get Samuel's permission to bring Kevin home.

Even before Aiden had stepped foot inside his office yesterday afternoon inquiring about the reporter's job, Kevin said he had planned all along to interview the Schrocks and Aiden. Kevin Hassler, the town's sole newspaper editor, had known all about Sunday's crash. It took him a mere few minutes to figure out who Aiden was. He declared it a true Divine providence, Aiden's walking into his office. A lot coming from a non-churchgoer like him, he joked during their impromptu interview.

Aiden liked his new boss. They hit it off like a reunited father and son. His receding hairline, thick glasses, and short stature made Kevin seem more like an amiable middle-aged man, rather than the hardened newshound that he was. When Aiden strolled into the cluttered two-desk office yesterday, grinning so confidently, there was little doubt the job was his. Aiden hadn't even needed to highlight his experience as a freelancer and reporter for his college newspaper; going "undercover" as an Amish man impressed Kevin enough. He said it showed "true journalistic spirit." His knowledge of German in a largely German-speaking community further made Aiden ideal.

Still, the tough-minded newspaperman was skeptical that a young man like Aiden would seek to give up life in the glamorous city for a small town. Aiden had to do some persuading. Being something of a square, Aiden could live without glittery nightclubs and theaters that showed foreign films. Besides, Henry wasn't such a Spartan town. There was a bookstore and a few cafes, diners, and bakeries, about half of them run by the Amish, which added to their charm. Driving through town yesterday, he remembered spotting a small art gallery and a community theater. Per capita, there were probably more places to patronize in Henry, Illinois than in Chicago. If Kevin still doubted his sincerity, he kept it to himself. He seemed happy to have Aiden on board.

On their way to the Schrock's, Aiden stared at the vast farmland. Henry was far from his dreams of life in a cabin nestled in the mountains of Montana, but it would make a good concession until his dreams could be realized. The area was quaint, a bit rustic even, a perfect fit for a "square" like him.

He was not fibbing when he'd told Kevin during their interview that he really did like the idea of moving to a rural community. Who would make up such a story for a mere thirty-two thousand dollars a year with no benefits? Aiden was used to no employer-provided benefits, and he earned roughly twice as much as a freelancer, but he figured in a small town like Henry, such a paltry paycheck would go far, much farther than his went in Chicago. While working at the paper, he figured he would continue to accept freelance assignments now and then to supplement his income.

The crunch of gravel under the wheels of Kevin's sturdy Buick grabbed everyone's attention when he pulled into the Schrock's driveway. Samuel, who was on the other side of the barn, popped around the corner. Grace peered out the kitchen window. The other children poured out from all parts of the property to greet Aiden as if he'd been gone for weeks, surrounding the Buick the same way they had when Mark pulled the Focus into the driveway with Aiden yesterday. They never seemed to tire of all the excitement. Mark, hands in pants pockets, strolled from the woodshop.

Out front there was a cauldron of commotion. Two English vehicles parked side by side, barefoot children running about, giggling and shouting.

Daniel was out front too. He was hitching Gertrude to the buggy Aiden had washed and polished.

"Going somewhere?" Aiden asked after he straightened out of Kevin's car. He tickled little Leah, held snug by Moriah, under her soft chin.

"I promised to take the kinner for a ride with the new horse before supper," Daniel said in his typical flat tone, strapping the trace to Gertrude's collar.

"Great, they delivered her." Aiden ambled up to the mare and stroked her long, black, shiny muzzle. "She's prettier than I remember."

"She's a good horse." Daniel tightened the straps. "I can see she'll be a hard worker for us."

"Do you mind if I come along with you? I've never been in an actual buggy before, only your wagon."

Daniel shook his head, his mouth taut. "Nay, you can come."

While the children buzzed about a drive with the new buggy horse, Mark wanted only to give Aiden's rental car another spin. Aiden promised to let him drive him around when the after-supper chores were done. The younger children also wanted to come. They wanted to check just how good an English driver their older bruder made.

Mark handed Aiden his cell phone. "You got a text message. I didn't read it, thought it might be personal."

Aiden glanced at the message. It was from Conrad. He had not heard from his ex-boyfriend in two years. The message was short. *This you Aiden? Call me. Conrad.*

His name no longer appeared after "sent from." Aiden had deleted his number from his address list a year ago. He'd heard through the gay community's gossip channels that Conrad had been living back home in Michigan with his new boyfriend. What could he want now, after all this time?

KEVIN stayed behind with Samuel to interview him about Sunday's incident. Rachel and Elisabeth were out, but everyone had assured Kevin they'd be home shortly. The rest climbed into the family buggy. Grace, Moriah, Mark, and David ran their hands over the smooth wooden interior and leather seats, impressed that Aiden had had the initiative to clean even the inside.

"It's real nice," Grace whispered. The strings from her white kapp brushed against her cape bib as she gazed around.

"Smells nice too," David said.

Daniel also thought it was all very nice, but refrained from saying so.

Rather than go to the pond like Moriah and Leah wanted, Daniel decided to drive Gertrude along the roads, to familiarize her with the routes she would be taking on a regular basis. She was smart, he could tell, and he sensed that in no time she would be able to find her way along the usual tracks with little prompting from her drivers. Dexter had been good at that. Daniel recalled one autumn when he was twenty, coming home after working long hours at the sawmill, when he had awakened, startled, to find himself stretched out on the front seat of the buggy, parked in his family's driveway. Dexter, still hitched to the buggy, had stood like a sculpture, waiting to be led to the barn. The shrewd gelding had found his way home all on his own while Daniel had slept

Dexter had proved to be a faithful friend in a horse, the one he'd always gone to when he needed to drive anywhere. Gertruce would prove just as loyal. There weren't that many good friends he had anymore, horse or human, not since his marrying Esther. Two of his childhood friends had moved with their wives to Amish districts in Missouri, where land was cheaper. Another had left for rumspringa to New York City and never returned. He had found glitz more enticing than manure. Last Daniel had heard he was dating a fashion model.

And Aiden? He glanced at him, sitting on the other end of the seat with Leah on his lap, David between them. Both were smiling at the passing corn and soybean fields bronzed by a late afternoon sun. Aiden pointed out two white-tailed deer trotting through a soybean field and little Leah, once spotting them, slapped her hand over her mouth to muffle her giggles. Was Aiden a friend Daniel could count on? So far he proved to be a good person. It was sweet of him to have bought him that baseball magazine, even if he already did have the same issue, and his siblings those other gifts from the IGA… and to have washed the buggy so finely. The way he coddled little Leah also nuzzled his heart.

But what did it matter? What good could come of a friendship between them? One being Amish and the other English was enough of an obstacle, but that was a mere trifling compared with the other issues. Nothing but trouble could come from Daniel and him getting any closer.

Best he avoid the Englishman as much as possible once he moved to town. If Aiden stopped by the shop or the farm, he would be polite, but nothing more. Daniel had no problem being firm when he needed to be. He did not have to be too cold to emphasize his points. In this case, that he and Aiden were strictly acquaintances, nothing more.

His family had expressed their gratitude in many ways for his veering his car in front of Bobby Jonesboro. There was no reason for any of them to do more. So what if he even chose to move right next door to them? Daniel would have little if anything to do with him. There were plenty of people in the community he rarely interacted with. Small as the county was, he wasn't friends with everyone. He didn't need to be friends with Aiden, either.

Chapter TEN

BEFORE Aiden knew it, he was backing his sixteen-foot U-Haul into the driveway of his new two-bedroom, one-bath 1920s bungalow. Nestled among sycamores and elms on a small corner lot on the southwestern edge of Henry, the house looked as if it were waiting to be occupied by none other than Aiden.

Kevin had found the single-story bungalow just in time, a mere four days before Aiden left Chicago. The owner, a widow retired in Alabama, was looking to sell, but after sixteen months on the market she'd agreed to rent it at $450, month to month. According to Kevin, she hoped Aiden might want to eventually buy. When Kevin had called with the news, Aiden had said yes to the house sight unseen. A few hours later, he'd read through, signed, and returned the facsimile of the lease agreement the homeowner's realtor had expeditiously sent him, and the house was his.

Looking at the squat white house with robin's-egg blue shutters, he was certain Kevin had made a decent find. He remembered seeing the house when he had walked the tree-lined streets looking for rentals. He had liked it then. How perfect things sometimes worked out.

The house was a bit shabby, especially the lawn, which showed bare spots skirting the trees, but Aiden was unfazed. The thought of having outdoor space to spruce up appealed to him. The past few years living in the city, he had missed having a lawn to care for, outdoor work to hone his muscles instead of needing to go to a gym. Compared to his 650-square-foot studio, which he'd been renting at $930 per month, the bungalow was a palatial bargain. Best of all, he was a short two-minute drive straight up Ivy Street to the *Blade* office.

He found the set of house keys where the realtor had said she would leave them, behind a juniper shrub by the front door. Peering around inside, he fell in love. It was a perfect fit. All 1,200 square feet of it. He didn't even mind the 1970s color scheme, or the wood paneling in the small dining area. Already the bungalow fit him like one of his well-worn fleece hoodies. Raddled, but warm and comfy.

Reading through the original copy of the lease agreement the realtor had left for him on the kitchen counter, he wondered if he should have bought the house. At $125,000, which, after living in Chicago, was a giveaway, it was definitely something for him to consider. But even at that low price, Aiden could not just fy buying without knowing if he would be staying in Henry long term. The house had been difficult for the owner to unload; Aiden did not want to be stuck with it either. He still had his sights set on that rustic cabin in the mountains of Montana.

He had subleased his studio apartment to a young woman from Oshkosh, Wisconsin, for $800 a month. He took care of all the other particulars, as well. Once he learned of his new address, he notified the post office, all his utility companies, and important correspondents. He even filled out the official "accident report" with the State of Illinois to have Bobby Jonesboro's insurance company reimburse him for the used car he'd ordered from one of those online auto traders, shipped to a dealer in Unity for him to pick up.

Most importantly, he had finished writing his article, enthusiastically accepted by *Midwestern Life* for its November issue. To keep the article short and tight, he focused on the "green" angle, since the media liked that sort of thing. He highlighted how eco-friendly the Amish were, from their use of wind energy to their driving horse-drawn buggies.

Although he fought back a few tears as he drove his U-Haul south on I-57, leaving behind the few friends he'd made and even his tiny studio, which, during the past two years, had become his refuge, he was glad to let Chicago fade into his memory. Leaving Chicago would put

Conrad firmly into the past. He even deleted the text message that Conrad had sent him a few weeks before, without responding. That part of his life was over. The future stretched as wide and expectant as the flat, unbending roads of central Illinois.

He stared at the U-Haul parked in his driveway. Full of all his possessions, the U-Haul symbolized another new beginning. His things had made many trips in his short adult life, from his parents' house to his college apartment, from there to Chicago, and ultimately to Henry, Illinois. In this small town, surrounded by vast farmland and Amish wonder, a new life was opening to him. A fresh promise, like the corn in the field across the road, green and bursting with life, was unfolding to him, holding boundless possibilities.

The clip-clop of horse's hooves on the tree-lined street brought him out of his reverie. He smiled, watching Mark, with David and Grace next to him, steer the wagon into the driveway. They had arrived right on time. He had left a message at the furniture shop two days ago, letting them know when he expected to get back into town, so they could help him unload. His smile faded when he noticed Daniel was not with them.

"Where's Daniel?" he asked Mark, acting nonchalant.

"He's at the farm, choring," Mark said. "He's been choring from sunup to bedtime lately. Only stops to take lunch and supper."

"I guess that's a good thing," Aiden said, lowering his eyes to the blacktop driveway.

"When I grow up I want to live in town in a house just like this," David said as he stood on the front lawn taking in the bungalow, his straw hat pushed high up on his head.

"Stop being so shussly," Grace said, rolling her eyes.

"Ach, almost forgot." Mark rooted a box out from the back of the wagon and handed it to Aiden. "These are from Mom and all of us. A housewarming gift."

Aiden steadied the box on the rear bumper of the U-Haul and dug through it. Inside were eight four-ounce jars of Rachel's homemade goods. Corn relish, strawberry jam, and four jars of Aiden's favorite homemade Amish peanut butter. Rachel's hand-printed labels kindled his cheeks: "A gift for Aiden, who is a gift from God."

A few short hours later, Aiden and his crew had almost all his things—TV, kitchenware, bedroom and living room furniture, boxes, backpacking gear, and the office equipment he used for his freelance work—unloaded and placed about his new home. Where to put everything became simple, as the house was small.

The unloading went quicker than anticipated, for two of Aiden's new neighbors had strolled from their homes to introduce themselves and lend a hand. Both were retired-age men, yet strong and useful and unafraid of lifting heavy boxes and cumbersome furniture Aiden was glad to have met some of his neighbors and to find them obliging. An hour later, Frank Burger and Lyle Keating said their goodbyes and left Aiden and the children to unload the smaller items.

The last of his things carried into the house, Aiden realized that he'd just begun to settle in. Sorting everything would be the most difficult part. For now, he needed to return the U-Haul and pick up the used car he'd ordered online before the auto dealer in Unity closed.

Mark, eager to drive the U-Haul and to check out Aiden's new car, insisted he come along. He too had been shopping for cars for his big trip to the Texas shore in December and thought himself a semi-expert. Aiden offered to take all the kinner and treat them to supper as a reward for their hard work.

Adelaide, the children said, would be happy with the bucket of water Aiden had given her and some hay the Schrocks had stowed in the back of the wagon until they returned.

A straight shot into Unity, Mark navigated the bulky U-Haul like a master while Grace and David egged him on. He handled the machine as well as Aiden had on the one hundred seventy-five miles from Chicago. They went to the auto dealer to pick up Aiden's car, a spiffy 2005 Chevrolet Aveo, nearly the identical color of the light-blue shutters on his new bungalow. Aiden drove the U-Haul to the rental office as Mark followed behind in the new car. The Schrock kids wanted to eat Mexican, so Aiden let Mark drive them to their favorite taqueria for a much-deserved meal. They laughed and chatted while eating, yet Aiden's laughter lacked its usual cheeriness. He was still disappointed Daniel had not come along.

BACK at the Schrock farm, Daniel tensed as his father walked up to him, where he labored by the buggy shed. He had been choring harder and longer the past few weeks than was usual, and expected his father would eventually question him. His latest project: replacing the ratchet on the reel of the old McCormick, normally a two-man job.

"You chore diligently, almost too diligently, as if you're hiding in it," Samuel said, stroking his graying beard.

Daniel, stiffening on his haunches, tried to keep his attention on his work. "Choring's got to get done." He sighed. "Why put it off?"

Samuel remained silent a moment. "You can't suffer forever the loss of Esther and Zachariah, Daniel," he said, lifting his bearded chin. "God has given you many other things to be thankful for. Too much grieving is selfish."

"I'm okay, really. I'm just trying to get needed work done, that's all."

"Don't use choring as an excuse to hide," Samuel reasserted, using his fatherly tone. "Things are hard for you, I know, but the Scriptures don't avow the virtue of hard work just for a means to hide from our troubles."

"I'm not hiding."

"Then you're using the sweat from your choring as an anointing to cleanse yourself of something?"

Daniel suppressed a shudder. Tightening a screw with three firm yanks of a wrench, he squared his shoulders and said, "We don't believe in anointings."

"Ach, there have been some."

A moment more of heavy silence, then Samuel said, "You're courting Tara now, ya?"

"We're not courting."

"But you drove her home from church last Sunday. Your mom was happy to see it. I have to say, I was too. It's good that you're starting to date."

"It was only one drive home; I wouldn't call it a date." But Daniel knew that, in his old-fashioned community, offering a girl a ride home from church meant more than a friendly gesture. Often it was the first step to courting. When an Amish man drives a maydel home in his carriage on Church Sunday, the community talk has them practically married in no time.

Tara Hostetler would probably relish such talk. She'd had an infatuation with Daniel for as long as he could remember. She was five years younger than he, but that never seemed to bother Tara, mature beyond her years. Everyone knew she was strong-minded. The middle daughter of eleven siblings, she was the type who knew how to get what she wanted and never look back.

Daniel was eighteen when he had first noticed the determined adolescent gawking at him in church. Although he had shrugged off her flirting as just a girlish crush, one of many he'd tolerated from the girls in the community, her gazes through the years never lessened. With his tall frame and sharp handsome looks, Daniel had always been the object of coy glances and muffled giggles. Yet his stubborn aloofness kept the other maydels at bay. Not Tara.

As she grew older and bolder, she would follow him around the singings and other youth gatherings like a fox, peering at him from behind trees or over the rims of her punch cups. Even when he officially courted Esther, she kept him in her sights. During his and Esther's short marriage, she of course backed off, but even then he sensed her attraction for him scarcely diminished.

She dated a handful of men in the community, but nothing ever came of their brief courtships. Once a man she'd been corresponding with in Iowa traveled to Illinois just to meet her, but that, too failed to take root. Since no man was ever good enough for her, the community assumed, even at twenty, she was destined to become an old maid.

Independent of mind and spirit, Tara never seemed to worry over the label. She always held her slender neck sturdy, her pointy nose aloft.

Then in March when Daniel's world collapsed so suddenly, losing his wife and baby son, she refrained from acting like a hawk sweeping down on an unwary field mouse. Daniel appreciated her self-control. In proper modesty, she gave him the appropriate amount of time to mourn.

Last Church Sunday when she glanced at him more often and more penetratingly than usual with her indigo eyes, Daniel knew she decided she'd waited long enough. Shuffling over to her after the sermons, he figured he should make the first overture. Her smile stretched to the brim of her black church bonnet when, after so many years, he offered her a ride home.

"Maybe this weekend you're going out with Tara again? To one of the gatherings?" Samuel grinned tightly, watching his son tinker with the binder. "She likes you, we think. The way she ogles you." He snickered.

"Gatherings are for kinner," Daniel said.

"You should go out with her. It would be good for you, Daniel. You're always by yourself."

"I'm fine; you have nothing to worry over. Now, I really do have to get this reel fixed before the binding tomorrow, don't you think? Or we'll be stuck with a field full of fallow oats."

Daniel felt his father's gray eyes penetrate his hunched form. With a grunt, Samuel got on his knees and grasped the reel. "This is a two-man job," he said with an air of authority. "Let me at least help."

Daniel did not refuse his father's support, or shake off his dependable manner. He appreciated his father's concern. Yet he knew he could not speak with him about relationships, not the way he would have wanted. Not ever. Nonetheless, his father's sage words echoed inside him.

Tilting his straw hat higher on his head to get a glance at his father, Daniel mulled over his advice. Take Tara out again? Even last Sunday, while she had sat so squarely next to him during the carriage ride to her family's farm, the idea had skimmed across his mind. His father's prodding encouraged him to set into motion more quickly, something he'd already considered.

Tara Hostetler wasn't so bad. She was cute in her own way, a woman of first-rate standing in the community. If God wanted him to remain leddich, then why would He have planted her in his life? She'd been nearly stalking him for seven years. The clues were clear. Surely da Hah did not intend for Daniel to spend the rest of his days as a bachelor.

Yes, he would ask her out again. It was the proper thing to do.

Chapter ELEVEN

ONE of the first responsibilities Kevin Hassler had assigned Aiden was to organize the cluttered *Blade* office. The task of sorting through so many boxes, old files, and stacks of newspapers was taking longer than Aiden had expected. With so many past issues of *The Henry Blade* lying about that Kevin wanted stored into some kind of accessible filing system (he insisted on having hard copies along with the computer files), some dating back more than ten years, Aiden found himself reading through each issue. He became absorbed by the stories, as inane as some of them were, as if he were taking a stroll through the past, like thumbing through an old yearbook or photo album.

Convincing himself he was acquainting himself with the newspaper's style, he perused through more and more issues, day after day, eager to take to the boxes whenever his small reporting assignments were complete. So far his reporting duties were meager: covering obscure community events, writing up notices for upcoming festivals or fairs, or waiting for Kevin's police scanner to shriek with anything interesting. Primarily, he was responsible for ensuring all the stories were inputted into the computer's layout template before Tuesday's midnight deadline. Even for a small weekly like the *Blade*, when deadline loomed, commotion seized the two-man office as if it were a major daily. The two deadlines Aiden had worked through, each time Kevin had managed to send the PDF files to the printer in Decatur just in the nick of time.

After two full weeks on the job, Aiden fit in well. At times the reporting work seemed trite, but he was acclimating to the lightness of the stories. Small town fare was interesting in its own way. The stories encompassed a personal scope not always present in larger newspapers, or even the college daily he had worked for in Maryland. He was learning to focus more on the people in his writing, rather than the actual events that surrounded them. Residents of small towns want to read about their neighbors, Kevin had told him, not faceless events.

He tried to heed that advice when considering the press releases that flooded the office floor each day from the fax machine. He spent many hours on his hands and knees, sifting through the curled facsimiles to see if any stories sent by the dozens of public relations firms could be shaped into anything of local interest. Kevin expressed his appreciation for his initiative and ambition. Each morning by eight Aiden was at his desk, and rarely did he leave the office before six. If an assignment lured him from his desk—taking a picture of Mrs. Miller's cow with a spot on its neck the shape of a question mark or interviewing the Henry High School marching band about its upcoming trip to Springfield—he almost always returned for a few hours before heading home, just down the street. He was eager to write up his stories.

And to read through more back issues of the *Blade*.

One evening, working late, he sat cross-legged on the floor before a large box, sorting through some more back issues of the yellowing newspapers and reading a few at a time, when an issue from 2006 caught his attention. On the back was a large ad for a rodeo in Urbana with a half-naked cartoon cowgirl. The provocative ad triggered his memory. Tucking the newspaper into his new chronological order system, he turned to his boss.

"Hey, Kevin...."

Kevin was working at his computer, typing an article into the template using the index finger only method. An old Mr. Coffee machine dripped in the background behind him, sighing and gurgling, filling the tiny utilitarian office with the comforting aroma of brewing coffee. He finished typing what looked like a lengthy sentence before responding. "Yes?"

"What's the deal with that huge X-rated store?" Ever since passing the adult superstore on the way to the horse auction with Daniel a month ago, he had wanted to ask someone about it. Kevin, twice divorced with three grown daughters living in nearby states, was no neophyte when it came to discussing such matters. A hardened newspaperman, Aiden had discovered it took a lot to make him flush.

"You mean the one by the Interstate?"

"Is there more than one?"

Kevin chuckled. "No. That's it."

"How did a place like that get there? I mean, in a community like this?"

"It's a prime location along the Interstate," Kevin said, peering at a handwritten note. Crumpling it and tossing it into the wastebasket, he glanced at Aiden before setting back to his typing. "There's lots of trucker traffic between Chicago and western Kentucky. It's one of the largest employers in the area."

"Really? How long's it been there?" Aiden thumbed through more newspapers, but he kept his ears pricked toward Kevin.

"About twenty years. There was controversy when they first built it, of course. The Southern Baptists organized to have construction halted, but court hearings ruled in favor of the business owners. A few months after it went up, the Southern Baptists got the county to pass a sign restriction, requiring signs to be only so large. I'm sure you noticed the sign of that place."

"How could I miss it? It's taller than some of the silos around here."

"Well, eventually the sign ordinance failed in court too, as you can see."

"What about that billboard, the one with a picture of Jesus looking down on the store?"

Kevin leaned back in his swivel chair, as if taking more interest in the conversation. Cleaning off his thick glasses with his shirt he said, "After losing twice in court, the Southern Baptists decided to work with what they could. They rented the billboard right across the interstate and put up that sign. It's been there ten years now. Rumor was the porn shop owners kicked themselves for not thinking of renting it first. It's all kind of funny, when you think about it."

"It seems strange to me, a place like that being in a community like this. The sign, the store. They stand out like sore thumbs."

"Yeah, well, people have learned to tolerate them over the years, I suppose." Kevin replaced his glasses and leaned back toward his computer. "Us locals don't even notice it anymore. Kinda blends into the background. Most of the tourists coming from Chicago don't use that exit anyway. They get off further north. I figure it's far enough away from the main Amish center here, businesses don't complain. Not much they could do about it anyway. The law wasn't meant to be one-sided."

Aiden was about to say more about the adult superstore when another back issue of the *Blade* grabbed his attention. Eyes and mouth gaping, he folded it in quarters and read through the page-three story.

"Wow, this is something," he said after he finished reading the article.

"What?" Kevin asked, but he seemed to pay only half attention while he typed.

"This story from 2002, about an Amish kid. He killed himself." The newspaper, dry in his hands, fell limp as he lifted it closer to his eyes. He gave it a cursory flex so that it would stand firmer. "He was found hanging in his family's barn. A seventeen-year-old boy named Kyle Yoder."

"Gee, I forgot about that. Pretty much shocked the whole community. First time I ever heard of anything like that happening to an Amish kid, at least around here."

Aiden scanned through the article again. "They never found out why?"

"Does anyone ever know why someone commits suicide?"

"Did you do any investigation into it?"

"Investigation?"

"Yeah, like what might have caused him to do it?"

"This is a small town newspaper; we don't do investigations." Kevin snickered as he uttered the word "investigations." He shook his head. "Besides, like I said, no one would've been able to answer why. The parents couldn't. No one could. Not even his friends. I left it at that. There's not much investigation involved in reporting on gossip, especially when it could hurt people. That's why I ditched Indianapolis."

Aiden concurred. He appreciated his boss's ethics. Too much of the media reported on speculation, he believed, and not enough on concrete facts. Kevin had mentioned lack of ethics as one of the reasons why he'd moved back to Henry, his hometown. He had worked as an editor for a large Indianapolis daily until, after fifteen years, he'd had enough. Conjecture, outright lying, getting too buddy-buddy with local politicians—all had sickened him to the point he'd seldom made it into work each morning without pouring two shots of bourbon into his orange juice. When he'd learned the *Blade* was for sale during a visit back home ten years ago, he'd taken most of his savings, bought the newspaper, and happily resigned from his editorial post in Indianapolis.

Aiden gently slipped the newspaper into his order system, as if to show respect for the poor deceased boy whose short life was summed up in a mere six-paragraph article. And, being Amish, he had not even a photograph to accompany it.

"Weren't you ever curious why he did it?"

"I'm always curious," Kevin said. The blue computer screen reflected in his thick glasses. "That's why I got into the news biz. But that doesn't give me the license to plaster speculation about people's personal lives all over for the whole community to read. For what? Just to sell newspapers? I saw too much of that in Indianapolis. I watched how it ruined people."

"But didn't you ever have any guesses why he might've done it, just offhand?"

Glancing out the window, where the western sky across the street lit up in a blaze of orange and pink from the setting sun, Kevin shrugged and said, "I figured it had to do with a girl."

"A girl?"

"Yeah. Unrequited love. That sort of thing. Why else would a young, good-looking Amish boy kill himself?" After a moment of quiet, he said, matter-of-factly, "He was a relative of the Schrocks, you know."

"Kyle Yoder? A relative of theirs?"

"Yeah. Mrs. Schrock's niece's son or something like that. Most of the Amish are pretty much related to each other one way or another anyway."

"Wow, the Schrocks really have had a lot of tragedies to live through," Aiden whispered.

"You'd think living in a rural community would shield a person from all that stuff, right?" Kevin stood up with a discordant screech of his swivel chair and went to get some coffee. With a full mug in hand, he grinned and moved back to his desk. "Bad news will find you anywhere, even in Amish Country. That's what keeps people like you and me in business."

"I guess so." Aiden, the sides of his mouth turned down in reflection, continued sorting through the newspapers, wondering why a seventeen-year-old Amish boy would want to hang himself.

Chapter TWELVE

DANIEL called Aiden at the *Blade* office several days later from the furniture shop. In the three weeks Aiden had lived in Henry, Daniel had talked to him maybe four times. He noted the surprise in Aiden's voice.

"Daniel? I'm… I'm glad to hear from you."

"We're hosting church this Sunday." Daniel was firm and to the point. "Mom wanted me to invite you."

"Oh? That sounds nice."

"Should I tell her you'll be there?"

"Of course, yes, I'll be there."

"Fine."

"Okay…. See you then."

Daniel hung up the phone and thought about Aiden. He hated thinking about him, but it was hard not to. He was always so considerate, and, well, handsome in his English clothes. The way he looked in his jeans always made his throat swell. He even liked the tone of his voice. It was wrong to think of such things—very wrong. He knew that. The thoughts flowed nonetheless.

Why did that Englishman have to move to Henry?

What was the point in dwelling on it anyway? No way would Aiden want to reciprocate his feelings. Even if he was "one of those," Daniel had dodged Aiden enough to leave him uninterested, he was sure. He figured he should be grateful for that. How much more complicated would his life be if Aiden actually saw him the same way he saw Aiden?

It was best to keep his distance, in any case.

Four times Aiden had had supper with the family since moving, and the one time Daniel had bothered to eat with them, he'd stayed silent. Just like that first supper after Aiden's release from the hospital, Daniel acted as if Aiden were invisible. When Aiden gave the family a printout of his Amish article for *Midwestern Life*, everyone but Daniel expressed enthusiasm. The article was a just portrayal of their community, Daniel thought at the time, but he refrained from complimenting the Englishman. All he mustered was a shrug. And just like last time, he hid out in his woodshop after supper. He was still hiding out when he spied Aiden from the window a few hours later, sleepy and sad looking, twist into his Chevy and pull out of the driveway.

One time Aiden stopped by the family's furniture shop when Daniel and his brothers were working. Daniel insisted he was too busy to chat. He heard Aiden, Mark, and David catch up on things from behind the storeroom's door. He felt like a fool hiding away, but he knew no other way to deal with such awkward emotions.

At the town's Fourth of July celebrations, Daniel kept his distance from Aiden still. Aiden was there taking photographs for *The Henry Blade*, but Daniel saw him mingle with his family and many others in the crowd. After watching the parade pass down Ivy Street, Daniel left to check on Uncle Eldridge at the furniture shop before Aiden could try to talk with him out on the street in front of everyone.

Silent and aloof. This was Daniel's stance whenever in Aiden's presence. Guilt pulled on him for hurting the Englisher's feelings. But he knew his coldness was for the best. For both of them. For however long Aiden lived in Henry (and Daniel was sure it would be short), they both would have to get used to it.

THE smell of beeswax filled the Schrock's home when Aiden entered that Church Sunday. Rachel had put much effort into preparing for the hundreds of fellow worshipers who would be gathering in her home. She and the family must have spent an entire week just dusting, scrubbing, and polishing. Aiden had never seen the mahogany floors so shiny. The windows were so clean he was unable to distinguish the openings from the glass.

Rachel introduced him to a few community members who had yet to make his acquaintance. Talk was hushed and abrupt, for chatting before church was frowned upon. David tugged on the sleeve of his olive sports coat and led him to one of the many benches, transported with the other church accouterments in the community's Church Wagon, parked by the side of the house. He sat with Mark and David as the benches filled. As far as he observed, he was the only Englishman present.

Most of the Schrock's furniture, including Samuel's beloved recliner, had been pushed against the walls and covered with white sheets; the benches were set up in the sitting room, hallway, and even into the kitchen. The males sat on one side of the rooms and the females on the other. Small children of both sexes sat with their mothers or older female siblings.

Aiden squirmed and tensed when the stalwart Daniel, smart looking in his dark dress pants, vest, and crisp white shirt, sat next to him. He took his seat reluctantly, Aiden sensed. David had patted the only available spot, which happened to be between him and Aiden.

Aiden smiled at him in silent greeting, but Daniel's ebony eyes remained fixed near the front door where a lectern and two benches were set up. Aiden assumed this was meant to be the "pulpit." Daniel sat firm and erect. His mouth taut, his hands stiff on his knees. Sweat beads formed on the smooth shaved skin above his upper lip. Aiden did not expect to strike up a conversation with Daniel, since it was considered improper to speak in church, but he would have appreciated at least a nod or even a glance to acknowledge his presence.

When Daniel had telephoned him to invite him to church, Aiden had been honored. But he had not looked forward to another cold shoulder treatment by him. He was unable to grasp why Daniel disliked him so much. Was he uncomfortable in front of all the English? Did he dislike journalists? Or was it something particular about Aiden he loathed? Did Daniel have little doubt he was gay and abhor him for that? He enjoyed his time with the Schrocks. He considered them his second family. Too bad Daniel did not share his feelings.

David whispered to him that upstairs the ministers were meeting in a bedroom. It was customary before each gmay, church gathering, for the ministers to discuss important issues affecting the community in private, usually in one of the host family's bedrooms. Hymnbooks were passed out, and the flock sang in High German while waiting. Their voices, unaccompanied by musical instruments, were droning and low.

At first Aiden hesitated to sing from the *Ausbund*, the Amish hymnal, thinking perhaps it was inappropriate. But as he noticed that even eleven-year-old David sang unabashedly, he joined in, his voice gaining volume along with his confidence. Aiden learned the somber melodies by following the others. He was quick to catch on.

Aiden noticed Daniel stiffen as his voice, rising louder, flowed around him. Daniel clenched onto his knees, his dark eyes unmoving from the pulpit, mostly mouthing the lyrics. Aiden quieted his voice, thinking maybe Daniel was offended by an Englisher singing centuries-old Amish hymns so loudly.

Aiden saw the dark shoes of the ministers come off the last steps of the enclosed staircase. Gradually, the singing stopped. The gmay gently closed the hymnals and placed them in their laps. Aiden followed suit.

The four ministers took their seats on the benches by the lectern. After a moment of self-composure, one minister, clearly the eldest, with a scrappy silver beard hanging to his front pant flap, stepped up to the lectern. Keeping his eyes fixed to his Bible, he began his sermon.

For most of the sermon the old minister's head remained downturned. The one time he lifted his head for a glance at the gathering, Aiden could not help but notice his stabbing blue eyes. They cut into Aiden like blue lasers. When their eyes met, Aiden turned away, embarrassed, almost before the minister did.

That same predictable guilt he experienced while living with the Schrocks poked him. Here he was, at a church gathering surrounded by some of the most ultraorthodox people in the United States, people's whose old-fashioned ways enthralled him, yet he knew he could never share their religious devotion. He felt like a hypocrite.

Attending Baptist services as a boy with his family, he'd also doubted the minister's words, yet he did not recall being troubled with shame. To admire the Amish lifestyle without believing in God was a strange paradox. It was like praising animal rights activists while wearing a baby seal fur coat, direct from the slaughtering grounds of Newfoundland.

Lunch break was a well-received reprieve. He almost jumped to his feet when he noticed the congregation move from the benches. After more than three hours listening to the sermons, much of them spoken in Pennsylvania German (he had related to the toddlers' yaps of displeasure while squirming in their caretakers' laps), he was more than ready to get up off the hard bench.

Most of the men headed toward the backyard, where picnic tables brought in by the Church Wagon had been set up, while the women gathered in the kitchen. Boys and girls leaped about outside, tossing a football someone had found in the barn and running around the field where the oat shocks provided perfect obstacles for chasing each other in circles.

The women served lunch to the men first. Since limited seating meant that not everyone could eat at the same time, the males were split into two groups: married men first, then the teens and single men. Samuel, as a show of honor, insisted Aiden sit with him with the first group of married men. Bologna sandwiches, noodle salad, and pickled beets were piled onto their plates. He noticed that Daniel waited to eat with the second group of teenagers and single men rather than with the older men. Widowers, he was sure, must have the same standing as married men. His choosing to eat apart from Aiden seemed deliberate.

After lunch there was a half hour more of singing, followed by another three hours of sermons, Scripture readings, and silent prayer. Aiden was exhausted by the time it all ended in midafternoon. He leaned against a porch post by the footpath out front and watched as everyone gathered on the Schrock's lawn, waiting for family members to hitch their horses, stabled in the barn or tied to posts. The dozens of buggies were parked along the blacktop lane or in the gravel driveway.

Aiden had never seen so many Amish in one place, other than at the horse auction. He watched, fascinated, the orderly progression of so many people climbing into horse-drawn buggies and carriages.

Next to the Schrock's mailbox, Aiden spotted Daniel, boosting a tall, thin woman into a carriage. Samuel, who had just stepped out of the house, stood next to Aiden and squeezed his shoulder.

"Ach," he said, smiling, his gray eyes twinkling in the afternoon sun. "Daniel is giving Tara another ride home. That's goot."

A strange feeling pushed into Aiden. He shook it off and, after watching Daniel climb into the carriage next to Tara and command Gertrude forward, followed Samuel back into the house to see if he could be of any use loading the benches and other things onto the Church Wagon.

Chapter THIRTEEN

"I NEED your help."

"Where're you calling from?"

"Phone shack down the lane."

"What's wrong?"

"I don't know where Mark is, his bike's gone. I'm worried about him."

"Why?"

"There's been some talk, I'm worried. Can you drive me around to look for him?"

"Of course, but—"

"I don't want the others to know. Meet me at the end of the lane at the corner of County Road 100."

Aiden found Daniel waiting against a wooden fence post, tugging fitfully at his beard, as he pulled his Chevy Aveo to the gravel shoulder. The pale light from the quarter moon showed that he had dressed in a hurry, not even bothering to put on his suspenders or wide-brimmed hat, important parts of Amish identity. Near one in the morning, Aiden thought it unsettling to see an Amish person out so late. Daniel leaped toward his car and opened the passenger door before Aiden could even come to a full stop.

"Daniel, what's going on?"

"It's Mark, the rumspringa. I'm worried he might be into something bad."

"What is it?"

"Let's go, please go back the way you came, then turn right at Highway 11."

Aiden did what Daniel commanded, his mouth taut and his heart pounding in his throat. As they drove down the deserted, darkened lanes, Daniel craned his head from side to side, turning in his seat as if desperate to find something.

Aiden could no longer stand it. "Please, Daniel, tell me what's going on."

Daniel hesitated. "Promise me you won't report on this," he said, keeping his eyes out the window.

"Report? Of course I wouldn't do that. Whatever it is, you can trust me. Just forget that I work at the *Blade*, for once."

"There's been talk... talk of some parties." Daniel massaged his beard, a habit Aiden had become accustomed to whenever Daniel grew anxious. "Bad parties... with the rumspringa and English youth."

"Bad parties?"

"Drugs, drinking."

Aiden gripped the steering wheel tighter.

"Please promise me you won't report on this," Daniel said again, fixing on him now.

"Of course I won't, Daniel." Aiden was flustered that Daniel did not fully trust him at this juncture of their relationship. When Daniel had called him for help, he was more than pleased; it proved that he was viewing him as more than a simple acquaintance. More than some nuisance he tolerated for the sake of his family. He only wished he'd yield more to his trusting side.

Four days had passed since he'd last seen or heard from Daniel. After spying him leaving with that Amish girl, Tara, on Church Sunday, he'd given him a wider berth. He'd wanted to visit the furniture shop, but had talked himself out of crossing the street. Had jealousy held him back? The thought crossed his mind. But he didn't want to believe it. Like Samuel and Rachel, he was happy for Daniel, that he was persevering past the death of his wife and baby son and living his life.

No doubt Daniel's handsome features singed Aiden's cheeks at times, but he wasn't so shallow as to let a man's good looks manipulate him. And he wasn't so stupid as to fall for someone as unobtainable as an Amish man. After his negative experience with Conrad, he was leery about falling for anyone. Sure, he liked Daniel. Who wouldn't, considering all he had lived through? Losing a wife and baby. Such a horrible tragedy. But he harbored deep emotions for all the Schrocks.

He was more than eager to reciprocate Daniel's first real attempt to reach out to him. Now he could show his compassion through friendship and good will, since Daniel had yet to mention his personal losses. He'd been reading in bed when Daniel had telephoned. Snapping his cell phone shut as soon as Daniel had hung up, he'd tossed his silly paperback aside and had scrambled to dress and meet Daniel, just as he'd instructed. Still, he worried that Daniel viewed him as an outsider.

"Don't you think you can trust me by now?" Aiden wanted to lay out his feelings once and for all, to let Daniel know he had no reason to distance himself from him any longer. He spoke in German to emphasize his sentiments. "I am your friend, Daniel. I would never do anything to hurt you or your family. Not in a million years."

CHEEKS burning, Daniel stared through the windshield as the headlighted road disappeared under Aiden's hatchback. He understood about half of Aiden's strange textbook German, but enough to get his point. Aiden was right. It was not fair to treat him like a criminal when he'd done nothing to warrant it. If only Aiden knew the real reason why he always acted so harsh whenever in his company.

He thought back to when he'd last seen Aiden, during the gmay at his family's farm. Aiden's voice had sounded almost angelic when he'd sung from the *Ausbund*. He'd captured both the somberness and joy of the lyrics, as perhaps the original hymn writers, imprisoned for their beliefs five hundred years ago, had felt them. Daniel had stiffened as Aiden's voice caressed him. He had wanted to look at him in admiration, as many of the parishioners furtively were, but he had forcibly kept facing the pulpit, afraid that his tender feelings would be too obvious to all.

He'd promised himself he would avoid Aiden as much as possible, to avoid any gossip from the community; yet, when he'd realized he needed a car to search for Mark, it was Aiden, not his English or Mennonite neighbors or Joe Karpin, whom he'd first thought of to call. He was grateful for Aiden leaving his cell number with the family before he'd left for Chicago, something he had jeered at, at the time. He was suspicious of outsiders by nature, but the truth was, at that moment there were few people in God's creation other than Aiden Cermak whom he could count on.

"I think there may be some illegal drugs going around," Daniel said. "Eli Rupp's son, Milo, was picked up a couple of weeks ago with crystal meth. The police claim he was trying to sell it."

"Yes, I know."

Daniel peered at Aiden. Of course he would know. He was sure Aiden had written an article about Milo Rupp's arrest for *The Henry Blade*. Aiden probably knew more about it than he did. Simultaneously unsettled and relieved, he decided to utilize Aiden's expertise in the matter to its fullest.

"I'm worried Mark might be caught up in it somehow," he said. "The last few weeks he's been staying out far later than is proper. Mom and Dad speak to him, but he says nothing. I'm sure something's going on with him. It's his rumspringa, I know; he's acting different."

"He seemed fine at church on Sunday. He was kind of quiet, but seemed fine."

"I can't explain it, there's something going on, I just know."

"Do his eyes look dilated?"

"Dilated?"

"Are his pupils really big?"

"I don't know. I... I don't remember."

"Does he seem hyper?"

"No, not really. Do you have any idea where these bad parties could be?"

AIDEN ran through the database in his mind. The article he'd written last week about crystal methamphetamine abuse in the Amish community was brief, since he had few facts to support it. Nothing more than a sidebar to accompany his story about Milo Rupp's arrest. Aiden did not want to be one of those journalists who placed assumption above facts to sell newspapers. His boss Kevin held the same principles. He refused to write an article making wide accusations about an entire community because of the arrest of one teenager.

Still, there were certain realities that he could not ignore: that in some cases across the country, rare as they might be, Amish were caught either using or dealing drugs. Those rare incidents had been the premise of his short sidebar. From what he'd gathered in his research, crystal methamphetamine was the drug of choice.

He was surprised to have learned that people in rural areas are more likely to abuse crystal methamphetamine than even those in the inner city. It turned out to be a matter of supply—the chemicals needed to make crystal methamphetamine are common ingredients found in farming fertilizer, and could easily be bought at local hardware and farming stores. Realistically, he supposed some Amish youth, chiefly during their rumspringa, could be tempted to use or sell the drug, although he had no idea how pervasive the practice might be.

"I'm not sure where they have parties," he said, his voice sounding more wavering than he had wanted. "Milo Rupp said that he used to get the drugs from an English farmer over by Hindsdale. But that's all he would say, he never would tell police where exactly, or from who."

"Hindsdale? That's the eastern district."

"Do you want me to drive there?"

"Ya, please." Daniel nodded. "Maybe there's something going on that way tonight."

Aiden hoped there was nothing going on. Hard to imagine Mark Schrock getting involved in anything illegal, like drugs. Undoubtedly the teen was enjoying his running-around time, but Aiden knew that he was as bright a boy as they came, with a firm grasp on commonsense and good values. But if there was trouble, he hoped they found Mark before trouble found him.

Hand over hand, Aiden turned into the direction of the main artery that would take them quickly to the eastern part of Frederick County, or the "eastern district," where a smaller Amish community lived. He'd learned to navigate many of the roads in the area, since his job as a reporter required he sometime drive out to farms and the little villages scattered about the area for interviews and to photograph special events. Strange how just over a month ago he'd gotten lost traveling these same roads, trying to find his way back to Chicago. Now he knew those roads rather well. They weaved past his own house.

They passed I-57—and the notorious adult superstore, its parking lot brightly lit and a quarter full of cars and trucks—and he waited for Daniel to instruct him where to go. Daniel told him to turn right on a gravel lane where he knew most of the Amish lived. Several minutes later, Daniel told him to shut off the headlights and pull over.

"I see some lights flickering in that barn," he said, the veins on his neck like twine.

Without hesitation, Aiden heeded Daniel's instructions. As soon as Aiden stopped the Chevy, Daniel silently got out. Aiden followed him across the gravel lane that glowed like a long gray ribbon in the night.

"What is it?" he whispered, scurrying closer to Daniel's side.

"It's the Lapp farm. I think I saw some lights in their barn. Flashlights or lanterns, maybe, or maybe something else. Mark sometimes hangs out with the Lapp boy, Jeremy. I never trusted him. I seen him smoke cigarettes a few times at the flea market when he thought no one was looking."

"Do you think something's going on in there?"

"Not sure, I don't see any buggies or Mark's bike. Maybe they hid them inside."

"I don't hear any rock music or anything."

"Maybe it's just the two of them. Besides, no Amish would be up this late in their barn, choring, especially not the Lapps. They're faul."

"Faul?"

"They're lazy."

"Do you think the Lapps would be involved in anything illegal? Milo Rupp said that he got the drugs from an English farmer; this is an Amish farm."

Daniel stopped just as they crossed the gravel lane and looked firmly at Aiden. "Now remember, you promised no reporting, you're here with me as a friend. You're not on the job."

"Yes, I promise." Aiden resented how his position as reporter had given Daniel reason to distrust him. Yet a lump filled Aiden's throat. Daniel had referred to him as a friend. His first verbal acknowledgment of their friendship. Aiden's heart fluttered like a chick.

They sidestepped the driveway to avoid the crunch of gravel under their shoes. They walked slowly, yet steadfastly, on the grass toward the barn. With only a quarter moon concealed behind intermittent corncob-shaped black clouds to light their way, Aiden stayed close to Daniel's side. With his sense of sight dulled, the smell of livestock seemed all the stronger. The taste of farmland was thick on his tongue. He was certain he could hear every minute sound too.

A dog barking in the distance gave him a start. Daniel indicated he also heard the barking. Stopping to gauge where the barking was coming from, they decided the dog was far enough off not to worry about and continued toward the barn. There was a rustle closer by. Daniel stopped and held Aiden back by grabbing onto his arm. A frisson of electricity shot through Aiden as the heat transferred from Daniel's large, calloused hand to Aiden's bicep.

"I hear something," Daniel whispered.

"Me too. What do you think it is?"

"Not sure, hope it's not that hound coming to check us out. We shoulda brought something just in case, like a stick."

"I could look for something in the car—"

"No," Daniel said, still in the alert position. "Let's just get this over with, hound or no hound. Besides, I think it's just a field mouse. Sounds like something rustling underneath some straw, can't be too big."

Aiden had faced much larger fears than field mice and overzealous hounds when backpacking in the woods. Lying in his tent at night, he had imagined every creak or rustle to be that of a bear or coyote—or even a psycho. Why would he feel that kind of paranoia now, in the middle of Amish Country?

They continued along the grass, careful to make as little noise as possible. Nearing the barn, Daniel, with Aiden on his heels, made a wide berth, circling the barn like a cat after its prey. The light through the cracks flickered, though there was no sound.

They closed in on the barn; another rustling sound made Aiden's heart leap. This time it came farther to their left, near the house. Daniel scanned for lights or any shadows.

"There's nothing there," he said.

There was a stir inside the barn. Daniel put his ear up against the planks. He listened for a good minute, then peered into a small crevice, but said he was unable to see anything. Standing erect, he brought his finger to his lips to insist that any questions Aiden had be deferred, and motioned for him to follow.

They skulked the length of the barn. Daniel used his hands to feel for the front as Aiden held on to his sleeve. As they neared the swing door, Aiden heard something from inside. It might be a horse or a cow, he tried to allay his fears, or any number of farm animals or rodents that live inside barns.

"Do you hear that?" Aiden whispered.

"Shhh." Daniel glanced at Aiden and nodded, indicating that he too heard the same strange noise.

Hearing the noise grow louder—it sounded like a combination of humming and heavy breathing—Aiden stopped and pulled at Daniel to stop him from going farther. But Daniel gently pushed him off. His arms stiffened by his sides and his hands clenched into tight fists. He inhaled, as if forcing all his strength into his body's core. Standing in front of the barn door now, he gestured for Aiden to stand back. With one swift motion, he kicked open the swing door and hollered in Pennsylvania German to startle whoever was inside.

The sniveling of a little boy caught Aiden and Daniel unprepared. The shaking boy's gas lantern swung in his small hand from when he had jumped up in alarm, casting eerie, oscillating shadows about the barn. With tears streaming down his round face, the boy begged Daniel for mercy.

Aiden and Daniel looked down at the boy, speechless. A diminutive lamb, feeble and unmoved by the commotion, lay next to the boy's bare feet.

"It's little Danny Lapp," Daniel said to Aiden, his eyes wide in distress.

"I… I was just… looking after my lamb," Danny sniveled. "He's sick… and I didn't want to leave him alone. Please… please don't hurt us." The little boy, so distraught over his helpless lamb, said between sniffles that he had snuck out of his home to sleep with it in the barn. He was rewarded for his compassion by Daniel's bursting in.

Daniel was clearly appalled by his frightening a poor little boy caring for a sick lamb. Aiden stepped in and soothed Danny.

"It's okay," he said, squatting next to the quivering and weeping boy. "We were worried about you. Your dad was wondering where you were and he wanted us to find you. We thought you were a thief, we didn't mean to scare you." Under the circumstances, using his reporter's skills to fudge his way out of such a predicament seemed appropriate, if only to mollify Daniel.

"We were worried about you," Aiden repeated, his arm on the boy's trembling shoulders. "And your little lamb."

Kneeling next to him, Daniel draped his arm around the shaking boy. With his free hand he patted the small lamb, too sick to stir from the ruckus.

"Go back to what you were doing, Danny," Daniel murmured, his fingers entwined in the lamb's fleece. "Go on, go lay down with your little lamb, everything's okay now."

AS THEY made their way back to Aiden's hatchback, disgusted by how they had frightened poor little Danny Lapp, the beam of a flashlight fanned across the front yard, followed by a man's gruff voice bellowing into the dark night: "Weir is datt? Who's out there?"

They scurried for Aiden's car and drove off just as the beam from the flashlight struck the back of the hatchback. Daniel was almost on the verge of relief when it occurred to him that Mark was still missing.

Despondent, Daniel said, "You might as well drop me home. I can have a talk with that Mark once I see him. He'll get an earful from me, for sure. What a mess. Look what he had me end up doing. It's all boogered!"

They were heading home in gloomy silence, passing under the I-57 bridge and approaching the one business that was illuminated at such a late hour for a farming community on a Thursday night, when Daniel, against his better judgment, practically yanked Aiden out of his seatbelt.

"There's Mark! He's getting onto his bike! Hurry! Pull over there! There he is!"

Mark and another youth had just climbed onto their bicycles and were peddling frantically from the adult superstore's parking lot when

Aiden pulled alongside them on the shoulder. They both fell off their bicycles and tumbled down a grassy ravine by a thin stretch of woods. Daniel jumped out of the Chevy and leaped for his brother.

He grabbed him up by his shirt and looked at him hard. Mark's companion was on his backside, scurrying backward like a crab toward the trees for safety. Both boys were wearing popular-styled jeans and T-shirts. Daniel recognized Mark's companion as a local English boy about Mark's age whom Mark often spent time with during his rumspringa.

"What were you doing in there?" Daniel demanded, still holding him by his collar, but refraining from doing anything more violent. "Mom would be sick if she knew about this." He shot a glare toward the other boy, who was trying to retreat into the woods. "And you, you get over here. Your mom would be sick too, if she knew about you, Alex Stadler."

"Go easy, man," Alex pleaded. "It's no big deal."

Tears spilled from Mark's eyes and he looked ready to pass out from the discovery. "It's not what you think," he said, shaking. "Honest, it's not."

By now Aiden had gotten out of the car and was looking down into the ravine where Daniel and the boys were sprawled. Daniel made sure to check his temper, if only for Aiden's sake.

"Is this what you think rumspringa is about?" Daniel pulled Mark to his feet by his shirt as if he were weightless and glared at him with burning eyes. Spittle trickled from the sides of his mouth and down his beard. "Is this it?"

"Daniel, please," Mark said. "It's not what it looks like, honest. Please, let me explain."

Daniel eased off just a bit.

"All right," he said, his voice still scathing. "Go ahead; I'd like to hear what you can come up with."

Mark straightened his shirt after Daniel released him, and confessed that he and Alex had been at the adult superstore, but not as patrons. They were employees. They began working there a few weeks ago to earn extra money. He rode his bicycle and wore English clothes so as not to scare away patrons or attract the attention of those in the Amish community. Alex was able to drive them on some nights, but he wasn't always able to borrow his mother's car. Mark insisted that he did not even look at any of the adult-oriented material, and that most of it disgusted him. The reason he took the job was because of the large salary: sixteen dollars an hour. And since the furniture shop was bringing in less money than it used to, he needed some way to earn cash for his big road trip to the Texas shore in December.

"You think that's an excuse?" Daniel's eyes burned like coals. "Working at a place like that for a worthless trip?"

"But, Daniel—"

"Get in the car!" Daniel pushed Mark into the backseat. He grabbed for the trembling Alex and nudged him in after Mark. "Help me with these bikes." Daniel and Aiden managed to fit the two bicycles into the back of the small hatchback, Daniel unconcerned whether he damaged them.

The drive to Alex Stadler's home on the western edge of Henry was fraught with penetrating silences mixed with piercing lectures. They dropped off Alex and his bicycle with a final warning from Daniel (and a hesitant promise not to say anything to Alex s mother) and then headed for the Schrock farm. Once at the bottom of the Schrock's driveway, Daniel ordered Mark out of the car and to wait for him by the barn. Daniel sat wordless in Aiden's car a moment, not moving.

"Hope you don't think all us Amish are this crazy," he said, gazing through the darkened windshield.

"No." Aiden said. "I just think you're human, like the rest of us. Didn't you say that once yourself?"

Daniel turned to look at Aiden. He wondered how so much warmth could flow through his veins after such a tumultuous night. But as he looked into the compassionate honey-brown eyes of the Englishman, he reckoned that perhaps now was the perfect moment after all. He placed his large hand on Aiden's shoulder.

"Thanks for driving me around," he said. His mouth was taut, but his insides were warm with affection.

"Anytime," Aiden said. "That's what friends are for."

AIDEN watched Daniel walk toward the barn where Mark waited (even in the dark Aiden could see Mark's silhouette shaking). Then he pulled away and left them privacy. Driving back to his bungalow along the dim back lanes, he still felt the heat on his shoulder from Daniel's touch. It was the first genuine physical gesture of friendship Daniel had shown him. He relished the sensation.

Chapter FOURTEEN

"YOU like Aiden Cermak now, don't you?" David said to Daniel at the furniture shop a few weeks after Aiden and Daniel had found Mark sneaking out of the adult superstore.

Daniel rolled his eyes while he sat at the back desk, trying to focus on tallying the few sales receipts they had from that week so far. "Mind your business, won't you?" He shook his head, annoyed.

"He comes by here for lunch a lot and you talk to him more."

"I don't talk to him much," Daniel grumbled.

Yet, in fact, Daniel had seen more of Aiden Cermak since that crazy Thursday night than he cared to admit. If they weren't popping across Ivy Street, lunching with each other on the days Daniel manned the shop, as David had pointed out, Daniel often drove Gertrude to Aiden's bungalow in the evenings and on weekends, after he finished his chores.

Daniel had wound up at Aiden's front door stoop more often than he thought he should have, as if he'd been pulled by an invisible lead. He found it difficult to fend off the mounting desire to be near Aiden. He wanted to sit near him, to talk with him, to look at him.

There was no denying their search for Mark had cemented a bond between them. Vulnerabilities had been exposed. They had openly declared each other a friend. Though Daniel wouldn't say their burgeoning relationship was without sudden setbacks (he sometimes slipped into his old aloofness), he understood it was impossible to go back to the way things were.

They never spoke about their search for Mark, although once in passing Daniel had mentioned that Mark had quit his job with the adult superstore. He had figured Aiden would want to know. When Aiden had reassured Daniel that at least Mark hadn't been involved in the drugs like Daniel had feared, Daniel had marveled at his wise thinking. So many clever perspectives this Englishman had. He had wanted to flatter him, but the words had lodged heavy in his mouth.

Samuel and Rachel had suspicions something had gone on with Mark, but Daniel had promised Mark to keep the entire episode between them. Aiden had also promised to keep quiet. Daniel and Aiden sharing a secret further strengthened their nascent bond.

He worried people in the community were noticing how much closer they had become. But who would suspect anything unusual in their friendship? There wasn't anything to speculate. He and Aiden were friends. Nothing more. What was wrong with that?

Everyone in the community knew by now that he and Tara Hostetler were courting. And Tara would never suspect anything. He was lucky that the Amish stay clear of most kinds of physical contact when courting, unlike the English. Many Amish couples do not even experience their first kiss with each other until their wedding day. He was glad that in his strict culture he was not expected to show romantic overtures of any kind. His standoffishness with Tara would not give him away.

But if David had realized that his feelings for Aiden had changed, then who else might have? Gossip in the Amish community spread like a hayfield on fire. Fear of such talk had stopped him from seeing Aiden a few times before.

"I remember how you were even before Aiden went back to Chicago," David said. "The way you told us all not to let him know about Mom and Elisabeth going to Bobby Jonesboro's funeral. You were looking out for him then yet. You like him for saving us, and because he's nice, admit it."

"Only thing to admit is you're slacking off on your choring," Daniel said. "Now get to dusting those shelves."

Daniel thought back to Bobby Jonesboro's funeral. It was the day Kevin Hassler had come to the farm with Aiden for interviews, just before Daniel took the kinner on Gertrude's maiden drive. He'd made everyone promise to keep their mouths shut about the whereabouts of Rachel and Elisabeth. He worried that if Aiden knew they were at Bobby's funeral, Aiden might become crushed with guilt. He didn't know why he'd felt so compelled to protect Aiden. Or even why he'd cared nothing that his family might question his motives. Now, he cared too much. Especially with David pestering him.

David turned back to the shelves with his feather duster. But his choring did little to keep him quiet. "I'm glad Aiden Cermak moved to town," he said, as if everyone on God's earth would agree.

Daniel, keeping his eyes on his receipt book, shrugged off his brother's praises of Aiden. "He's just another Englishman."

"Maybe he'll live here forever and marry someone local and buy a farm."

"Sure, sure." Daniel tried to foster a laugh. "That'll be something, Aiden Cermak buying a farm."

"Why not?" David said. "He wants to live in a cabin in the woods, that's kinda like living on a farm. Maybe when I grow up I can buy his bungalow and he can buy the farm from me after I inherit it."

David's comment made Daniel scrunch his forehead. "Dad wouldn't care much for that, for sure. Mom and him are planning on retiring in their daadi haus on the farm. Besides, Aiden doesn't own that bungalow, he rents it."

"He said he's thinking of buying it. He said it's real cheap compared to the houses in Chicago."

Aiden Cermak living in Henry permanently? Daniel had never considered that before. He'd always assumed Aiden's stint of living in Henry was just an experiment in small-town living. Just like his move from Maryland to Chicago had been an experiment in big-city living. Isn't that why Aiden had moved to Chicago, just for kicks? Aiden had never mentioned why he had moved from Maryland to Chicago, and Daniel had never thought to ask. Until now. At this point in their relationship, he supposed he could. They were close enough friends these days, just like David had stated. And what had really persuaded Aiden to move to such a small town like Henry?

Thinking how much David understood, Daniel was again seized by a numbing dread. He was always amazed at how shrewd his youngest brother could be, as wise as a fox. How much else did David comprehend? The thought made him shudder.

Perhaps he needed to lay off seeing Aiden for a while, at least until it did not become so obvious to even an eleven-year-old that they were becoming fast friends. Yet how many times had he tried to talk himself into doing just that?

How could he keep a simple friendship with Aiden if he were to remain in Henry forever, for the rest of their lives?

What if things with Aiden turned out the way they had with… with his second cousin Kyle Yoder? What if he were responsible for destroying another human being? Not to mention himself? The last thing he wanted was to hurt Aiden.

"Never mind about Aiden Cermak," Daniel said, his mouth dry from apprehension. "Just keep to your choring."

Chapter FIFTEEN

KYLE YODER'S death was never too far from Aiden's mind. Ever since reading about the boy's suicide in a back issue of the *Blade*, he had wondered why—why would a seventeen-year-old Amish boy hang himself?

Just another topic that he could not broach with the Schrocks. Asking about a relative's suicide, no matter how distant, would be improper in any culture. Besides, he did not want to don his reporter's cap with the Schrocks. They were his friends, his second family. Nevertheless, his curiosity—that fire that was never fully extinguished, always smoldering below the surface—scorched him.

Kevin had said something about unrequited love. Aiden supposed any adolescent boy, whether Amish or English, would feel the dramatic pangs of a shattered romance. It wasn't impossible to imagine that he'd taken his life after facing a lover's rejection.

Yet hanging oneself required some planning. Unlikely Kyle was standing in his family's barn with a rope in hand at the precise moment the sword of rejection pierced him; he must have been caught up in his anguish for quite some time. A prolonged suffering that he could no longer endure.

Kevin's newspaper was for small towners, maintaining a mawkish tone (a tone Aiden hoped to change), but some of the larger newspapers might have had more details about Kyle's death. He surfed the Internet for archived articles about the 2002 suicide, but after a half hour of searching he found only one from the regional newspaper. The article was as succinct and vague as Kevin's. He was not so surprised to get only one hit. The Amish lived insulated lives, largely untouched by the Internet. It was unlikely to find much information on them floating through cyberspace. Not everything they did caught the attention of the outside world.

Aiden decided there were other ways to douse his reporter's inquisitiveness. Packing his notepads and sharpened pencils into his knapsack, he drove the fifteen miles to the County Records Office, in the county seat of Overton, to do a little extra background research on Kyle. The County Records Office would have the coroner and police reports, with more information about why he might have committed suicide. Even the Amish could not stay clear of government documentation.

The middle-aged woman who worked at the Records Office was pleasant and helpful. She provided Aiden with a heavy three-ring binder containing the coroner and police reports for the relevant time frame, which he carried to a small table by a window.

Sunshine laws made it simple to look up whatever information he needed, information that was recorded, at least, provided he put the effort into digging for it. Although he appreciated the Internet for its research value, he preferred the old-fashioned way: touching the laminated pages with his fingertip as he scanned down the reports, the tactile feel of the cardboard pages as he turned each leaf of the binder.

He came across the coroner's report first. Within the top five lines of the document the boy's entire identity was summarized. Decedent: Yoder, Kyle C. Race: White. Sex: Male. Date of Birth: 05/10/1985. Age at Death: 17. Home Address: East County Road 325, Frederick County, IL. Height: 5'10". Weight: 165 lbs. Eyes: Blue. Hair: Dark blond.

Further down the page was something even more unsettling: a description of the body at the scene. Kyle was found hanging from a rafter inside the barn fully clothed: suspenders dangling from trousers, right boot still on foot, left foot covered with sock—left boot missing.

Aiden gazed out the window overlooking the small parking lot. Left boot missing? That seemed odd. He took out his notepad and pencil and jotted down a few notes. For what purpose, he really didn't know.

He continued reading the coroner's report: "External Injuries on Body: 1) On left parietal ridge, pink linear laceration, 2cm length. 2) On left crown, 1.5cm light contusion. 3) On neck, 8 1/4cm length x 1cm width linear contusion, likely caused by rope. 4) On anterior neck, 1cm laceration, likely caused by shattered thyroid cartilage protrusion...."

Most of those injuries, with the exception of the neck contusion and shattered thyroid caused by the rope, could have occurred at any time, either when Kyle was in the process of hanging himself or even before that. Farm work entailed much manual labor, and one received many cuts and bruises as a result. Aiden had experienced it himself while working on the Schrock farm back in June. Most of the Amish he knew, male and female, had many scars and nicks. And he had seen more people in Henry hobbling along on crutches than in any one place. All part of a semi-subsistence lifestyle.

The coroner's report contained a front and back outline drawing of the human body, depicting the precise location of each injury. The drawings made Kyle's death all the more real. Aiden had come across enough death while in Amish Country.

Below the drawings the coroner had written in an abrupt script: "Manner of Death—self asphyxiation." Aiden braced himself for the coroner's description of Kyle's internal neck injuries. But what he read surprised him. The coroner described limited neck trauma; he merely repeated the words "shattered thyroid cartilage" and "8 1/4cm length x 1cm width linear contusion around neck," clearly caused by hanging from a rope. Nowhere did the coroner mention that Kyle's neck was broken, or that he suffered any severed spinal nerves.

The more he thought about it, the more strange it all seemed. He thumbed through the next few leaves of the binder until he came to the police reports. Perhaps those would explain the coroner's findings.

According to the police reports, Kyle had hanged himself by jumping off the barn's loft. The image of the teenager leaping to his death, then dangling in midair, made Aiden cringe. But from that image it became even clearer that Kyle could not have escaped a more serious neck injury.

He uncovered another interesting fact, one he would have expected to have made it into the *Blade* or the regional newspaper, if for no other reason than its human interest angle. According to several of the police reports, Kyle Yoder's father had been the one who had found him hanging in the barn. A police photograph of the father accompanied one of the reports.

At first he did not recognize the man with piercing blue eyes and a scraggly silver beard. As he narrowed his eyes at the photograph, he gasped. The records lady, lowering her bifocals, glanced at him. Aiden smiled at her to ease her concern. He pretended to have a slight cough, and she went back to her work.

Turning back to the photograph, Aiden brought the binder up to the window to utilize more natural lighting. The photograph revealed the old minister who had preached at the Schrocks when they had hosted Church Sunday last month. He was the one who had given the opening sermon with his eyes glued to his Bible. Aiden had been introduced to him briefly, between the sermons. There were so many Yoders in the community, of course he had not assumed he was Kyle's father. The photograph was eight years old, but there was no mistaking the somber-looking man with the piercing crystal-blue eyes.

So far nothing in the police reports mentioned anything suspicious. Still, Aiden could not get the missing left boot or the fact that Kyle had no broken neck out of his mind. Perhaps he had misread. He read further, his fingertip firm to the laminated pages, taking many notes as he scanned for any clarifications.

Not a single mention of a broken neck anywhere, or any other spinal injuries. No mention of the missing boot, either. The next few pages revealed grim color copies of the photographs taken at the scene. Several wide shots from different angles showed Kyle's body hanging lifeless from the barn's rafter. Aiden was grateful none of the photographs exposed Kyle's face, for his head slumped to his chest. Indeed, it was clear from the photographs he had on only one boot.

If Kyle had lost his boot in the process of hanging himself, wouldn't it have been lying around the barn somewhere, perhaps in the loft where he had jumped, or on the barn floor, possibly knocked off from the force of the fall? Yet there was no sign of it in any of the photographs, and none of the police reports mentioned finding it. Shouldn't the police have been suspicious of his wearing one boot?

But there was more.

Kyle was hanging from the highest rafter of the gambrel ceiling, which someone had marked along the edge of one photo as being "16 ft." in height, indicating it with two arrows pointing in opposite directions from the top to the bottom. The loft was several yards to Kyle's left.

This all looked odd to Aiden. Kyle could only have managed to tie a rope to the center rafter while standing on the loft if he were made of rubber. Curious, Aiden again scanned through the police reports, thinking he had missed something in his initial readings. But nothing mentioned the implausibility of Kyle tying a rope to a sixteen-foot rafter so far from where he would have been standing before leaping to his death.

Aiden considered the possibility that Kyle had used a ladder, like the aluminum stepladder in the photographs that was mounted on the wall to the horse stall. But no way could Kyle have managed to climb the ladder (which looked to be about twelve feet in height in comparison to the ceiling), tie a rope to the rafter and his neck, climb back down the ladder, replace it neatly on the wall, then climb up to the loft where he jumped to his death.

Even if the police were wrong about his jumping from the loft, and he had instead jumped from the ladder, there was still the mystery of who had mounted the ladder back on the wall.

When Aiden set out to quench his reporter's thirst, he never expected to find so many missing pieces. The more he uncovered, the more his blood heated with suspicions.

He closed the binder, realizing there was only one thing to do. He needed to interview the police officers and coroner who had worked on Kyle's case and see if they could fill in any of the holes they had either purposefully or inadvertently left open.

More importantly, he needed to go to the scene of Kyle's death itself—to the Yoder farm and the barn in which the Reverend Yoder had found his son hanging from a rafter.

Chapter SIXTEEN

"WOULD you like another slice of applesauce cake?"

"Danke." Daniel handed Tara his crumb-covered plate, and she disappeared with it into the kitchen around the corner. Itchy eyes focused on the wooden floor, he wiped his hands on the thighs of his broadfall pants and tried to bite down on his boredom. Walling off a yawn, he forced himself to stay alert, to concentrate more on Tara. Leaving now would give her the wrong impression. He took another sip of his black coffee and set the cup on the coffee table, hoping time picked up its pace.

"Here you go," Tara said, strolling into the room a few minutes later with a fresh slab of cake.

"Danke." Daniel took the plate from her small hand and ate a few forkfuls of the moist cake, careful to avoid dropping crumbs onto her mother's sofa.

"It's real good," he said, for what he thought must've been the tenth time that night.

"I'm glad you like it."

"You can make real good cake."

Tara's mouth seemed to stretch to the brim of her kapp. She always grinned like that when he complimented her. Still grinning, she poured herself a cup of coffee from the pot on the coffee table. The strings of her kapp dangled like cobwebs in a barn caught in a draft. He thought she wore her head covering farther over her face than was necessary for a woman her age in the community. She always dressed far more conservatively than the other maydels. Daniel thought he had liked that in her. Lately, he found it dull.

"Do you want more coffee?" she asked, flashing him her indigo eyes.

"Ach, nay." Daniel shook his head. "I'll be up the rest of the night for sure as it is."

Settling back against the sofa, Tara held her cup and saucer delicately over the lap of her white cape. "All that coffee hasn't kept your mouth awake. You been awful quiet tonight, more than usual."

"You keep filling me up with this wunderbar goot cake," Daniel said. "I can barely keep my mouth free." He caught a glimpse of their reflections in the darkened pane of the awning window, tilted up just enough to release the day's heat. The two of them looked so stiff sitting on the sofa, the glow of the gas lantern on the coffee table like an eerie orb. They looked like ghosts, he thought. Shussly ghosts.

Doubt filmed over Tara's eyes when she turned her slender neck and gazed at him. "Is that all that's keeping you quiet, my wonderful good cake?"

The right words failed to come. He squirmed, hoping they'd rise to his head. He did not want to offend her. He liked having her as a distraction, yet being attentive to her did not come easy. The past few weeks he'd sensed she was wanting more assurance from him. Assurance that his interest in her was genuine.

Intimate gestures in the Amish faith were uncommon (for which Daniel was grateful), but holding hands in private after an appropriate period of courtship was expected. They had been courting a little more than a month. Enough time had passed for him to at least hold her hand, even for someone as conservative as Tara. Daniel could barely compel himself to do it.

"I figure I got many thoughts tonight," he said, averting his eyes to the floor. "With the threshing coming up day after tomorrow, I haven't been able to concentrate much on anything else." He was partly telling her the truth. Threshing was the highlight of the season, and anticipation of its return preoccupied his mind. Yet he knew he had been quieter than was typical, even with the threshing. Even for him.

He always felt a bit tongue-tied in Tara's presence. What was there to say to her? There wasn't even farming to discuss, as much as he would've liked to. Her family had stopped commercial farming several years ago when her father and three older brothers began working for the English wooden beam manufacturer. Word was they brought home hefty paychecks. Daniel had thought about applying for a job there; everyone said he'd be accepted. But Daniel valued his independence and working at his own pace.

"You always think too hard." Tara giggled. "Sometimes I think I can see your thoughts pouring out your ears."

Daniel, glancing at her, dropped his fork onto his empty plate with a clink. "What a thing to say." He worried she was being literal, and really somehow could see his thoughts floating out of his head, although rationally he knew that could not be. But was she astute enough to read his face? Were his thoughts so obvious to her and everyone else in the community, as clear as words written across a blackboard with the starkest white chalk?

"Well, it's true." Tara lowered her head, her cheeks pink. "But that's why I like you; you're smart, some men aren't. I like how you ponder things."

Daniel grinned. He remembered how Aiden had once said the same thing to him. Picturing the two of them sitting on Aiden's sofa watching the Chicago White Sox when he had told Daniel he was the most—what was the word he had used?—"ruminative" man he'd ever known made his own cheeks flush. Daniel hadn't really known what the word meant, but it had made him smile nonetheless. Next day at the furniture shop, he had looked up the word on the Internet. He'd smiled even further, and had felt another burning flush. The word had seemed fitting, especially for a farmer like him.

Tara turned as red as a radish. He wondered if she had misread his grin from what she had said, when in truth he had been smiling over Aiden's words. Guilt rapped his brain. He shouldn't be imagining himself sitting next to Aiden while with her. He needed to train himself not to think of such things. It was unfair to everyone. Awfully unfair. And wrong.

Saturday night when Aiden had had supper with the family at the farm, Daniel had been more talkative, but he'd still had a tough time looking at him without the crushing shame. He'd hoped spending more time with Tara would help lift some of the weight. But whenever he was with her, all that he wanted was to be with Aiden.

He had promised himself he would try to avoid him. Promises to oneself. They were sometimes as difficult to keep as dandelion seeds in one's palm. His determination to steer his mind from running off into those dark ravines filled with Aiden hadn't made it any easier. Sweeping him from his mind was a daunting chore.

As Tara sipped her coffee, he wondered what Aiden was doing at that moment. Was he watching that television contraption, baseball or some silly DVD? Or reading in bed the way he'd said he liked? He was probably still at the *Blade* office, bent his desk getting his latest story typed. It was a Monday. Tomorrow would be the newspaper's deadline. He remembered Aiden telling him that Tuesdays were so hectic. He probably wanted to ensure he got as much done as possible to lighten tomorrow's load. Aiden was industrious like that.

Two of Tara's barefooted younger siblings peered around the corner at the two "lovebirds" sitting on the sofa. Tara saw that Daniel had spied them and she shooed them away.

"Get up to your beds, and stop being so nawslich." After they ran off giggling, she turned her attention back to Daniel. "The kinner can be an armful. I'm so glad the rest are gone and married, but I still don't get all that much peace. Being the oldest left in the house, I get all the responsibilities that come with it."

"Ya, that can be trying." Daniel was glad that Tara's older siblings were out of the house and married too. Five fewer pairs of peering eyes to have to contend with. They were all settled with children, living in homes of their own. Tara, the middle child, was next in line. Daniel sensed that whenever he came over for visits, Tara's parents were eager to marry her off. The way they always looked at him, as if he were a prized hog. He hoped they didn't expect oo much. Thank goodness they were visiting Tara's aunt for the evening and he wouldn't have to face their gushing smiles.

"Do you want to go sit out on the porch?" Tara asked. "It's a pleasant night, and we can get away from the younger ones."

"Ya, that would be nice." Daniel was grateful just to leave the balmy confines of the house with the pesky children. Also, it was a few steps closer to Gertrude, waiting for him tied to a hitching post in the driveway.

They sat on the porch bench, a good arm's length between each other. Tara set the lantern on the oak side table next to her and gathered her hands into a ball on her lap. She smiled at Daniel.

"So you didn't work the furniture shop today?"

"Ya, that's the case," Daniel said. "I work tomorrow."

"You chored in the field?"

"It was too hot for the horses. I worked in my woodshop."

"That's good."

"Did you have a good day at the fabric shop?" Daniel often had a difficult time remembering that Tara worked at the English owned shop in Unity. He prided himself on being able to think of it out of the blue for conversation.

"I work Wednesdays through Saturdays," Tara said. "Don't you remember? Today's Monday."

"Ach, ya. That's right. Sorry." Daniel cringed. "So, how's everything going there? Business been good?"

"It's going good," she said. "Not too busy."

"Anything interesting happen lately?"

"As a matter of fact," Tara said, "last Saturday was an interesting day. There was this English woman who came in, never seen her before. She actually wanted to barter down the price of ribbons and buttons. Can you believe? Just because we're Amish doesn't mean we barter down prices in commercial stores. Don't you hate that? Mrs. Chandar laughed when I told her about it. She says everyone in India barters down prices, even in the nicest shops. You remember Mrs. Chandar, don't you? She's the Hindu woman who drives me to and from the shop sometimes. She's a maid at the motel near the fabric shop. Her family's from India. She's very nice. Daniel? Daniel...."

Daniel jerked up and feigned a smile. "I'm listening. Mrs. Chandar? I remember her, she's a real nice lady. She's Hindu, isn't she? Her family's from India, right?"

"Ya. A goot woman, very easy to talk to. Easier than you, I have to say." Tara gave Daniel a sidelong look.

Daniel gripped his knees and squared his shoulders. He could feel Tara's eyes burning into his knuckles. She wanted him to take her hand, he knew it. He flexed the fingers on his right hand, warming them up, willing his hand to rise up off of his knee.

Slowly he raised his hand. He held it there, as if he were about to swat a fly. Staring straight ahead at the shadowy elms in the front yard, he took a deep breath and placed his hand on top of hers, balled in her lap.

A sigh left Tara, light and airy like the breeze. Mockingbirds sang in the trees, filling the awkward silence that followed.

He glanced down, still holding his breath, wondering how it looked. Was it authentic enough? Her hands nearly disappeared under his large one. His were so much darker compared with her pallid, store-sheltered skin. Her skin almost glowed, especially in the flickering light of the lantern.

Tara, her eyes downcast, placed her free hand on top of Daniel's. They sat like that for several minutes without speaking. The birds singing, Gertrude nickering from the driveway. Daniel could feel the pulse beat in the veins in his palms. Fearing sweating, he pulled his hand away and pretended he had an itch on his nose.

"It's a nice night out, for sure," he said, scratching. "Kinda cloudy, but not too bad."

"Ya, it's a nice night out, despite the clouds. I can sit out here all night, listening to the birds. Aren't birds a beautiful gift from God?"

"Ya, birds are a beautiful gift."

Tara's hand rested by her side on the bench, as if she were waiting for Daniel to take it again. This time, he let it be They sat, quiet, staring into the dark yard. Daniel again wondered what Aiden might be doing.

Chapter SEVENTEEN

THE days sandwiching Labor Day, the entire county seemed to buzz with excitement. Almost everyone was focused on the threshing. For the Amish, it was a community affair.

When time came for the Schrocks to harvest their oats, Aiden was there to help. Samuel had invited him when he'd had supper at the Schrock's last Saturday. He was more than eager to join forces. So were neighbors Gunny Rupp and his two sons and Micah Yoder and his wife, in addition to three of Samuel's older nephews, one niece, two good friends, four cousins, and an uncle.

Without the modern combine used by English farmers, threshing was a laborious undertaking, involving several exhaustive steps. Amish farmers would not be able to compete on the market without those in the community lending each other a hand.

Aiden knew that each season Kevin reported on the harvest with large color photo spreads (it was one of his best-selling issues), but Aiden was hesitant to act as the journalist around the Schrocks. As it turned out, Kevin had told him he did not have to don his reporter's cap this time. He could cover another Amish family's harvest later in the week.

He was glad to be helping the Schrocks as a friend rather than a reporter. Helping them would also give him a good excuse to redeem himself after his embarrassing tumble from the binding machine. He'd never forgotten that hot day back in June, working the Schrock's oat field for the first time, and his miserable attempt at driving the Belgians.

Images of his fall from the McCormick regularly flashed across his mind. What a humbling experience that had been. Threshing would be a good way for him to prove he was as sturdy in the field as any Amish farmer, not "city soft."

Things were already underway when Aiden, dressed for hardy farm work and wearing his latest Oakley knockoffs, showed at nine thirty in the morning. A few straggling English tourists were leaning on the fences in their shorts and sandals, watching the old-fashioned method of harvesting grain.

Spread out in the field, Amish children and adults were filling three grain wagons with sheaves from the shocked oats. Pitchforks poked into the overcast sky. An armful of toddlers, too young to be of any real support, rode up and down the oat field in a kid-sized handcrafted wagon led by the Schrock's two mini horses, Jake and Frieda. Aiden couldn't pass up taking a few sneaky snapshots with his cell phone. Boris, the Schrock's new hound they had purchased from the Troyers in August, trotted about the field, his tail wagging, barking and getting into the spirit.

A fourth grain wagon idling by the thresher was loaded with what looked like a ten-feet-high tower of oat sheaves. Aiden feared the load might fall; it was so top-heavy. The full wagon dwarfed even the two enormous draft horses hitched up front.

"Hi." David came up to Aiden, a grin stretching his face.

"Hi, David. Everyone looks so busy."

"There's a lot to get done yet; we'll need to make at least forty trips back and forth from the field to the thresher before it's all over."

"Wow, that is a lot of work."

"If we used the combine like the English farmers we'd be done in no time, but the ministers won't permit it."

There was some sign of automatic machinery: an ancient coal powered steam engine. David told Aiden it was owned by a co-op of a dozen local Amish farmers, including his father. The old Advance Rumely spun the belt to the threshing machine. Aiden guessed there was no bypassing its use.

The Rumely was warming up, pulsating with loud claps as the steam pressure built inside the valves, sweet music to the ears of the Amish farmers who stood around it like anxious schoolboys. Gray exhaust sputtered into the ashen sky as an English volunteer fed coal into the firebox.

The children and adults finished loading one of the grain wagons in the field with oat sheaves. Mark eased the Belgians through the corrugated field back to the thresher. Children rode atop the cumbersome-looking load, giddy with the work and camaraderie. They cheered and laughed. Boris chased after them, barking and running circles around the wagon.

Daniel was standing by the thresher, talking with a bearded young Amish man and an Englishman as Mark drove the heavy wagon into place behind the first. Samuel and a few of the other elders inspected the steam engine. The Rumely thrashed as it conveyed the thresher belt. With the sides of his mouth pulled toward his grizzled beard, Samuel signaled a "thumbs up."

Daniel and the two men he'd been talking with climbed up the wagon like spiders and began feeding sheaves into the thresher with pitchforks. Samuel motioned for Aiden once he spotted him.

The Schrock's patriarch was happy to see Aiden and instructed him to help out atop the grain wagon. With a little nudge from David, Aiden hoisted himself up the sheaves. Aiden was glad that Samuel had confidence in him to stride high atop another old farming contraption after losing his balance the first time.

A clear view of the flat farmland and all the activity below tickled him. He understood why the children liked riding on the loaded wagons so much. Daniel was polite to Aiden, but exchanged minimal words when their eyes first met. It had been nearly a week since he'd last seen Daniel—at the Schrock's for supper. Lately, he had slipped into his old moody self. Aiden had grown accustomed to his sudden bouts of aloofness.

The other two men worked the far end of the wagon, while Daniel and Aiden found themselves side by side on the other end. The September day was hot. The white sun burned through the overcast sky. Aiden had read on the Internet earlier that morning that the heat index would climb to ninety. Their shirts were already spotted with wetness, and sweat beads formed on their upper lips and foreheads as they forked sheaves into the thresher.

Golden grain heads separated from the stalks and came out through the chute into the barn's storage loft. Immature green heads shot into a smaller wagon. Above the rumbling of the thresher, the clip-clop of a horse-drawn wagon passing below on the blacktop lane caught Aiden's attention. The middle-aged driver was hauling in more coal for the Rumely.

The oat stack grew smaller as the men labored. Aiden and Daniel chatted very little. Before long they were down to the bare bottom. They gathered the loosened sheaves with the pitchforks, using them like push brooms as the sheaves gathered in the tongs, and tossed the remainder into the thresher. The men climbed out of the wagon and Micah Yoder hopped into the driver's position and drove back out onto the field for more sheaves. David drove the second wagon into position. Daniel and Aiden climbed up with the other two men and fed the thresher the same as before.

Halfway through the second load, Daniel, without pausing in his choring, said to Aiden, "Do you plan on staying in Henry forever?"

Aiden snickered. He thought it a strange question to ask so out of the blue, especially since Daniel had been so quiet. "Why do you ask?"

"Just curious."

"Well, I'm not sure. I still have my heart set on living in Montana." He chuckled with a self-effacing shrug as he hoisted the pitchfork full of sheaves over his shoulder. "In my dream cabin."

"If you like rustic living so much, why did you ever move to Chicago?"

Aiden squinted toward the milky sky, his pitchfork light in his hands. He took the occasion to rest his burning muscles. In the background the sound of the Rumely churned. He felt the rhythmic vibration of the thresher. Leaning on his pitchfork, he thought about his former boyfriend. When Conrad had abandoned him in Chicago two years ago, he'd assumed he'd move back to Maryland. But the more he'd considered his options, the more practical it had seemed to stay put. He'd had a good part-time job and had steadily built his freelance writing portfolio. There had been no reason to leave. A few months after Conrad's leaving, he'd had so many freelance assignments he'd been able to quit his part-time editing job and devote himself full-time to writing.

He wondered if he could ever tell Daniel all that, the full truth, that he was gay. What would happen if he did? Could Daniel deal with it? He had feared Daniel might've figured him out already (it would explain his rough behavior), but lately he wasn't so sure. If Daniel thought he was gay, would he spend so much time with him? Or maybe he suspected and didn't care?

Leaving out specifics, something he'd grown accustomed to when discussing his personal life with the Amish, he said, "I moved to Chicago to chase after a love."

"Ach." Daniel nodded. "So why did you move here to Henry? Not just for that reporter's job; I know it doesn't pay much."

Aiden minded little that Daniel asked him personal questions. He liked that he wanted to get to know him more. Still, he knew he was treading barefoot on that hot sand with all those thorns. No way could he speak his mind as he would have liked.

He turned back to pitching sheaves into the thresher, averting his eyes from Daniel. "I guess to erase the memory of everything in Chicago. Things didn't work out like I had planned." He supposed that was as good an explanation as any.

DANIEL could understand Aiden's reason for wanting to leave Chicago. His life hadn't gone as planned either. There were times when he wished he could up and leave everything in Henry, take flight like a raven from a field. To run from his sorrows like Aiden had and never look back. It was one aspect of English culture that he both envied and scorned. Being able to just go, far away, wherever and whenever one wanted, without a care for another soul. He often fantasized about running off to Glacier National Park in Montana, to hide among the hemlocks and mountains like he had just before his marriage to Esther. But too much responsibility held him back. Unlikely he could ever travel that far again.

One of the reasons he always kept a current driver's license was to have access to places like Glacier, even if he knew he would most likely never return. Even in the face of his parents' disapproval. Just knowing he could leave was enough. The license meant more to him than access to rental cars for his backpacking trips. For Daniel, it allowed him to keep one foot outside the community while the other remained planted in centuries-old customs and the tenets of his denomination.

Frowning with sympathy, he looked past Aiden's bent form toward the house. Rachel and his aunt had just stepped off the stone footpath from the small garden and were carrying glasses of what looked like lemonade on wooden platters. Grace and Moriah followed behind with boxes he was sure were filled with his favorite homemade donuts. Rachel and the girls made them for the threshing each season. It had become a tradition.

When Aiden straightened from pitching sheaves and followed Daniel's gaze, he lost his balance and stumbled, heading straight toward the edge of the wagon. Daniel dropped his pitchfork and grabbed him just in time.

"Watch it!" he said, holding Aiden by the waist.

"Oh, I'm such a klutz." Aiden straightened his sung asses. "At least this time I didn't fly over the side. Thanks for catching me in time."

"Don't worry," Daniel said, releasing him and wiping his hands on his broadfall pants. He picked up his pitchfork. "Takes a while to get used to being on top a pile of oats. The kinner fall sometimes, gives everyone a harmless laugh."

"I'm just glad no one was watching." Aiden flushed.

Aiden was incorrect. Someone had been watching.

Daniel had noticed his father watching when Daniel had caught the Englisher just in time before he went flying over the edge. He saw Samuel continue to scrutinize them as they climbed down from the wagon and headed to the picnic tables where Rachel and her helpers were laying out the refreshments. It bothered him what his father might be thinking.

Daniel kept clear of Aiden the remainder of the day.

Chapter EIGHTEEN

AT THE *Blade* office the following week, Aiden had been aware for several minutes that his boss was studying him from his desk. He wanted to write his latest article about a small house fire that he'd just come from, but Kevin's staring sideswiped his focus. "Is there something you need, Kevin?" he finally asked.

"As a matter of fact, there is." Kevin stood. "We need to talk, Aiden."

"About what?" Aiden noticed the deep worry lines etched across his boss's forehead. He was certain they were about to discuss something he would rather avoid.

"This Kyle Yoder business. It's got me concerned."

Yes, he was right. It was a topic that he did not wish to broach. At least not with his boss. Aiden had worried Kevin would eventually find out about his investigation into Kyle's death and chew him out for it. He sighed, accepting the inevitable.

"All this investigating you've been doing," Kevin said. "You need to back off. We're just a small-town newspaper."

Aiden pushed his swivel chair out from under his desk and looked at his boss squarely. He had no idea how Kevin had learned of his investigation, but he worried little about that now. Folding his arms across his chest, he chose to deal with the matter as if his boss had known all along. He played no elusive games. "You want me to back off what could be a murder story?"

"You don't know it's a murder."

"But that's why I'm investigating; I'm trying to find out what happened."

"We know what happened. The police themselves and the coroner all officially say the boy committed suicide."

"But Kevin, if you saw the reports, you'd realize—"

"Aiden, quit acting like you're Bob Woodward."

"Who?"

Chuckling, Kevin shook his head. His grin failed to mask what Aiden saw as frustration staining his face. "Aiden, it just looks like you're going after the Amish, like you've got some vendetta against them."

"Vendetta? That's ridiculous, I love the Amish."

"You already printed that story about that Amish boy, Milo Rupp, the one arrested for dope. And I let you print that sidebar about drug abuse among the Amish. Even that was pushing it."

"But that was news. They reported the Milo Rupp story in the county paper too. I think it even made the national wire. My sidebar, if anything, made us out to be the bad guys, tempting the Amish with our 'evil English ways.'"

"You made too many speculations about something we don't know much about. Drug abuse and the Amish? I should've known better than to let you print it."

"I didn't write anything horrible. Everything I put in there was based on fact. I was just trying to make the newspaper more interesting."

"Aiden—"

"They're not immune from this stuff, Kevin. The Amish are like people that way. We shouldn't be so condescending toward them. I know for a fact that they don't like that."

"It's not the Amish I'm concerned with."

"Who then?"

"It's the English," Kevin said. "They're the ones who con't want the Amish to look bad. To a lot of people they are the last decent people on earth. Our last connection to a time when, frankly, we weren't so screwed up. The truth is most the complaints have been coming from the English, not the Amish."

"Complaints?"

Kevin nodded. "People think you're making the Amish look bad, like you're out to get them. They think you're picking on them. They've been calling, writing, even stopping by. A man just stopped by this afternoon before you got back from that house fire. He was pretty upset. People here like to think of the Amish as, well, as perfect as those cute little Amish dolls they sell in those souvenir shops."

"And you're taking their complaints seriously?"

"I have to; I'm a businessman. I have a business to run. At this rate I might start losing subscribers."

"Kevin, I want you to see something…." Aiden rummaged through one of his desk drawers. Finding what he wanted, he waved a folder of papers before Kevin's eyes. "While I was going over some old police reports on Kyle Yoder, I came across something else about an Amish man a few years ago who was found dead. I don't think you even wrote a story on it. It just so happens a few months before, the police were called out to his farm after some English lady reported a disturbance at their house. The police suspected he was beating his wife, but she refused to press charges. Since the Amish don't believe in divorce, the ministers shipped him off to some mental hospital in Michigan for treatment. I asked Joe Karpin about it, and he told me that while the husband was gone, another Amish man started to help the wife with her farm work. A few weeks after the other man came back from Michigan, he was found dead, headfirst in a cistern. The police wrote it off as an accidental drowning. No further questions. Doesn't that seem a bit strange?"

Exhaling, Kevin dropped into his chair. He rubbed his graying temples. "Aiden, I want you to back off this investigative kick you're into. This isn't the *Chicago Tribune*. Our biggest priorities are recipes and farmer's markets."

"They have a newspaper like that, it's called *The Budget*."

"I'm asking you as a friend, Aiden, but I'm also telling you as your boss—stop this. Stop this now."

"Whatever happened to you wanting someone with 'true journalistic spirit'? Isn't that why you hired me?"

"Aiden, this is not Chicago, it's not Indianapolis. Hell, it's not even Springfield. It's Henry. This entire county has had one homicide in the past thirty years."

"Possibly three." Aiden again sifted through his paperwork. This time he brandished a notepad, full of dog-ears and flagged pages. "I've got information about Kyle Yoder's death that would make you question everything you think you know about it. Check this out. Kyle was found hanging in the barn without a broken neck, hardly any neck injuries at all. And one of his boots was missing, wasn't found anywhere. Yet nothing in the police reports ever mentioned—"

"I've already read them."

"The reports?"

"No. Your notes."

"You read my notes?"

"While you were gone this afternoon I read them. It's my responsibility to read your notes, especially with all the complaints we've been getting."

"If you've read my notes, then you have to agree with my suspicions."

"I don't have to agree with anything. And I definitely don't agree with your theory that Kyle Yoder was murdered by his father."

"I know I haven't proved anything yet, but he's the one who found his body. Why didn't you mention that in your story on Kyle's death? It was in the police reports."

"I chose not to for the sake of the family."

"But what about the other stuff? All the gaping holes? Even the sheriff couldn't explain some of the strange findings. Kyle's missing boot is just part of it. I was doing some research about asphyxiation. Have you ever heard of something called petechial rash?"

"Aiden—"

"It's what happens when a person chokes to death. Tiny blood clots pop out all over the face. Kyle didn't have that, which means he might've been killed before he was hung. And if you saw that barn, you would know there was no way Kyle could've tied a rope to the rafter, and then to have jumped—"

"You had no business snooping around the Yoder property."

"What?"

"You heard me. The sheriff wasn't too thrilled with your snooping, either. He was the man who stopped by today to complain. I wasn't going to mention it, but I think you should know Someone reported you snooping around Reverend Yoder's barn a few weeks ago. At first the sheriff just dismissed it as the meddling of a bored English neighbor, but then when you interrogated him at his office last week, asking all those questions, he decided to say something about it."

"I haven't done anything wrong."

"Aiden, you've wasted too much time on this nonsense already. For crying out loud, Kyle's suicide was eight years ago. Besides, this is the reason why I left Indianapolis. Too much speculation and gross hearsay."

"But I haven't even printed anything yet. I'm being cautious about speculation and hearsay. That's why I'm investigating I want to make sure. At least let me keep looking into it. What's wrong with some harmless investigating on my own free time? Who could worry about that?"

"This is a small town, Aiden." Kevin narrowed his back eyes. "Everyone knows everything. Word spreads quickly. People even know you've been to the County Records Office. Originally I dismissed those complaints, too, but now...."

Aiden chucked the notepad he'd been holding onto his desk and leaned back in his chair with a heavy sigh. "What's the point of having a newspaper in this town if everyone always knows what's going on before you print anything?"

"Listen, Aiden. The cornerstone of democracy in this country has always been two things: freedom of expression and privacy. You doing investigations at a public records office is one thing, but you snooping around people's barns without their okay is an invasion of privacy. You should've known better."

Aiden brooded. He had no idea how he should feel. He was angered, angered about so many things. Mostly because he knew on some level Kevin had a point. But he still wanted some kind of victory. He looked at his boss with a roguish smirk. "You snooped in my notes, isn't that an invasion of privacy?"

"Not when they're in my desk and in my office, it's not, and especially not when people like the sheriff have been coming around making complaints."

Grumbling, Aiden shook his head. He chortled, frustrated.

Kevin softened his tone, but his sentiments were clear. "Just back off the hardcore investigation kick, Aiden. I don't want to see you or anyone else get hurt. Any more time wasted on stories like those,"—he nodded toward Aiden's notepad—"about drug abuse and alleged murders and wife beatings, and I'll have your backside. Understand? Just back off, please. Find some nice horse auction or flea market to write about. That's what I hired you for. This is your final warning. Don't disappoint me."

Chapter NINETEEN

"WE'RE becoming more English every day," Daniel said the following Saturday as he and Aiden strolled a paved footpath by a pond at a popular county park.

Evening twilight had just set in. The trees and bushes were forming into colorless shapes. Canada geese took off in flight to their sleeping ponds. Triangular ripples pulled across the smooth surface of the pond as they took to the cobalt sky where faint stars emerged. Bullfrogs splashed by the pond's bank and mockingbirds and warblers, fluttering from treetop to treetop, twittered, as if rejoicing mischievously in the encroaching nightfall.

Aiden was unable to see Daniel's expression in the descending darkness; not that it would've mattered. Gauging Daniel's temperament was difficult even under the full brightness of the sun. Yet Daniel's spirit most of the evening had been pleasantly buoyant.

He was glad when Daniel, after closing the furniture shop early that afternoon, had crossed the street to the *Blade* office and suggested they go for supper at the corner diner. It was nice to get away from the office, especially with all the pressure from his boss to back off the Kyle Yoder story. And Aiden was happy to see Daniel emerge from his old aloofness. Lately he'd ratcheted it up. During the Schrock's threshing a few weeks before it seemed to have come out of nowhere. Aiden had a tough time guessing when his moods would swing. He was pleased to see him rebound. He was even more delighted when Daniel had agreed to go for an easy car ride after supper.

How funny when Daniel had reached for the door handle on the left side of Aiden's Chevy. Aiden had teased him. "Are you going to drive?" he'd said, in mocking disapproval.

Daniel had looked confused at first, his short beard pulled toward his pondering eyes. But then he had beamed.

"I figure I deserve that," Daniel had said, chuckling as he got into the right-hand side of the car, as any passenger in an automobile should. Neither could keep from laughing, remembering when Aiden had climbed up the wrong side of the wagon before their drive to the horse auction back in June and Daniel had given him the evil eye. It had made an already pleasant evening turn into something even lighter. A flirty sparring had sprung up between the two.

They ended up at the park, where hickories and elms and scarce prairie grass surrounded a tranquil pond. Ancient wild onion, once common throughout the Midwestern prairies and collected by natives for their medicinal value, still grew in protected clusters in low-lying areas slumping toward the pond. Aiden could smell the onions' odor carried by a gentle breeze that combed through the prairie grass from the south. The late September evening was mild. They were alone mostly; a few straggling shadows of couples were idling back to their parked cars. They sidestepped the goose poop that littered the footpath, some hidden under the yellow and orange leaves that had fallen from the trees.

"How are you becoming more English?" Aiden asked.

"Just last week Dad brought home flowers for Mom."

"I think that's sweet," Aiden said. "What's wrong with giving someone flowers?" Even in the spreading darkness Aiden sensed Daniel enjoyed their little sparring. Aiden was enjoying it too.

"I don't remember him ever doing that before," Daniel said. "It's very English."

"He was just showing her he loves her, that's all."

"Every day he shows her that," Daniel said, "with working hard, taking care of the family."

"Sometimes it's nice to show people how you feel by doing nice extra little things, like giving them flowers."

"It's shussly. Flowers! Nothing but trouble."

"How could flowers be trouble?"

"Very haughty," Daniel said. "Toying with people's emotions. A waste of money, too. All it does is put money into the pockets of florists."

There was no awkwardness as they strolled through the soft touch of descending darkness. Aiden enjoyed catching glimpses of Daniel's dark, shiny eyes when he turned his head in a certain way so they'd glow like the eyes of a white-tailed deer at night. He held that sensation even as he sidestepped a cluster of annoying goose poop.

"What if your father got the flowers for free, hmm?" Aiden chuckled. "Maybe your dad cut them from somewhere. What would you say to that?"

"It's still shussly," Daniel said again.

Aiden could tell that Daniel did not think it silly. He could tell Daniel liked that his father had given his mother flowers. He smiled in the twilight. Blithely he watched as the first super-bright stars emerged in the sky.

"I sometimes wish someone would give me flowers," Aiden dared to say. He gazed toward the indigo sky, almost afraid to catch Daniel's expression, even in the dark. Was he giving away too much? Was he risking scaring Daniel off again?

"Give you flowers?" Daniel blurted a laugh. "But you're a man."

"What would you know about that, anyway?" Aiden quipped, still evading Daniel's look, yet his grin stretching his face to new limits. "To you it's not right for a man to even give a woman flowers; what difference does it make?"

Daniel tugged at his beard. Aiden could see the whiteness of his teeth when he smiled, his eyes as dark and shimmering as the pond.

"If anyone is to give someone flowers, it should be the man to the woman, not the woman to the man," he said.

Aiden baited him. "To be honest, I'd rather get them."

"You English," Daniel huffed, teasing in his voice. After a pause, he said, "That'll be the day when Amish women buy their husbands flowers. Then what? They'll make us cook supper and do the washing and sewing. We'll be more English every day, see, I told you."

Aiden rustled up his courage. "Doesn't have to come from a woman."

Daniel stopped in his tracks. Aiden continued to walk ahead impishly. As if choking on his chuckles, Daniel said, "You mean… you mean for a man… to give another man flowers?" He advanced one step to catch up with Aiden. "And what reason would that be for?"

"Same reason your dad gave your mom flowers."

Night birds singing and bullfrogs gurgling filled their tiny space of silence. A bat flew by so close that Aiden could feel the tip of its wing brush his nose. For some reason it only made him giggle.

Daniel, too, started giggling. His giggles mingled with Aiden's, until both their giggles turned into loud laughter, drowning out the sounds of the birds and the frogs, rising up past the crowns of the trees toward the iridescent stars.

Daniel slapped his thigh, his belly laughter bending him over. Aiden fell into Daniel as his guffaws set him off balance.

A FEW days later, Daniel was at the flea market hoping to buy some good Swiss-made woodcarving tools when he found himself in front of a flower kiosk. Transfixed, he approached the kiosk inchmeal, tugging at his beard. The English vendor, a cheery elderly woman, spotted him as he neared and asked if she could be of assistance. At first Daniel was not sure he had heard her. She repeated herself. Finally, Daniel took notice.

He looked up, anxious and embarrassed. He tried to force a smile, his lips twitching. He told the vendor he was only browsing and then marched off. Stopping, he turned and gazed back toward the kiosk. The flowers were teasing him, beckoning him like tiny coquettes

This time he approached the kiosk from the side so that the vendor would not see him. Concealed behind hanging and potted flowers, he gazed at the array of colorful blossoms. He thought about his father giving his mother a bouquet. Rachel was at first embarrassed, but he noted that after Samuel had handed her the flowers she'd blushed like a girl courting. Didn't all women want to feel like they were forever courting? Even Amish women?

Why did Aiden want flowers? Not to feel like he was courting? What was it that he had said? He would like for a man to give him flowers for the same reason Samuel had given them to Rachel? What had he meant by that?

Surely Aiden had been teasing. Both had been in a playful mood all that evening, poking each other and acting shussly. Aiden's words had struck Daniel as comical when he'd spoken them; now, he dissected them in his mind like he did the old McCormick to figure out what made the reel stick.

He fiddled with the maroon and white mottled blossoms of an orchid, which he was certain smelled like chocolate.

"Back again?"

Startled, Daniel realized he'd been spotted behind a hanging basket full of fall-colored mums.

"You thinking of buying something?" The vendor smiled at him solicitously, almost maternally, in that manner common among older English women when they interact with the Amish.

"Maybe," Daniel said, holding himself steady, accustomed to such patronizing behavior.

"I didn't know Amish men bought flowers for their wives." She of course would presume Daniel was married because of his beard, as many people did.

"We don't. I mean, not often."

"I think it would be sweet. Want to buy a bouquet? I bet your wife will love it."

Daniel thought of Tara. She wasn't his wife, but they were courting, whether he admitted it to her or anyone else. He was expected at her family's farm in less than an hour, in fact. What would she say if he were to show up with a bouquet of flowers? Was Tara the type who would be receptive to such a gift? She was as Old Order Amish as he, and as dedicated to upholding the Ordnung. She had been baptized when she was sixteen, much younger than most. Even Daniel had waited until he was twenty-three, the year before his marriage to Esther, before joining the church. Tara was too conservative to want flowers. Wasn't she?

He'd never bought Esther flowers. Never even thought of it before. Why was he thinking of giving anyone flowers now?

Amish men were not expected to do such things.

Shussly English ideas.

"Well?" The old vendor was still grinning at Daniel. "Decided on anything?"

He pulled a twenty from his black jacket and laid it on the counter. "Whatever I can get with this," he said.

THE bouquet of yellow, orange, and purple daisies joggled in the backseat of the buggy next to his newly purchased woodcarving tools. He drove Gertrude at a walking speed. No hurry to get anywhere. Tara would be waiting for him at her home, probably by now sitting on her family's porch, a bit impatient. He didn't care about that or his gnawing fatigue; he simply wanted to be alone. To think.

He drove the backcountry lanes, his mind rotating like the slow wheels of his buggy. The sun was setting beyond the fields. Unharvested corn stalks, dead as straw, silhouetted against the explosive orange western sky streaked with bold strokes of black stratus clouds. The earthy smell of the daisies filled the buggy Occasionally he glanced in the backseat, uncertain the flowers would still be there.

Would Tara even appreciate them, he wondered, yawning. His own father had given his mother flowers. Would Tara be as pleased as Rachel had been? Should he give them to her?

He should just toss them out of the buggy, into the passing cornfields.

His mind roved on, and on....

He woke up confused, cold. Rubbing his temples, he thought he was in bed. With a start, he sat upright. The understanding that he was still in his buggy hit him like a blast of dirt. It was dark. His eyes were not yet acclimated, and the large trees blocked the half-moon's light. Waiting unmoving, Gertrude blew air through her nostrils. She was still hitched to the buggy, undisturbed.

Understanding descended over him as his eyes adjusted to the dark. While driving he must've fallen asleep, and Gertrude continued to lead the buggy, to the place where Daniel had driven her so many times before.

He knew the mare had not taken him to Tara's farm or to his own, for the gray gravel of their driveways always emitted lightness at night. This driveway was black, as black as tar. Gradually he recognized the elms and sycamores, and the tiny white bungalow with robin's-egg blue shutters. And the Chevy Aveo of the same color parked in front of his buggy. Gertrude had taken him to Aiden Cermak's.

"Gertrude," he whispered, "why did you bring me here?"

The smell of the daisies in the backseat jostled his memory. He looked toward them, where they lay next to the carving tools, although only the yellow petals gave off a slight radiance. Dreamlike, he brought them under his beard.

When Aiden answered Daniel's light knock on his front door, he looked at the bouquet in his hands as if puzzled.

"Flowers," Daniel said, pushing a smile.

"I can see," Aiden said.

The fall-colored petals were brilliant under the florescent door lamp.

"I was napping," Aiden said, suppressing a yawn. "Who're they for?"

"You." Daniel nudged the bouquet toward him. "You said you wanted someone to give you flowers."

Aiden stared at the bouquet, his eyes groggy-looking.

"Remember?" Daniel said. "You said so when we went walking by the pond."

"Oh, yes. Now I remember."

Daniel pictured them walking side by side along the footpath in the soft night with the birds singing and bullfrogs gurgling and the smell of the wild onion. The pleasant memory brought a tightness to his throat as Aiden finally took the bouquet from his outstretched hand.

Chuckling, Aiden said, "That is sweet of you, Daniel."

Daniel, his face burning, was bewildered by Aiden's snicker. Fearful that he was laughing at him, he fumbled to explain himself.

"It's a joke," he said, flashing a grin he knew must look as if it were seared to his face. He wanted to chuckle, but it came out more like a cough. "I'm playing a joke on you, just like your joke from the other night. About wanting a man to give you flowers." He forced a tight smile. "That's what you get for playing games."

"A joke?" Aiden stood looking from Daniel to the bouquet. Dazed-like, he brought the flowers to his chest and instinctively smelled them. "It's a nice joke," he said.

Daniel's head reeled. He did not know what he was doing there, standing before Aiden Cermak, having handed him a bouquet of flowers. What had he been thinking? Sleepiness weighed on him. He wanted to flee without words, but it would make him look all the more ridiculous. What a dummkop Aiden must already think of him.

Aiden stepped aside and gestured with the bouquet for him to enter.

"Nay," Daniel said, almost too rapidly, raising his hand. "I was just on the way through and wanted to give you a good laugh. I see that I was able to." Daniel turned to leave for his buggy. Halfway down the driveway, Aiden called out his name.

Daniel stopped and, squaring his slumped shoulders with all his might, for they felt as if they scraped the driveway, slowly turned to him. His eyes met Aiden's from across the blacktop. He savored the golden highlights of Aiden's brown irises as he stood under the door lamp.

"Thanks for the flowers. I meant it when I said I always wanted someone to give me some. It wasn't a joke. You're the first."

This flustered Daniel. His thoughts could not be shaped into words. He blew out a floundering chuckle and waved his hand to dismiss the silly ordeal. With a nervous grin he climbed into his buggy and, calling to Gertrude, disappeared into the night.

THREE miles away Daniel drove Gertrude down the back lanes, taking the turns at higher speeds than he should have for such a dark hour— for any hour—especially now that a drizzle had begun to fall. He was not rushing to meet Tara. Already two hours late to her family's farm, he had no plans to go there. Pictures of her sitting on the porch bench, growing angrier and angrier at his tardiness, slogged through the haze in his mind. None of it mattered. He wanted only to get home and to the sanctuary of his woodshop.

Gertrude, galloping down the darkened lanes, panted in the damp night. She needed no commands from Daniel to get her back to the farm. Already the mare, just over three months with the Schrocks, knew her way through the grid of roads without any real prompting from her drivers. Her taking Daniel to Aiden's bungalow after Daniel had fallen asleep was proof of that. Faster she went, back to the farm and to her dry stall with oats and water.

As Gertrude raced home, Daniel's mind also raced.

He had given Aiden Cermak a bouquet of daisies.

None of it seemed real.

What a mockery he'd made of their friendship.

But hadn't Aiden stopped him just before he was getting into the buggy to say he liked the flowers? That he wasn't joking? Hadn't he repeated what he had said when they had gone for that stroll at the county park, that he wanted flowers from… from a man? Had he been joking both times? Taking a gag too far?

Again he wondered if Aiden was "one of those." Was it possible? In the past he'd thought he might be. He wasn't sure why. Perhaps it was some kind of twisted wishful thinking. Lately, he'd dismissed such notions from his mind. Nothing Aiden had ever done indicated he could be, or was interested in Daniel other than as a friend.

Until the last few weeks….

How boogered things had gotten.

He could see Tara one moment in his mind, standing like a statue by his side, then, just like in the DVD he'd once watched with Aiden— what was the name of it?—with the soaring cluster of lights that dazzled a small Indiana town, she would be swept away into a vast vacuum of the universe, and Aiden would emerge in her place, set beside him as if by an angel. Or by a demon?

He tugged on the reins, encouraging Gertrude to get home… faster… faster….

They were about to take the left turn onto the blacktop lane where the Schrock farm was when Gertrude reared up. Daniel slapped a hand on top of his black hat and held steady to the reins as the buggy came to a jolting halt. The buggy veered to the side, skidding on the slick compacted gravel. Instinctively he braced himself with his feet against the dash. Gertrude, kicking out her forelegs, screamed. Daniel held onto the seat to keep himself from falling out. The hydraulic shocks absorbed most of the energy from the sudden stop.

"What is it, girl, what is it?"

Peering beyond Gertrude's collar, he spotted through the mist in the buggy's LED lights, that his mare had halted just in ime before striking a deer carcass that lay in the middle of the lane.

Shaking his head with both relief and dismay, Daniel thought the entire episode symbolized his life up to that point. Obstacles always seemed to be scattered before him. The deaths of Esther and Zach. Now his relationships with Tara and Aiden, both having started cff innocent enough, were galloping out of control as well. And there lving before him was the bloody remains of a young buck, struck down b a car.

How fitting.

His face sagging into his beard, he jumped out of the buggy, dragged the darkened mass of flesh and bones to the side of the lane, and hopped back into the buggy, letting Gertrude walk the few hundred yards to the farm. His only wish was to get back to the sanc uary of his woodshop where the tears that burned behind his eyes could be spilled in private.

Chapter TWENTY

AIDEN thought about his boss's words from a few weeks before while he sat at his dining table sipping his morning coffee. He had replayed the lecture many times in his head. Maybe Kevin was right. He was being foolish. Playing an overzealous reporter, like one of those on television. The missing boot? Could've been anything. Maybe Kyle was so distraught before hanging himself he had forgotten to put it on. And the implausibility of Kyle's hanging himself from a rafter so far from the loft? Who knew what had really taken place that day?

Aiden did not want to believe the Reverend Yoder had killed his own son, like some kind of Amish Ivan the Terrible. Just speculation he had jotted down in his notepad while he'd been brainstorming. He hadn't meant for anyone to read it.

So far Reverend Yoder was the one name on his crude list of suspects. There wasn't another soul in the community who could've been responsible for such a horrible crime. To kill Kyle and make it look like a suicide? The thought was absurd.

Yet there were so many holes, so many incongruities surrounding Kyle's death. Too many unanswered questions. The missing boot, the hay loft, the lack of any severe neck injuries or petechial rash.

And there was that other Amish man's bizarre death, the one found headfirst in a cistern. Aiden suspected he'd been drowned by his desperate wife and her lover. Was that just another fantasy?

He was chasing ghosts.

He put down his coffee and shook his head in defeat.

It was all a game, something to keep his mind from going sour. Living in a rural community had proved lonelier than he had anticipated. There weren't many people his age in Henry to do things with other than the Amish, and they were so closed off from his world even with his reporter's responsibilities taking him deeper into their lives. The few English his age married straight after high school and moved away, looking for more opportunities and excitement elsewhere, like Chicago or Champaign. His neighbors were kind enough, but they were much older than he, in their golden years. Maybe his investigation into Kyle's death was nothing more than a distraction. To keep himself from succumbing to the cold reality of his loneliness.

If it wasn't for Daniel's friendship, much of his personal time would be spent in despair.

He looked to the bouquet of fall-colored daisies on the dining table. He had put them in a glass vase soon after Daniel had given them to him, making sure to set them on the table where he could see them from any corner of his tiny house. The petals were wilted and had lost their fresh color, but he was not yet ready to toss them into the trash.

Daniel. His head was full of him, more than usual. More than Kyle Yoder's death. Over and over he reflected on Daniel's bringing him that vibrant bouquet that strange night.

He'd meant it when he'd told Daniel he wanted a man to give him flowers. Unable to hold himself back, he knew it had been a daring thing to have said. That night by the pond there had been something whimsical in the air. Even the birds had seemed extra bold with their playful chatter and capricious fluttering about.

Never in a million years did he expect Daniel to take him up on it. The somber Amish man had a peculiar prankster in him, Aiden guessed. He was just acting shussly, as the Amish would say.

Why else would Daniel have brought him those flowers?

Aiden had asked himself that question many times since Daniel had showed up on his front stoop with the bouquet. He wanted to understand, to believe. But it all seemed too implausible. Like Kyle Yoder's suicide....

Daniel had been married and fathered a child. He had mourned their tragic deaths. He courted that Amish girl, Tara Hostetler. Aiden had seen her a few times. She seemed nice. They made a cute couple. Everyone had said so. Daniel seemed to like her. He acted aloof at times, but Amish men always acted detached with their sweethearts in public. That was their way.

He wanted to laugh at the outrageous things he was thinking.

It couldn't be true. Daniel was Amish.

But what if it were true? How jarring would that be to Daniel, a stoic man with such staunch religious convictions? He knew that the Amish viewed homosexuality as a sin—he didn't need to do research to discover that. He couldn't imagine them even discussing the topic in private.

But then there was that time four months ago, when he'd first visited the Schrock's furniture shop in Henry and had overheard those Amish boys playing the arcade game at the IGA. They'd teased each other using the word "faggot."

The Amish weren't so far removed from the twenty-first century not to know that even certain members of their own community might be gay, or bisexual, or whatever the current academic terms were. They must know homosexuality was not confined to the English world.

His mind went back to that night when they were standing by the door, the air cool and soft, Daniel holding in his large hands the yellow, orange, and purple daisies. He'd been so impish when he had told Daniel he wanted a man to give him flowers. He admonished himself for that now. How unfair to have teased Daniel that way.

Daniel's gift of the bouquet had made Aiden realize something else that he admonished himself for. Something that he had been hoping to dodge for some time. Something that had pestered him since their ride to the horse auction in June. There was no hiding from it any longer.

He was in love with Daniel.

He'd gone so long without any love or romance. Without anyone touching him in that special way. Not since Conrad had he met anyone he'd want to be with. Until now. He should've known how vulnerable he would be near someone as needful and profound as Daniel. Not to mention handsome. He was a fool to think his feelings for him had only to do with sympathy.

His compassion hadn't evolved into longing—the longing had been there all along.

The hard truth was he had moved to Henry to be near Daniel. That unwelcome fact brushed up against Aiden like a spindly oat shock. It irritated him. He had rashly followed one man halfway across the country before. Here he had done it all over, and after he'd sworn to himself he would never do it again. He would never have moved to such a small, isolated town—a village in technical terms—taking such a measly paycheck, if Daniel had not lived mere miles away.

Bad enough to allow silly emotions to motivate his actions. But to fall in love with someone as unattainable as an Amish man? He would've been better off if he had fallen in love with a Catholic priest.

Shaking his head, he understood he was jealous of Tara Hostetler too. Ever since spying Daniel boosting her into the carriage that Church Sunday at the Schrock's, what seemed like ages ago, the hot spices of jealousy had pickled him.

He closed his eyes and sighed, wondering if it could ever be. Daniel? What if it were true? What could come of it? Confused and even angry at himself for making himself wish for something he couldn't have—or shouldn't have—Aiden laid his forearms on the table, overcome with tiredness.

It was times like these when he wished he believed in God. That way he could have someone to blame all his troubles on.

If Daniel were gay, he knew it would be an utter nightmare for him. He would rather Daniel be one hundred percent heterosexual than for him to live with such a weighty secret in a culture like the Amish.

Being homosexual wasn't easy for anyone. Those who were less "visible" and defied the stereotypes often faced the most internal turmoil, people like himself, perhaps. But Daniel? Unfathomable.

Steam from his mug of coffee washed over his troubled face. Rubbing his forehead, he eyed the bouquet of daisies. No man had ever given him flowers, not even Conrad after more than a year together. Though he'd been drowsy from a nap that night Daniel had stood at his front door holding the bouquet, the image was as clear as if Daniel were at that very moment standing before him.

What a mess one little bouquet could cause. No wonder the Amish eschewed such sentimental nonsense. He understood Daniel's derision.

He wished the steam from his coffee would forever fog his mind so he would not have to feel or think so much.

A harsh thud on the front of his house jerked him from his deep thoughts. He raced to the dining room window overlooking the front yard and peered out. He saw nothing. Puzzled, he hurried outside.

Orange and yellow slime oozed down the front of his white house. A pumpkin lay smashed open in his garden, where last month he'd planted black-eyed Susans. Two of the thick flower stalks were snapped in half from the pumpkin having fallen on them. He nudged the desecrated pumpkin onto the grass with his shoe to inspect it. Seeds and pumpkin innards trickled out. He squatted, lifted one of the broken flower stalks. They were dying anyway, he thought miserably, letting the broken flower drop lifeless to the ground.

Seed splatter on the house covered a radius of about three feet from the center of impact. The basketball-sized pumpkin must have been thrown from the street, he surmised. By someone strong enough to have hurled it with such velocity. He stood and looked about for a sign of anyone. He saw nothing: no people, no cars, no bicyclist racing away. Not even a horse-drawn buggy. All his neighbors, typical for seven o'clock in the morning, were as quiet as chipmunks. The sun was just nudging above the roofs of their houses. The older inhabitants were probably comfortably sipping coffee at their kitchen tables, wondering how to fill another day. He wondered if whoever threw the pumpkin wasn't trying to aim for his window. He'd lucked out, he supposed. It could've been much worse.

Whoever threw it may have been playing a random prank. Halloween was a couple of weeks away. English youth were gearing up for the celebrations. Maybe they had chosen his house because his was the last one on the street, making it an easier getaway onto the main thoroughfare.

He carried that thought, along with the pumpkin's remains, to the trash receptacle by the side of the detached garage, ready to forget all about it. On the way back to the house, he stopped in his tracks. For the first time he noticed the writing on his front door. Someone had spray-painted in red block lettering: GET OUT OF TOWN.

Chapter TWENTY-ONE

DANIEL, choring with his father in the horse pen on a brilliantly sunny afternoon, noticed his father studying him. He was thankful the early weeks of autumn brought another warm day, so that his father would not take his sweating as a sign of nervousness. They were cleaning the concrete water troughs, and much exertion was needed to scrub them free from the grime that could make their horses sick. Boris, their hound, lay in the shade of the barn while his masters toiled.

"You're spending a lot of time with that Englisher, don't you think?" Samuel finally said.

Daniel tensed and tried to compose himself. If only there was a way he could just run. He chewed on his lower lip, wishing he were anywhere other than with his father. He had dreaded the day when his father would mention his relationship with Aiden. He had smelled it coming for weeks.

After catching his father eyeing them so suspiciously during the threshing, the haunting fears kept rearing up like those huge English eighteen-wheelers barreling down the road. He could never face the community's shunning, much less his father's. But as the days passed, keeping away from Aiden was not so easy. He'd tried to keep on the cold exterior. To shrug him off. Yet, whenever he did, he would be gripped with guilt. It had even kept him up at night. The last thing on earth he wanted was to hurt Aiden Cermak. He was such a fine man, after all.

Such a turbulent ride of emotions—guilt for being with Aiden, guilt for staying away.

Lately he had heeded nothing of what those voices in his head warned. Even visions of his father's disapproving gaze at the threshing had failed to blot out his good feelings. But now, with his father's eyes burning new holes into him, those feelings turned to alarm.

He knew he should have been more cautious and avoided the Englishman. Picturing in his mind his giving Aiden those shussly flowers made his throat tighten. Why hadn't he practiced more discretion?

"What do you mean, that Englisher?" he asked, feigning ignorance.

"Aiden Cermak. You're with him a lot these days."

Kneeling by his trough, Daniel scrubbed with excessive vigor, as if trying to scrub away Samuel's worrying words. "I don t know what you mean."

"Your mom and me think you spend too much time with him,' Samuel said. "I notice you're with him more and more."

"I thought you liked Aiden," Daniel said, eyes on his scrubbing "He saved our lives, remember?"

"Ya, I like him a lot." Samuel sounded annoyed. "And I remember all that he's done for us. I'm grateful to him. But we wonder why you're with him so much."

Daniel tasted the bile in his mouth. "I'm not with him that much," he said, forcing firmness into his voice.

"Your mom and me, we worry."

"There's nothing to worry about."

Samuel's scrubbing was less enthusiastic. Daniel knew the harsh October sun made the difficult chore wearing for his middle-aged father. Wiping the sweat from under his straw hat, Samuel sat on his haunches. Boris lifted his head and stared at his master, his tail wagging. When Samuel failed to move, the hound gently lay his head back down.

"You're close with him now," Samuel said, "maybe too close."

"He's just a friend of the family," Daniel said. "We run into each other a lot, that's all. He works across from the shop. It's hard to avoid him sometimes. He even has supper with us. First you complain that I'm being rude to him; now you complain I'm being too friendly."

"No one is complaining."

"Then what's wrong?"

"We worry."

"There's no need to."

"People see you parked at his house a lot. They mention it, in passing."

Had anyone spied him handing Aiden a bouquet of daisies, spotlighted by his door lamp? Trying to control his nerves, Daniel said, "Shouldn't they mind their own business? They're all nawslich."

"No one is being nosy; you can be friends with whoever you want. It's just that they, your mom and me, we all worry. We worry that you'll leave the church."

Daniel's hand froze over the scrub brush. He looked up at his father. "What?"

"We worry that you being with Aiden so much might make you, well…. We worry that maybe he's tempting you with the fancy ways and you'll want to leave the Amish."

Daniel began scrubbing again, turning his grinning face from his father.

"Don't worry," he said, giddy with relief. "Aiden isn't tempting me to leave the church." He almost wanted to laugh out loud as the sickness in his stomach eased. Thank goodness that was all this was about, and not what he'd feared.

"We like the Englishman," Samuel said, "but we worry; we don't want you to get too comfortable with the English life."

"If anything, we're probably tempting Aiden to become plain." Daniel snickered. "You know how he admires us Amish."

"That may be," Samuel said. "But you know almost no English become Amish. It's as common as fireflies in January."

"It's uncommon for Amish to become English too."

"Ya, but it happens, that's my point. The community has lost four of its youth rumspringa this year."

"That's still a small number, and they may yet come back."

"Ya, but we want our children to stay in the church, especially after they been baptized. You know, once you been baptized and you leave the church, there's the shunning. That'll be hard on you, hard on the whole family. Think about that," Samuel said, and he bent back to his scrubbing.

"I'm not leaving the church," Daniel asserted.

"We know how hard it's been these last few months." Samuel said into the trough. "It's been hard on all of us, but these are the times when we keep our faith, and build on it, make it stronger."

"I haven't lost my faith."

Samuel waved a horsefly from his face. "Just remember, da Hah has His own plans for us; we can't complain about it. Losing Esther and Zachariah and your farm, I know how that's been hard for you. It will be hard for your mom and me to lose Leah someday too. Sometimes we don't always understand God's will, but you must know that He's doing what's best for us. He knows us well. God, too, lost a child. He sacrificed His only son so that those who follow Him could have everlasting life in Heaven."

Daniel was not annoyed as he listened to his father's frets. He was just so relieved that Samuel's concern was about apostasy and nothing else. "I'm not leaving the church," he said.

"Goot."

A moment later Samuel stood up with a crack of his bones. He tossed his brush into the trough, startling Boris. The hound jumped up, shook himself then wobbled to a shadier spot near the buggy shed and lay down, this time uninterested in following his master anywhere.

"I'm done with this scrubbing," Samuel said, stretching his back. "Ach, to be young again."

Watching his father lumber toward the house, Daniel marveled at his faith, as sturdy as the concrete troughs he was scrubbing. Daniel's faith proved not so strong. He believed in God, but he often wondered why so many of his prayers went unanswered.

Seldom did he ask God for anything material. He simply asked for answers. What were the reasons why the things that happened to him happened, and what was he to glean from them? And more and more since Aiden Cermak had crashed into his life: Why was he the way he was? Did God make him that way to test him or was he bad in some way? He'd always looked for the clues that he had asked God to provide him, though he had found none.

Questioning God's will he knew was hochmut, haughty, yet he wondered why there were so many sinkholes in his life to circumvent, so many obstacles to avoid, when he thought himself a good, God-fearing man.

He hadn't rejected God. But at times he wondered if God had not rejected him.

He looked to Boris, still resting in the shade of the shed without a care in the world. If only his life could be as uncomplicated as a dog's, Daniel mused.

Turning back to the water trough with a sigh, he began scrubbing the grime with extra resolve.

"THERE'S talk of your English friend," Tara said Church Sunday as Daniel drove her home from the Plank's, where services had been held. Gertrude led them at walking speed along the blacktop, which was plastered with wet leaves from an earlier rain. Autumn's first real chill nipped at them as they sat in the carriage with a woolen blanket laid across their laps.

"What do you mean, talk?" Daniel tightened his grip on the reins, anxious. Up until now, Tara had been quiet. He knew she was percolating with something, ready to singe him with her words. She'd become testy with him lately. He could hardly blame her. His remoteness was trying even Tara's old-fashioned values. Scrunching his nose, he braced himself.

"People are saying he's trying to harm our community," Tara said.

"Trying to harm our community?" Daniel brought his shoulders to his ears. He feared another lecture about his friendship with Aiden. "How's he doing that?"

"He's reporting in that paper bad things about us." Tara flashed Daniel a sharp look. "Writing things like we abuse drugs."

Daniel relaxed, lessening his grip on the reins, and sniggered. "Is that all?"

"Is that all?" Tara lifted her pointy nose toward the gray sky. "Isn't that enough?"

"He's not trying to harm our community," Daniel said, trying to ease Tara's mood, as chilly as the weather. "He admires us."

"Is that what he's been telling you? If that's the case, why is he reporting all those bad things about us?"

"What do you mean, us? He reported on one boy who was doing something he shouldn't have. How is that about all of us? The regional newspaper reported on Milo Rupp's arrest too. Besides, that was a while ago. Most what he writes is good; I read some of it."

"He just puts in those good stories to fool people into thinking he's not trying to make us look bad."

"Who's putting such unsinn in your head?"

"It's not nonsense. Writing about us Amish doing drugs; it's horrible."

Daniel peered ahead at the slick, leafy blacktop. He'd grown tired of this conversation even before it got underway. "Maybe he's trying to help the community by reporting those things, ever thought of that? The fact is it does happen; why should we pretend it doesn't? We're not saints, you know, Tara."

"I know that, but what about that other stuff? He's been trying to dig up dirt on Kyle Yoder. I heard he's trying to make Kyle's suicide look like a murder. What proof does he have anything like that?"

Daniel remained wordless. He didn't know what proof Aiden had, yet the thought concerned him. He, too, had heard rumors of Aiden's investigation, but had hoped nothing would come of it. He wished too much that Aiden would drop the entire Kyle Yoder story. He realized he partially agreed with Tara and many others in the community, and this disturbed him.

"You should stay away from him," Tara said.

Daniel glanced at her, forcing his respect for Aiden to resurface. "You forget what he did for my family, that he saved us from tragedy?"

Tara folded her slender arms across the bib of her white cape. "He didn't do all that."

"He for sure did, and you know all what my family's been through."

"Daniel, of course I do," Tara said, softening her tone. She leaned toward Daniel. "I don't mean to sound like a dummkop. I'm grateful what he's done for you and your family, really, but maybe you're letting him get too close. Maybe he's taking advantage of you so that he can report bad things about us. You know how those reporters can be."

Tara's nudging words forced Daniel to sit up. He did know how reporters could be. Pushy, judgmental, even deceitful. Was Aiden any of those things?

Leery of Aiden at first, Daniel had grown to trust him. He had shucked aside those old distrustful feelings. Aiden had proved to be a worthy friend. Someone to even admire. Still, nagging feelings had emerged anew whenever he was with him. Aiden was "studying" him, looking at him as a project. He hated those thoughts, but couldn't help thinking them.

He found himself trying to defend Aiden while at the same time believing some of the absurd gossip Tara was recounting. "He's just doing his job," he said with a sigh.

"He's nawslich," Tara grunted. "Sticking his nose in other people's business to make us look bad."

"He might be a bit nosey, but I can tell you for sure, if he's making us look bad, he's not doing it on purpose."

"What difference does it make? He's an outsider butting in."

Daniel listened to her words. An outsider? Wasn't Daniel a bit of an outsider himself? Lately he felt like one. Perhaps he always had.

"It will all come to pass," he said. He tugged on Gertrude's reins, encouraging her to go faster, to get Tara home and be done with this conversation.

Tara settled back in her seat and gathered her black shawl around her shoulders. "Just best you stay away from him in the meantime. He's bad news."

Chapter TWENTY-TWO

HE HANDED Daniel another cold can of Dad's Root Beer and sat next to him on the sofa. He made sure to always have Daniel's favorite pop on hand for whenever he stopped by. They were watching television, a bowl of microwave popcorn between them. The television's volume was low, since Daniel always complained about the jarring racket. Aiden respected his feelings whenever he visited by keeping the sound low, or shutting the set off entirely.

That evening Aiden left the television on, sensing they both could use the distraction. When he had answered the light knock at his front door to see Daniel standing there, he was elated, but Daniel was visibly disturbed about something. Three weeks had passed since they had last spent any significant time together. He only wished Daniel wasn't so preoccupied. It seemed the entire community was edgy lately.

Neither had ever mentioned that night Daniel had given Aiden flowers. There was a tacit agreement, no matter how difficult it was for Aiden to accept, that both needed to forget it had ever happened. When Daniel had stepped inside the house, Aiden caught him eyeballing the wilted bouquet that still sat in the vase on his dining table. He was uncertain what his grimace had meant. He supposed he should have tossed the decayed flowers out; he still could not bring himself to do it.

They sat as still as oat shocks. Only their arms and mouths moved as they munched on popcorn and sipped pops, Aiden not even knowing quite what they were watching on television. They made small talk now and then about the spring oat crop and the new curio cabinet Daniel had just custom crafted for a judge in Champaign. Aiden talked about his reporter's job, refraining from mentioning anything about Kyle Yoder.

"I'm worried, Aiden," Daniel said finally, popping open a new can of root beer, foam spitting out. He took a sip before resting it on his thick thigh.

"What is it? I could tell something's been on your mind "

"It's you." Daniel settled back in his seat, gripping his can of root beer as if it were a club, his left hand clasping his knee.

"Me?"

"You got people upset. A lot of people."

"Don't I know it." A snicker fluttered from between Aiden's lips, itching with salt and Diet Sprite.

Daniel shifted to look at him. "Why are you harping on Kyle Yoder's suicide? You could get a lot of people into serious trouble snooping around like you been."

"Not you, too, Daniel. Why does everyone think I'm out to cause trouble? I'm just trying to uncover the truth. There could be a murderer out there, maybe more than one. Doesn't anyone care about that?"

"Just leave the story alone," Daniel said. "The community is talking about it more and more, English and Amish. You should worry what it all could lead to. Kyle hung himself, that's all there is to it, people do things like that. There's not always a clear reason why, quit looking for one."

Aiden hugged himself in his fleece hoody and squirmed in his seat. He was annoyed with everyone trying to thwart his efforts to find the truth behind Kyle's death. He had tried to put the story aside, like Kevin had wanted him to, like everyone wanted him to, but his curiosity proved too overpowering. The latest discovery had convinced him something was just not right with Kyle's death.

Last week he'd talked on the phone with the county coroner, retired in Arizona. The coroner, thank goodness, remembered Kyle's death. Who could forget an Amish boy found hanging in a barn? Unresponsive mostly, the cranky coroner did say one thing that interested Aiden. Kyle had been dead between eighteen and twenty-four hours when his body was brought into the county morgue. Aiden thought this was odd. A barn on a busy Amish farm usually doesn't go without someone entering it for more than overnight. Wouldn't Kyle's father have found him hanging in the barn much sooner? Unless, of course, Kyle had died from another cause.

Aiden was a man who embraced the truth. But not everyone shared his convictions. For Daniel's sake, he was willing to listen to his concerns. He trusted Daniel. Respected him. Loved him even.

"Everyone is so worried about the truth," Aiden chirped. "Why is that?"

"The truth? You mean your version of the truth, right?"

"No, that's not what I mean. You know I'm not stupid, Daniel, I've got a lot to support what I believe."

"What you believe, huh? And what you believe happens to be the truth, just like that?"

Aiden hesitated, wondering if he should go on since Kyle and Daniel had been second cousins. But he decided because Daniel had brought up the investigation, he needed to tell him what he'd uncovered. Maybe if Daniel understood more, he would be more willing, perhaps even eager, for Aiden to continue probing Kyle's death.

"Daniel, I've done some serious investigating into this. Nothing is adding up the way the police and the coroner reported. I tried to ignore it, leave the story alone like you said. I never intended to find so many incongruities, but a boy might've been murdered and I think I can prove it. The autopsy report shows that he didn't even have a broken neck. I saw the barn. Not only is it near impossible for someone suicidal to have gone through so many steps to successfully hang himself, but even if he did, no one could leap from the loft that high and not break his neck in the process. And there're other facts too. It's looking more and more like a setup. Don't you think it's important to find out what really happened?"

Lowering his head, Daniel looked ready to hand himself to the executioner. His shoulders slumped forward, his eyes glassed over with lethargy. Aiden wanted to comfort Daniel, but he was unsure what for.

"Uncovering the truth can sometimes cause more trouble than it's all worth," Daniel said under his breath.

"Daniel, that's shussly."

"Is it really so shussly, Aiden?" Daniel said, his mouth taut. "You're the one who said you didn't want to be a haughty reporter, yet you insist you're right and everyone else is wrong. You think that dragging out everything will make us all feel so much better? Isn't that just a bit hochmut?"

Aiden wanted to tell Daniel about the threats, the spray painted message on his front door—which he'd since painted over—and the pumpkin smashed against his house. And most recently, the threatening letter someone had left in his mailbox, hand-delivered, with a skull and crossbones drawn where a stamp would go. The note had the same warning, written in the same block lettering as the one on the door. But this message went one step further—it was addressed "to the sodomite." He had chortled when he'd read it. Doesn't one have to be sexually active to be a sodomite? When was the last time he'd been intimate with anyone? More than a year ago, with someone he hadn't even felt a connection with. Some man he'd met online out of desperation.

As unsettling as it was to receive threats in such a small community, Aiden had no fear. Whoever it was, he reasoned, was just out to scare him, not cause any real harm. Difficult to believe otherwise. He had taken pictures of the threatening message on his door with his digital camera before painting it over and stowed away the note for evidence. He considered showing Daniel. But he decided against it. Daniel was upset enough without having to deal with that ugliness. He'd even refrained from telling Kevin and the police.

Whether the threats stemmed from the Kyle investigation or, based on the letter he found in his mailbox, from someone disliking homosexuals living in the community, he could not say. Either way, he refused to be swayed by intimidation.

"It's not hochmut wanting to know the truth, Daniel." Aiden took a handful of popcorn and popped it into his mouth. Chewing, he said, "Whoever did this needs to be brought to justice."

Daniel set his root beer on the coffee table and concealed his ashen face with his large hands. Inhaling, he rubbed his temples.

"Then you better have the police arrest me," he said.

AIDEN'S startled gape did not surprise Daniel. He exhaled. Where to begin? He had never imagined he'd ever reveal his secret to anyone. He came close once to telling Elisabeth. She was always so much wiser than most of the women he knew—most of the men he knew, English or Amish. Yet the words had never parted from his lips. Though he thought sharing the story with Aiden might come easier. He was a good friend, a special friend. He felt for some reason that Aiden would understand. And he was English. It was easier to open up to the English.

"If anyone is guilty of Kyle Yoder's death," he said, looking away from Aiden to hide his shame, "it's me. I'm the one who did it."

"What are you talking about? Daniel, what do you mean, you did it?"

"I killed him."

"That's nonsense; how could you have anything to do with it?"

"I drove him to it."

Aiden shook his head. "Daniel, stop talking cryptic. Please, tell me, what are you saying?"

"Kyle Yoder and me. We… we were friends, good friends. Kyle killed himself because of… because of me."

"Because of you?"

Daniel looked toward the ceiling, beseeching God for guidance. Hard to believe he was on the verge of telling Aiden the truth—telling anyone the truth. Other than Kyle, he had never exposed his real self to another soul, but with Kyle he had needed no words to convey his feelings. Now, however, he had little choice. He needed Aiden to back off the Kyle Yoder story before the entire community learned the horrible truth about him—about Kyle. About what they had done.

Gazing toward the television, where some sort of situation comedy filled the screen, Daniel spoke as if someone else were speaking for him. "Kyle and I... we... we were the same age. Growing up we spent a lot of time together, we fished, hunted, backpacked, did everything. When we were about seventeen... something in our friendship changed, we both could feel it. I know we could, it wasn't just me, it was a feeling we both had."

He looked to Aiden to check for his reaction. So far, Aiden seemed unmoved. He kept his head riveted on Daniel. His eyes unblinking. He wondered if his telling Aiden would spur him to run. Or would it cause an opposite reaction? What would Aiden do when he learned Daniel harbored such feelings?

The room buzzed around Daniel. Holding onto the armrest, he managed to keep himself steady. His mind fluctuated between delight and disbelief as he told his tale. The light murmur of canned laughter came from the television set, but he barely noticed.

"One day, in his family's barn," he went on, mustering his courage, his eyes on the carpet, "after we got back from fishing, we... we kissed, a little kiss. We couldn't help it, it just happened. But Kyle, well, he didn't take it too well, he avoided me after that. I knew he wasn't thinking clear. If I wasn't so worried about myself, what people might say if they found out, I might've said something, maybe helped him. People knew he was acting strange. He wouldn't talk to me about it. Whenever we were near each other, he... he would look at me like... like I was the devil, and run away. Maybe he saw something in me that was really there. I figure he just couldn't take the guilt anymore. A few weeks later... well, you know what happened."

AIDEN stared at Daniel wide-eyed. He licked his dry lips, his eyes rapt on Daniel. Frozen in attention, he was unable to even scratch the itch that came to his nose. He wanted to reach out and comfort Daniel, but he did not yet feel at liberty to do so. Keeping his hands in his lap, he tried to soothe him with words.

"Daniel, I don't know what to say. I'm so sorry you had to go through that." Daniel did not respond. He remained silent, staring, trancelike.

Daniel had just confessed to Aiden a tremendous secret, one which for many would have been difficult to disclose. That he was Amish made it all the more poignant. Yet Daniel's confession did not give Aiden license to show him love.

Aiden did not know if it was appropriate at that moment to declare his own sexuality. Was Daniel even "coming out" to him? Lots of teen boys kiss each other, none of it really meaning anything. Just some kind of sexual test. Gay men, even those who were comfortable with their sexuality, had intimate relationships with women. He knew of some. They were still homosexual. In reverse, heterosexual men could be intimate with other men and not be gay. Human sexuality was a rollercoaster ride of confusion.

He was still hoping Daniel could care for him in that special way. Was his kiss with Kyle a one-time thing?

Reproaching himself for thinking of his own desires when Daniel suffered, he remained still, waiting for Daniel to collect his thoughts, to say something further. He had revealed to him something so intimate, so heartbreaking….

Daniel had mourned Kyle's passing alone, unable to let anyone know how much he had grieved. He had to keep his emotions concealed should anyone question why he would be so troubled. Everyone had known his and Kyle's friendship had run its course. In some ways his death had been much worse than Esther and Zachariah's. With their passing, Daniel had been able to openly mourn, gleaning support from family and community. With Kyle's death, he had suffered alone.

Wanting to show his deference, Aiden let his eyes fall to the shag carpet, but he kept a keen peripheral watch on Daniel. It was through this perspective that Aiden saw the slow shadow eclipse Daniel's face. His deep brown eyes turned black as coal.

"Why? Why? Why didn't I say something to him?" Daniel beat his fist on the armrest. "He wouldn't even let me talk to him after that. I should've forced him to talk to me. He was such a good person, so hard working. Why did I do it to him?" He turned away, hiding his throbbing, reddened face.

This time Aiden placed a hand on his shoulder. To his relief, Daniel did not shrug it off. He strained for the right words to add to his touch, the right expression to impart, desperate to make things better.

"I know whatever I say won't change what happened," Aiden said. "But everyone has times when they blame themselves for the tragic loss of a loved one." He hoped that making the issue more universal would assuage Daniel's pain. "Logically, you know you can't blame yourself—"

"There's nothing logical to any of this." Daniel shot Aiden a smoldering glare. Aiden flinched. His hand dropped from Daniel's shoulder with a thud.

Sighing, Daniel forced a tight smile. He lifted his hand to Aiden; it hovered in midair for what seemed an eternity.

"Forgive me," he said, his arm drifting back to his side. "I understand what you're saying. Thank you for your kind words, you always know the right things to say. But I can tell you for sure that Kyle's suicide is my fault."

"I don't understand how you can blame yourself, Daniel. All you did was share one kiss, one simple kiss. It's not so uncommon."

"His father saw us," Daniel blurted.

Aiden gawked at him. "The Reverend Yoder saw the two of you kissing?"

Daniel nodded slowly. "He saw us, he saw us that one time, that one time we kissed in the barn. He saw us that one time when we finally allowed ourselves to... to be closer to each other. That one little kiss, sitting on the bale of hay, Kyle's father saw us. I can remember it like yesterday. The sun pouring through the crevices. The animals calm after their feeding. A warm April afternoon. I looked up when we pulled apart, and his father was standing in the doorway, just staring at us like he was looking into the depths of hell. I had never seen a look like that on a man's face before. And those eyes of his, they were like blue torches burning into us. I'll never forget that stare."

"That must've been awful."

"When Kyle saw his father standing there, his face went completely white, every drop of blood drained from his face. I was afraid he was going to pass out. Then the reverend just left, he turned and walked off, like nothing happened, never said a word. Three weeks later, Kyle hung himself. Reverend Yoder has never said a word to me about any of it, not one word to this day. All these years I lived, worried he might say something to someone, reveal my secret. Every time I sit through church services, I sweat wondering if this time he's going to call me out in front of the gmay. But he never has, hasn't even said anything to me in confidence. Sometimes our eyes will meet and they'll be something there, some kind of silent threat, but that's it, he acts like nothing ever happened."

Aiden slapped a hand on his thigh. "I've been right all along. I knew there was something not right about him; now I know for sure."

"What are you talking about?"

"The Reverend Yoder. He did kill his son. He was the one who found him hanging in the barn. It was him who made it look like a suicide. I was right, I'm certain now. He had a motive."

"Motive? What?"

"He probably struck his son, maybe during an argument about what happened between you two. Kyle must've died from the blow, and then his father tried to cover it all up by making it look like a suicide. Everyone knew Kyle was despondent. It all makes sense now. The Reverend Yoder killed his son."

DANIEL peered holes into Aiden. How was he going to get Aiden to stop? To stop his rampage of seeking the truth? A truth, in whatever form, that could destroy Daniel's life as he knew it.

"Enough of this, Aiden, no more of this game of yours."

"Game? But Daniel. You're not to blame. You can stop hating yourself." He set the bowl of popcorn on the coffee table and switched off the television with a solid click of the remote. "You're not responsible for what Kyle did, his father is, don't you see? I even think I know how he did it. There's a part of the head that if struck just right you can die almost instantly, without leaving hardly any external injuries. I did some research on it. The coroner told me he never conducted a brain autopsy to check for internal bruising of the brain—"

"Do you know what you're saying?"

"This is all even more important now. Uncovering the truth is for you, Daniel." Aiden lowered his voice. "You don't have to feel guilty anymore."

"What difference does it make whether he committed suicide or was killed by his father? Either way I'm still to blame."

"But, Daniel, you can't blame yourself for someone else's crime, you're not the devil in all this. It's the Reverend Yoder who—"

"You keep up with this and I'll be shunned." Daniel's eyes felt like burning lignite. He willed back the hot, angry tears. "It'll be me who'll lose. Not the Reverend Yoder."

"I don't see how that can be—"

"You know how it is in the Amish community, in any close-knit community. Even among the English in Henry gossip spreads like a hayfield on fire." He looked away and shook his head. "Act, Tara was right about you."

"Daniel, of all the people, I thought you'd understand. Why are you being this way, don't you want Kyle's killer brought to justice? Don't you understand that I'm doing this for you now? Don't you see? It's all for you."

Daniel glared at him. "Don't you put any of what I told you in one of your articles. I told you all this in the strictest of confidence, I never expected you to use it against me. Don't you betray me, Aiden Cermak." With both hands he seized Aiden by the collar of his hoody. "Don't you betray me! Don't you betray me!"

His arms locked and he looked hard into the startled Englishman's golden eyes. He held him by the collar for what seemed endless minutes, motionless, Aiden limp and powerless in his grip. Daniel saw the deep iridescence of Aiden's irises, the gentle rounding of his nose, the curl of his lips like rose petals....

He knew at that instant. Just like with Kyle that warm spring in the barn. Aiden did not have to say anything, like Kyle did not have to speak to reveal the feelings that had been fermenting between them for months. He retraced Aiden's reaction to his story about him and Kyle. Daniel was sure he'd seen a flicker in those amber eyes when he'd told Aiden he and Kyle had kissed.

He knew. For the first time, Daniel knew. For sure.

Aiden was "one of those."

The sensation was exhilarating, as if he were floating and yet had the weight of three Belgians pressing on his back. His nostrils flared, desperate for oxygen as he panted for breath.

He wanted to go. Turn and leave at once. But it was as if his thighs were strapped to the sofa.

A quake shook inside him. The tremor traveled from his toes inside his boots to the top of his bowl cut. He remembered that sensation. He had experienced it just before he had leaned in to kiss Kyle.

Daniel pulled Aiden nearer, his eyelids closing as he submitted to the same power that had lured his lips to meet Kyle's.

Consequences from that one simple kiss streaked across Daniel's muddled mind. He jerked up, as if awakening from a horrible dream, and loosened his hold on Aiden. His arms dropped lifeless to his sides.

Spotting his black felt hat where he'd left it on the dining table, he grabbed for it, upsetting the bouquet of wilted daisies in the glass vase. Turbid water spilled across the table and trickled over the edge.

He bolted for his buggy parked in the driveway. Disoriented and frightened, he was unable to untie Gertrude from the elm tree fast enough. He thought he heard Aiden calling for him as he fumbled in the darkness, struggling to untie Gertrude's lead. Everything went fuzzy. Nothing seemed real as he climbed into the driver's seat and unset the brake. Getting Gertrude to trot speed, he was rounding the corner before he realized he'd forgotten to switch on his LED lights The driver of the Nissan Pathfinder failed to notice him in time.

Chapter TWENTY-THREE

TWO hours had passed since Daniel was brought into Decatur Memorial Hospital by ambulance. While Daniel went through the typical battery of tests, Aiden sat restless in the waiting room, paced the halls, drank coffee, and blamed himself for everything that had happened.

His mind churned with anxiety about how bad off Daniel might be. Things were horrible enough with the whole Kyle Yoder fiasco scattered at their feet. Now to have to face the possibility that Daniel might be critically injured. It was all too much to take.

He wished he had held Daniel back from rushing out his front door. Daniel had been so distraught. Too distraught to be driving. Everything had happened so fast. Aiden heard the sound of tires skidding and metal screeching while still standing on his front stoop, calling out Daniel's name into the night. Frantic, he bolted down the darkened street, his imagination playing out the most horrific scenarios.

He found Daniel's buggy overturned and an elderly man standing outside his SUV, shaken and confused. Rushing in to help, Aiden discovered Daniel inside the buggy, semiconscious and bleeding from his head. Aiden had his cell phone tucked in his jeans so he promptly called 911. He stayed by Daniel's side until the paramedics and police arrived minutes later, then rushed back for his Aveo to tail the ambulance for the thirty-minute trip to Decatur.

The uninjured driver of the Pathfinder told Aiden and the investigators at the scene he had sideswiped Daniel's buggy wheels just as Daniel's safety flashers switched on. He said Daniel's buggy emerged out of the darkness so unexpectedly, it was as if it had magically appeared before his eyes. The sixty-something-year-old driver could not stop in time. He had broadsided the wheels before he could react, forcing the buggy carriage to topple and the shaft to dislodge. Gertrude was found a half mile down the road, still dragging the shaft, startled but unharmed.

A weary-looking Rachel and Samuel hurried into the waiting room where Aiden sat wringing his hands. They looked around, appearing out of place as the Amish usually do when surrounded by modern English contraptions. Spotting Aiden, they hastened over. Concern marked their middle-aged faces.

They told Aiden they'd heard of Daniel's accident from a Mennonite neighbor who often received emergency calls on their behalf. Joe Karpin had given them a ride. When Aiden had no information on Daniel's injuries, they sat next to him, their heads low, mouths stiff.

With typical Amish composure, they asked how the accident had happened. Aiden told them what he could without mentioning the reason why Daniel had hurried from his house. They seemed understanding and nodded lethargically as they listened.

When the doctor appeared, they all rushed to their feet. With their eyes fixed on her, she told them Daniel had four bruised ribs and a pulled shoulder and had received sixteen stitches on his forehead. Other than that, there was nothing too serious. But the doctor wanted to keep Daniel forty-eight hours for observation. Injuries like Daniel's, she warned, could worsen if he did not remain immobile for a few days.

The doctor escorted the three of them to Daniel's room. Staring at him lying in the hospital bed with the IV stuck in his arm, Aiden thought he looked so fragile, so vulnerable. Above his right eye was a lengthy scar, painful looking with the fresh stitches. His right arm was in a sling, already loosened by the fidgety and stubborn Daniel. The bandage wrapped around his rib cage looked too fixed for him to mess with.

Neither could discuss what had happened that night with his parents hovering about his bed. Aiden yearned to reach out to him. To hold him. But it was impossible, not with Rachel and Samuel there. After a while, Rachel and Samuel insisted Aiden go home for sleep. He looked to Daniel for a reassurance. Daniel gave him a reserved nod. Aiden, forcing his arms by his sides, wished Daniel his best and left for home alone.

His mind rehashed over and over everything that had happened that night as he made the drive back to Henry.

Daniel had tried to kiss him.

Aiden had seen the change that came over Daniel's face just before he had leaned in with his eyes closed. It was electrifying, yet, for some reason, frightening. He now saw Daniel for what he was. The gift of the bouquet, Daniel's moodiness around him. Kyle had not been an anomaly. There was no longer any doubt.

Daniel Schrock was gay, and he had wanted to kiss Aiden.

Everything made sense then. Daniel's coming by his house for so many visits. Sitting by his side watching TV. Going for lunch together whenever Daniel manned the furniture shop. Yes. Ever since that night they had searched for Mark together, he and Daniel had been courting, courting like any Amish couple. The bouquet had underlined what had been taking place between them the entire time.

But what about Tara?

She had been nothing but a ruse, a "beard."

The realization sent shivers through Aiden's body, as if his system had short-circuited. Elation lifted his heart into his throat. His head felt inflated with breath.

Yet all Daniel had to show for it was a stint in the hospital.

Energized, he visited Daniel the next morning. He brought along a baseball magazine and Rachel and Samuel too. He wanted to come alone, but had felt he should swing by the Schrocks to give them a lift. No doubt they would want to see their injured son.

Daniel was visibly edgy. Whenever Aiden tried to comfort him with words or gestures, Daniel fidgeted and looked away. When Rachel and Samuel left for coffee, he relished the opportunity to tell Daniel he loved him, but Daniel's terseness deflected any chance for him to say anything, to get close at all. An hour passed when Aiden felt as if he were intruding. Rachel and Samuel said they would call Joe Karpin for a ride; they wanted to stay a while longer with their son. Aiden drove into work, alone and confused.

It was at the *Blade* that afternoon when he first heard the rumors. Kevin strolled into the office from a dentist appointment and casually mentioned it, but Aiden did not want to believe it. A short time later he overheard some Amish on the street talking about it. Finally, at the IGA, the store manager happened to bring it up. The gossip worried Aiden enough that it prevented him from going back to the hospital to visit Daniel.

As the evening passed and the stories spread, Aiden had no doubt they were true. In a way, he'd seen it coming. He almost understood Daniel's motives.

Difficult as it was, Aiden refrained from visiting Daniel the rest of that night. He worried Daniel would not welcome him. The next morning, though, he could no longer resist. He needed to speak to him, to see him, to hear for himself that the rumors were true. He almost brought Daniel a bouquet of flowers, but had stopped when he'd remembered how much trouble a bouquet had caused them.

"How do you feel?" he asked, standing just inside the doorway to Daniel's hospital room. No one else was there, thank goodness; he had feared Tara might be there. He swept aside his guilt for not asking Rachel and Samuel if they wanted a ride to the hospital. This time, he needed to speak with Daniel alone.

"I'm doing better," Daniel said. He appeared in good spirits, happy even to see Aiden. "I can't wait to get out of here. I never spent so much time in a hospital before."

"It's good your community will be helping you pay for your bills," he said, remembering when Joe Karpin had told him about how the Amish use proceeds from auctions and flea markets to help out those with medical expenses.

"Ya, they are good about that."

"So is it true what I've been hearing?" Aiden wasted no time asking. He had little doubt about the rumors, yet he needed to hear from Daniel himself to be sure. He averted his eyes to let Daniel speak more freely. He peered at the two lumps where Daniel's feet poked under the bed sheets.

"I figure you mean Tara and me?" Daniel said, his voice coarse and hollow-sounding. "Ya, it's true. We're to be married. Next June just before the oat binding."

He was unprepared for the sharp sting of Daniel's words. Although he'd known the rumors of Daniel's proposing to Tara to be the truth, to hear it firsthand smarted like the poke of a needle. Yet in some ways, his sympathies for Daniel strengthened. The Amish world was much different from his. A person had fewer options living in a rigid community. Hundreds of years of tradition and staunch religious teachings could not be discarded so easily.

Nonetheless, he accepted partial responsibility for nudging Daniel down the path he had chosen to take with Tara. If not for his overzealous need to know the "truth" about Kyle Yoder's death, Daniel would never have rushed from his bungalow, winding up in the hospital where he'd been so compelled to propose to Tara. Yet he supposed, one way or the other, Daniel eventually would have asked her to be his wife.

Rumor had it Daniel had proposed while Tara had sat by his bedside. According to the gossip, he'd asked for her hand in the characteristic, unembellished Amish manner: "We should marry."

Word was Tara had at first hesitated, playing coy. She'd wanted to ensure Daniel's intentions were sincere. But as everyone knew, Tara could hardly refuse something she'd wanted almost half her entire life.

Inhaling, Aiden squared his shoulders. He had to deal with the reality of the situation. Why sink into the fantasy of what could never be? One way or the other, he supposed a life with Daniel would've been impossible. Even if they lived in a society that completely accepted homosexuality, they still had too many differences to circumvent. They were from two different worlds.

"Congratulations are in order," he said, looking fully into Daniel's dark eyes with a tremulous smile.

"Danke," Daniel murmured.

"I hope it all works out for you." He adjusted the thin gold chain around his neck so that the clasp lay on his nape.

"It's for the best," Daniel said. "For all of us. There's been too much chaos, too much confusion. You understand, don't you? You're too smart not to."

"Sure, I understand."

A flashback of Daniel nearly kissing him rolled across his mind. He still felt Daniel's breath on his face. Raw, with a faint smell of root beer. His fierce dark eyes, burning with passion, penetrating him as he clutched onto his hoody. His beard so close he could feel the bristles like the scratch of an oat sheaf.

No use thinking about any of that now.

"Well," Aiden said, shaking himself back to the present, "I decided to drop that whole Kyle Yoder investigation. It's not worth it, I guess. I was in over my head anyway, I didn't really know what I was doing. Sorry I caused you so much trouble."

"You didn't cause me any trouble. It's not your fault, you know how small towns are. But I'm glad you're not going to investigate anymore, I didn't think you would."

Aiden considered something that had haunted him for some time. With Daniel helpless in bed, with no chance of he and Daniel ever being lovers, he decided to reveal what he had known for many months, since June. After everything that had happened between them there were no longer any personal barriers. Not really. He took a few steps closer to Daniel. Tilting his head, he said, "I've always wanted to say how sorry I am for your losses. For Esther and Zachariah."

Daniel flushed above his moustacheless beard. He turned away and seemed to quiver. "I figured you might know about that," he said, looking back Aiden's way. "Thanks for your kind words."

"I can't imagine how horrible that must've been for you. Losing a wife and baby in a tornado. I just always wanted to say I'm sorry."

Daniel lowered his head. "God has plans for us, I figure. He knows what He's doing."

Aiden caught the shame in Daniel's eyes, and dismissed his labored mentioning of God's will. "You don't blame yourself for their deaths, too, do you, Daniel?"

"If I hadn't made so many wrong choices, a lot of people would never got hurt."

"Daniel, you didn't cause Kyle's death, and you certainly didn't conjure up that tornado—"

"Aiden, please, let's not talk about this, not here."

Silent a moment, Aiden stared down at the tiled floor. When Daniel remained quiet, he checked his wristwatch. He supposed there was little else to say. With a tight grin, he said he had to go. Chortling, he added, "I have to interview some man about his 250-pound pumpkin."

Daniel shared Aiden's chuckle, perhaps understanding small town frivolities as well as anyone.

"I guess I'll see you then," Aiden said. "Hope you feel better." He turned to leave. Daniel called out to him before he reached the door. Aiden looked back at him, hopeful.

"Yes?"

"Thanks for keeping my secret."

Aiden shrugged, the sides of his mouth heavy. "What're friends for?"

"No hard feelings?"

"Sure…. No hard feelings."

HE RUSHED out of the room before the hot tears spilled from his eyes. Darting out of the elevator, he almost knocked into Samuel in the lobby. Face to face, they stood speechless.

Aiden cleared his throat and held back his tears. "_ was just coming from seeing Daniel," he said, flushing like a thief who had just been caught fleeing from the scene of a crime. He looked down so that Samuel could not see his reddened cheeks and eyes. "He's doing better. He looks good."

"We hope to be taking him home today," Samuel said, fidgeting with his black felt hat in his brown hands. "Just in time for Thanksgiving."

Aiden glanced up and noted Samuel's expression lacked the normal joviality. Perhaps the stress from another near tragedy had left its stain. "That'll be nice."

"We're grateful his injuries are minor. God has spared us."

"Yeah, it could've been worse," Aiden said, his tone hushed. "Lucky he was broadsided and not hit from the back. That SUV could've done some real damage."

"You told us the other night he was driving home from your house, ya?"

Aiden hesitated. "Yes, that's the case."

"We had thought he was with Tara at her family's farm."

"Well, he was supposed to go there from my house, but I guess he lost track of time."

"I'm surprised Daniel forgot to use his lights. He can sometimes drive the horses too fast, but he's very cautious otherwise. We even tease him about being too safety conscious. We're surprised he was so careless."

Aiden's stomach churned with acid. "I guess he had a lot on his mind."

Samuel dragged veiny fingers through his grizzled beard. "Maybe it's best if you stop seeing each other so much."

Aiden widened his eyes. "What?"

"It's not good for him… to see you, I think. Maybe you should stay away. We like you, and always will be grateful for what you did for us, but that doesn't make up for the differences between our world and yours. It's best if Daniel not spend so much time with you."

Aiden looked away. Worse than if Samuel had slapped him solidly across the face.

"Daniel will be married to Tara next year, by the second week of June. We're happy for him, that he's getting on with his life." Samuel fidgeted with his hat. "Maybe for Daniel's sake, for all of us, including you, it would be best if you leave Henry altogether. A small town, it can't be good for you. There's nothing in Henry for a single young Englishman like you."

Aiden lifted his face to meet the Amish man's stare. There he was. Standing before him. Just like that first time, many months ago, at that very hospital, where Samuel had visited him after he had swerved his Chevy Cavalier into the path of Bobby Jonesboro's pickup truck. He'd held his black felt hat in the same manner, his rough fingers clutching and unclutching the brim. Only this time, instead of inviting Aiden to his home, he was asking him to go away, to leave his family and community for good.

"Leave Daniel alone, Aiden," Samuel said.

Aiden's mind went blank, anesthetized. Whatever Samuel's pronouncement meant to Aiden, rebuffing him was impractical. As patriarch of his clan, Samuel was doing what he thought best for his son. His Amish ancestry almost demanded it from him.

Despite everything, Aiden reached his hand out to Samuel. It was a small solace that Aiden's hands were calloused now, though nowhere near as much as Samuel's, unlike that first handshake they had shared in the emergency room months ago when he had worried that his hands were so soft and underworked.

As he left the hospital, dazed and numb from rejection, Joe Karpin was pulling his van away from the main entrance drive-thru. Noticing Aiden, he grinned, his face crinkling, and waved. Good to see some people never changed.

Chapter TWENTY-FOUR

NO SURPRISE when the Schrocks did not invite Aiden to Thanksgiving dinner. He spent the day alone, watching the traditional football games and a DVD of his favorite movie. Alone on his sofa watching Richard Dreyfus struggle up the face of Devil's Tower, he realized Samuel was right. He did not belong in Henry. He never did. Just like the aliens in the film, he was an outsider on unfamiliar turf. He had encroached on a foreign culture and had tried to insert his ways into it. The result? A pathological contraindication, like an adverse reaction to medicine.

Samuel did not want him there. Whoever had written those two threatening messages and smashed a pumpkin against his house did not want him there. Daniel no longer wanted him there.

Even the pimple-faced girl who worked at the IGA no longer looked up to Aiden. Whenever he'd purchase anything from the store, she'd avoid eye contact and scowl. Not too long ago she'd treated him as if he were a rock star for having saved the Schrocks.

There was nothing keeping him in Henry any longer. The chief reason why he'd even moved there was out of his reach.

Daniel was engaged to Tara Hostetler and they were to be married in June.

His time in Henry had come to an end.

The following Monday, he resigned from the *Blade*. Kevin, who had just gotten back into town from visiting his eldest daughter and her family in Davenport, Iowa, seemed almost relieved. He accepted Aiden's resignation with a nod and a sturdy handshake. He wished him all the best and asked him to stay in touch. That was it. The job ended as easily as it had come.

Aiden wanted to say a formal goodbye to Daniel. He crossed the street to the Schrock's furniture shop, hoping he'd be there. But it was Uncle Eldridge and his two daughters' turn to man. They told him Daniel was home from the hospital, but he would not be manning the shop for a few weeks until he fully healed.

He did not dare drive out to the Schrock farm, not after Samuel's rebuking him at the hospital. He would've liked to have said goodbye to the entire family, especially the children, but he supposed it was all for the best to leave them be. To slink away from Henry like a wounded coyote to its lair. He'd caused enough trouble already.

Deep down, he hoped Daniel would come and see him once he heard the news that he was moving. Everyone had to know by now. Perhaps Samuel had told him about their conversation at the hospital. Each time he heard the familiar clip-clop of horse-drawn buggies pass his house while he packed the belongings he wanted to take with him, he'd rush to the window and peer out. No Daniel. All for the best, he supposed.

With his month to month rent, it was simple to terminate the lease. He informed the realtor by facsimile that he was leaving at the end of the week. He mentioned he planned on leaving most of his furniture behind. She could do what she wanted with the prefabricated junk he'd bought while in college. Probably wouldn't survive another move anyway.

Chicago seemed a million miles away, another world. Returning there would be futile. Everything Chicago represented for him was in the past, from another era. Like Henry, there was nothing for him there. No one to lure him back. No family. No real friends.

He considered heading west to Montana like he'd always dreamed. But the thought of such a drastic move alone sapped his mouth of moisture. He knew not a soul out west. With his meager savings, only the unknown awaited him in Montana. To up and move to an isolated part of the country on his own, where freelance work could only trickle in? His dream of living in a cabin deep in the woods surrounded by snow-capped mountains was just that—a dream. How many people his age could afford to make such fantasies come true?

The best option was to return to Maryland. Back to his boyhood home in St. Mary's County. A few of his high school and college friends still lived there. Besides, he hadn't seen his parents since he'd moved to Chicago, more than two years ago. Time he got back home for an indefinite visit.

LIFE back in Maryland wasn't so awful. The weeks passed slowly, but it was nice to feel he belonged. His parents, comfy in their midcentury rancher, were congenial, as always, and easy to live with. Quiet and smiling. No matter what life dropped into their laps, they always took it with a smile. Even when Aiden had come out to them six years ago during a weekend visit from college, they had merely smiled. No outrage. No questions. Never to mention it again. They were as malleable as the rubber fittings Aiden's father used to fix bathroom sinks in his plumbing business.

He saw his old college and high school buddies once in a while. They would do crabs, go for beers, hang out and chat sitting on the hoods of their cars like old times. Most were married with babies, and seldom could get away for more than a few hours a week. Being around his married friends made Aiden long for something he worried he would never have: love and commitment.

During the passing weeks, Aiden fell back full-time on his freelance work. He'd even earned a two-month assignment working on-site as a technical writer for a defense contractor in Lexington Park. Working there filled the yawning days.

Sometimes while driving the winding roads of southern Maryland, he'd spot a horse-drawn buggy from the region's small Amish population, and he'd watch with moist eyes as it jostled past an Amish-owned tobacco farm. Seeing the Amish forced to the forefront of his mind those persistent images of Henry. He'd picture Ivy Street and the IGA and the cornfield across the road from his squat white bungalow with the robin's-egg blue shutters. He'd reflect on the Henry High School marching band and the quaint villages scattered about Frederick County. He even started to see the adult superstore along I-57 as charming.

He wondered if Christmas had treated the Schrocks well. If they were preparing for the spring oat crop now that New Years had passed. He'd grin, thinking about Mark's rumspringa roadtrip to the Texas shore, and imagined he and his companions had had a fabulous time. He trusted he was staying out of trouble. He fretted over Little Leah, hoping she was battling bravely against her MLD. At times he could picture the family so clearly, nestled together in their sitting room after the evening chores were complete, going about their diversions by the glow and hiss of gas lanterns. He imagined he was there with them. Rachel crocheting a shawl, Samuel reading *The Budget*, David scribbling in his coloring book.

He'd think about *The Henry Blade* and wonder if his former boss had received any more complaints since his "ace reporter" had gone. Did Kevin really think Aiden's investigation into Kyle Yoder's death a waste of time? Aiden understood that Kevin had a business to run, after all.

Still suspicious of Kyle's death, Aiden had learned to let go. Although the image of Kyle Yoder's body hanging from a rafter in the barn continued to haunt him, as the weeks passed he was bothered by it less and less. He still believed his death had many unanswered questions—too many—but he accepted the possibility that he might have been misguided about the entire investigation.

The question of who had left those two threatening messages and hurled a pumpkin at his house still puzzled him. He considered that the Reverend Yoder himself might have done it, whether he was guilty of filicide, or manslaughter, or neither. One time he had laughed, thinking the threats had come from Tara Hostetler, jealous of his and Daniel's relationship. But he supposed that was unlikely. He even considered that the family of Bobby Jonesboro might have been the culprit.

Possibly they had wanted to frighten Aiden as revenge for their loved one's death.

Or maybe it had been an angry neighbor who wanted to prevent him from making the Amish "look bad." Kevin had said it was the English who had lodged the most complaints against him. Was it so strange that the English wanted to protect the Amish? To protect a seemingly more innocent era long past in American culture? Even Kevin and the police seemed to want to protect the Amish from "bad publicity" by overlooking obvious incongruities in the deaths of Kyle and that man found in a cistern. Hadn't Aiden himself risked his life to protect the Amish when he had swerved his car in front of the drunken Bobby Jonesboro? Would he have done the same if the Schrocks had been an English family in a minivan?

And, of course, Aiden never stopped thinking about Daniel.

The tall, dark, and brooding Amish man always hovered somewhere in his mind. Daniel had become such a fixture in his thoughts, he would appear without Aiden's realizing he was even thinking of him. Reaching for a drink from the refrigerator, brushing his teeth at the bathroom mirror, reading a paperback in bed. There he would be, as real as if he were flesh, like something he could taste. At times he was certain he could smell the musk from his hard-worked body.

So often he dreamed Daniel would leave Tara, give up on Henry, and rush to Maryland to sweep him away. He almost believed it true sometimes, and would insist he could see him coming toward him from the corners of his eyes. But when he'd turn quickly to look, it was always just his mind playing a cruel trick.

Many times he considered calling Daniel at the shop, but he'd talk himself out of it. What would be the point? They were from two different worlds, just as Samuel had said. To assume after everything that had happened between them they could go back to being simple friends, while Daniel led the life of a married Amish farmer.... There was no way.

He understood that their short juncture in life was over, yet forgetting about him was not so easy. Did he recover from his injuries fully? Had he absolved himself from the deaths of Kyle and Esther and Zachariah? Was he happy he was to wed Tara?

Daniel had never verbally stated he loved Aiden. But as Aiden replayed their relationship over and over in his head, from their first meeting when they shook hands so clumsily the day Samuel had brought him home from the hospital, to that moment when Daniel had tried to kiss him on his sofa, he suspected at some point Daniel had fallen in love with him. As tacit as it had been, undoubtedly he and Daniel had courted. For Aiden, it was a beautiful, old-fashioned, genuine courtship. One he would have difficulty forgetting.

Yet in the end, Daniel had made his choice. He had chosen his destiny. A destiny apart from Aiden's. It was as simple as that.

People always have choices. Despite all their talk of God's will, even the Amish have choices. Joining the church came down to a choice. One is free to stay or leave.

Social pressures could sway one's decision: fear of loss of livelihood, family, friends. Dread of the Amish shunning must work wonders in keeping even the most agnostic in their ranks. Even the gay community had its own ordnung, an unwritten code that dictated style of dress, beliefs, behaviors. In some ways, it was more fiercely enforced than that in the Amish world. Aiden had learned that firsthand. But, ultimately, everyone is at liberty to make his or her own way in life.

Daniel had made his.

As the months progressed and the mild and wet southern Maryland winter passed like a yearling leaping over a creek into a warm and dry spring, Aiden tried to put everything in Henry behind him. He forged ahead. He did whatever was necessary to avert his thoughts from it all. He worked at his writing, occasionally socialized with his friends, helped his parents with the upkeep of their rancher. Time was his best friend. If he got through the next year, everything would be easier after that. Daniel would inevitably evaporate from his mind.

Chapter TWENTY-FIVE

ONE night during the Memorial Day weekend, Aiden was working on a freelance writing assignment at his parents' dining table when he heard footsteps near the side of the house. His father was out on an emergency pipe break and his mother was upstairs in the master bedroom watching television. The house was dark, except for the hanging lamp spotlighting Aiden and his work.

The sound of footsteps was crisper, coming from near the detached garage. He could hear the sound clearly, for the house was still. Voices from his mother's television program were barely audible. He had turned off the air conditioning unit in the living room once his mother had gone upstairs; he was still unable to acclimate to the artificial coldness after spending so much time with the Amish. He'd even stopped watching so much television and rarely bothered to turn on his car radio while driving.

He thought at first it was his father returning home, but he hadn't heard his van pull up in the driveway. He was also familiar with his father's step. His gait was careless, less deliberate. These steps sounded furtive, like a prowler trying his best not to be heard.

He heard the steps shift closer, this time near the dining room window. There was almost no crime in this small part of southern Maryland, but the thought of a recent rash of burglaries in the area alarmed him. He nudged aside his laptop and, holding his breath, peeked out the window.

Light from the streetlamp was blocked by a large maple tree on the side of the house. He saw in the faint light that the driveway was empty where his father would park his plumber's van. More crunching of earth fading toward the back yard. Uneasy, he let the curtain dangle back into place.

He scurried into the kitchen and looked out the window above the sink. He saw nothing in the darkness. Rustling seemed to be coming from his left. Whoever it was, he was circling the house, heading for the front.

He made sure to make as little noise as possible when he opened the front door. There was a scant orange glow coming from the door lamp. The glass globe was covered in muck and filled with dead bugs. The streetlight was unhindered from this view; he could just see the rhododendrons bordering the driveway, dim and colorless in the night. Along the curb was the murky shape of his Chevy and an unfamiliar Jeep that he hadn't recalled seeing parked there before. He figured it belonged to a visitor of one of the neighbors.

He pushed open the door wider and scrunched his forehead into the night. A smack of late night mugginess made him wish he was back at his laptop, finishing his article about southern Maryland's African American crabbers. He detected a hint of the briny scent in the air, a smell he'd never grown used to even though he'd lived there most his life. Another crunching sound to his right.

He caught sight of something, a figure moving. His breathing stopped. He let go of the door handle, and, inhaling, balanced himself in preparation for fight or flight.

Out of the darkness the outline of a person came toward him, hovering closer. The streetlight hit the figure from the side, casting a long shadow over the tulips abutting the brick skirt of the house.

"Aiden?"

A man's voice. A familiar man's voice. Peering toward the figure, he tried to make out who it was.

"Who's there?" He wanted to force warning into his voice, but his words came out in a coarse, frightened whisper.

"I wasn't sure this was your house."

The figure came into focus.

"Conrad?"

"It's been a while, hasn't it?"

"What… what are you doing here?"

"I wanted to see you, Aiden."

"Why are you prowling around? Why didn't you just knock?"

"I wasn't sure this was your house. I remembered the street, but not the address. I didn't see your dad's van, so I went looking for your old Cavalier in the garage to make sure."

"I don't have that car anymore. I wrecked it about a year ago." Aiden's shock at seeing Conrad standing on his parents' front stoop momentarily overshadowed his disappointment that he was not Daniel coming to sweep him away like he'd so often fantasized. Unbelievable after nearly three years, speaking with his ex-boyfriend.

"Are you alone?" Conrad moved closer, looking more confident.

"Pop's gone for work, Mama's upstairs watching TV. Why?"

"Perfect. I was hoping we could talk."

"Talk?"

They sat at the dining table sipping canned beers Aiden had retrieved from the utility room refrigerator. He sat at the head of the table, his laptop and notepads pushed off to the side; Conrad sat catty-corner to his left. Ignoring his better judgment, Aiden had had no option but to invite Conrad inside. He hadn't wanted to hurt his feelings by refusing him. He'd travelled so far, all the way from Michigan, his home state. Aiden had learned a few years ago that he had been living there with his boyfriend, the one he'd dumped Aiden for.

He was still in disbelief, looking into the face of his ex-boyfriend. After so long apart, he looked much the same. Square jaw, pale blue eyes, reddish-blond hair cut in the same high-and-tight style he'd had ever since they had first met, when Conrad was in the ROTC program at college.

"What brings you back to live with your parents?" Conrad asked, his hand clasped around his can of Coors Light.

Dazed, Aiden said, "Just decided it was time to move back to Maryland. Been busy with freelance work, haven't had time to look for a place of my own."

"Are you seeing anyone?"

Aiden shook his head. "No," he said, suspicious of what it was Conrad really wanted to talk about.

"Neither am I."

"What about that man? The one you left me for back in Chicago?"

Conrad lowered his head. He fingered the tab on his beer can. "Things didn't work out with him. We broke up. Last summer actually. We were living back home in Michigan. I stayed on because of my job, but I got laid off in April."

Despite everything that had happened between them, Aiden was sympathetic, but apprehensive as well. Was Conrad there because he'd nowhere else to go? Was he desperate for money and shelter? Conrad had never been that close with his family in Michigan and would likely have few others to turn to. Aiden laid his arms across the polished ebony of the tabletop and folded his hands.

"Why didn't you just call instead of coming all the way out here?" he asked.

"I lost my cell phone a couple months ago, with all my numbers in it. Thanks to speed dial I can't remember peoples' numbers. Besides, you never returned my other calls."

"What other calls?"

"I left you messages."

Aiden recalled the one short text message Conrad had sent him about a year ago, the day he'd gone on a buggy ride with Daniel and the children to break in Gertrude. He wondered if Conrad had texted him that summer in need of companionship after his break-up. He never did bother to reply to Conrad's text. He had wanted to keep Conrad in his past. Now here he was, sitting at his parents' dining table, within arm's reach.

"Why didn't you just look up my parents' ground line?" he asked.

"I wanted to surprise you." Conrad showed his even white teeth.

"How did you know I was back home?" Aiden was guarded.

"I was in Chicago a few months ago and ran into an old friend of yours. He remembered me but I didn't really remember him. He told me you got some job with a newspaper in some small town I can't remember the name of now. I called the only newspaper in town, but the man who answered said you quit and moved back with your parents."

"You called *The Henry Blade*? Why?"

"I wanted to get ahold of you. What do you think I came all the way down here for? I never really stopped thinking about you, Aiden."

Aiden dropped his eyes. Twiddling his thumbs, he studied his blurred reflection in the polished table top. His mind came to a slow halt.

"I've really missed you, Aiden." Conrad inched his hand across the table toward Aiden's. "With my new job and all, I started thinking a lot about—"

Aiden jerked his head up. "You have a new job?"

"Yeah. A buddy of mine works for a software company. He set it up for me. I started last month. Awesome, huh?" Conrad beamed one of his double-duty smiles that used to make Aiden quiver. Did it still? "I was in the same boat as you. No prospects and nothing going on. I was just about to move back in with my parents like you when my buddy came through. Losing my other job was a blessing in disguise. I'm bringing in more money than ever."

Relieved Conrad wasn't desperate for money and a place to stay, but still defensive, Aiden said, "So why are you here? It's been nearly three years, Conrad."

"Like I was saying, I've been thinking about you a lot lately. About us. I was hoping we could maybe start over."

"Just like that?"

His mind traveled back to that day Conrad had left him so abruptly in Chicago after a short two months together in the city. He'd come home from his part-time job to find him practically out the front door and gone.

Now after all this time he wanted to come back.

"What do you say, Aiden? Another shot?"

Conrad had come all the way from Michigan to Maryland just for him. No man had ever chased after him before. He'd always been the one who did the pursuing. He had followed Conrad all the way to Chicago after Conrad had gotten that job offer; he had moved to Henry just to be near Daniel. It was nice to be the pursuee for a change. Still, he resisted allowing flattery to sway him.

"I don't know," he said. "It's so quick. A lot has happened since you left. We're not the same people anymore."

Conrad brought his hands closer to his chest and sighed. "I've never understood what that means. Of course we're the same people. I'm still me. See?" He framed his face with his hands.

"That's real deep."

"Aiden, you know what I mean." He leaned forward and reached his hands back across the smooth table. "We were together for over a year. In gay terms, that's like a lifetime."

"What about that man in Michigan?"

"I told you, that's over. It was over pretty much from the start, to be honest. I was an idiot to leave you. I admit that now; I made a mistake. We all do sometimes. It doesn't change the fact that I still want to be with you."

Conrad was someone he had once loved and with whom he'd assumed he would spend the rest of his life. It wasn't so much he was hurting about his running out on him so abruptly; he had gotten over that. But how could he trust him after he had abandoned him? He knew that Daniel was now in his past and that in a few weeks he would be married to Tara. He would recover from him fully too, he supposed. Nevertheless, he surely did not wish to spend the rest of his life alone. How many other chances would he get?

Other than Daniel, Aiden had yet to meet another gay man like Conrad who shared his love of the outdoors and backpacking—rugged outdoors and real backpacking, not backpacking through Western European capitals. Were he and Conrad meant to be together after all? Was it some kind of sign, a clue from God, the way the Amish always talked about?

"Come on, Aiden." Conrad lowered his voice. "Let's try again. What do you say, huh? The best part is we can stay here—we can stay in the DC area, I mean." His pale blue eyes widened. "Wouldn't that be great?"

"What do you mean, stay here?" Aiden eyed him. "What about your new job?"

"My job's in Alexandria."

"You mean you've been in Virginia all this time? The past month?"

"Yeah, since April. I remembered your old boss saying you moved back home. You were just down the road practically. How coincidental is that? I lucked out you were still here with nothing going on."

Aiden sighed. So Conrad hadn't come all the way from Michigan to Maryland just for him. He had been in the area the entire time. His coming to his parents' house was a matter of convenience, a mere whim. He never would have traveled all the way from Michigan just for him. It had taken him a whole month just to drive the forty miles from Alexandria. Conrad's old selfish ways were resurfacing.

"Aiden?" Conrad reached across the polished table and tried to take Aiden's hand in his, but Aiden pulled back.

"I guess you're right," Aiden said. "Maybe we haven't changed much."

He stood up, pushing his chair out with a discordant screech on the wood floor, and peered out the darkened window. He'd never felt more alone.

"Aiden, don't you see? It's perfect. We're both already here, with no connections to anyone or anywhere else. Chicago is in the past, for both of us. We can live in Alexandria. Start new, fresh. I already have a great apartment. Fourteenth floor! And there're gays everywhere—"

Aiden shot him a scowling look. "I don't care about that."

"You know what I mean. We can live happy there; we don't have to hide. We can be ourselves."

"You mean you can be yourself. I won't be happy there."

"Why not? It's practically where you're from. It's barely an hour from here."

"If neither of us have any obligations, with our entire lives open to us, why not move somewhere out west? Like Montana?"

Conrad slumped into his chair. His arm slid off the table and into his lap with a dull thud. "That again," he said, sighing heavily. "I was hoping you had grown up in the past few years. Hard to imagine you're still hanging onto that old fantasy. You're too much of a dreamer, Aiden. Move out west? What do you think it is? 1850?"

"I used to think you liked that sort of thing. Remember how we used to go backpacking in college?"

"Those were weekend trips, Aiden. You can't live like that every day. You're not being realistic."

Turning back toward the window, Aiden muttered, "It's realistic if you want it." The corners of his mouth hung heavy. He felt sapped of hope. Why did Conrad have to come back? Why did he have to magnify his loneliness? Just when he was getting past Daniel, past everything, Conrad brought back that razor-sharp awareness that he was destined to be alone forever. Why did he have to tease him with ideas that he could find love again?

"These romantic notions of yours are going to get you into big heaps of trouble one of these days, Aiden. Look at you. Twenty-four and—"

"I'm twenty-six."

"Even worse. Twenty-six and still living at home. So much for your ridiculous dreams, huh? A lot of good it's gotten you. With me you could at least have a life."

"Yeah, well, I guess I'm just not interested in that kind of life," Aiden said, thinking about Daniel's imminent marriage and the Montana mountains.

He wanted to say more but remained quiet. He was tired. He'd been in love with this man not too long ago; now he wondered what had attracted him so much that he had followed him all the way to a city he'd never set foot in before. Conrad had been the one who had introduced him to backpacking. Had he expected that to be enough? He had thought they had wanted the same things; now he realized they never did.

Lonely or not, he would not commit to someone out of desperation. He did not relay this insight to Conrad. He was too worn out to get into a quarrel with him. He knew from experience it would lead to nothing but personal insults and ego-driven accusations.

No. Conrad's double-duty smile no longer worked on him.

He replayed in his mind his own words from just a moment ago: *It's realistic if you want it.*

His dream was always to go west, to Montana. Why shouldn't he? He had as much chance of making something of himself out there as he did in Maryland or Illinois. Why not go where he'd rather be? If it didn't work out, he could always come back home, just like he had when things soured in Henry. No harm taking an extended trip at least. No reins held him back.

Let Conrad and the others scoff at him. What did he care? What made them such exemplars of how one should live?

Feeling more determined than ever, he looked deep into the glacier-blue eyes of his former boyfriend. A sense of resolve filled his chest. "I think we're done talking, Conrad."

Chapter TWENTY-SIX

TWO days after Conrad's surprise visit, Aiden packed his little Aveo with his backpacking gear, laptop, and other essentials, adequate for at least a month, and pulled away from his boyhood home, waving goodbye, once again, to his smiling parents. He wasted no time heading out on his western excursion. Too much time had already languished. If he waited any longer, he knew he wouldn't go through with it.

If things worked out and he found a suitable life out in Montana, he'd send for what was left of his belongings. His parents, who had never traveled west of Nashville, Tennessee, had said they might even want to drive them out for him.

He had never set off alone on such a long journey before. Fear could not hold him back this time. For once he needed to heed his own advice. No ties restricted him from doing anything or going anywhere he wished, just as he had told Conrad. His dreams could never come true if he didn't at least try. Stagnating in his old bedroom in Maryland was hardly the answer.

For the first time in his life, he was traveling to a place without chasing after someone. He had trailed after Conrad to Chicago. He had moved to Henry just to be near Daniel. Eventually, he'd even run back home to his parents in Maryland. This time, he was going off on his own, without the safety net of knowing someone would be on the other end waiting for him.

When he neared Pittsburgh, he almost turned back for home. The farther he pulled away from Maryland, the more his nerves pinched.

Driving through the western suburbs of Chicago his second morning out, he had to fend off the urge to postpone his trip to Montana entirely. The draw of the I-57 interchange stole his mind away from everything else. It was almost surreal. In two hours he'd be back in Henry. Out of fear, loneliness, longing, he wanted badly to take that exit. But as he drove, his eyes peering through the rain smeared windshield, he used all his strength to keep heading west. He sat on his uncertainties, forcing himself to keep the steering wheel straight.

He knew going back to Henry would prove pointless. Daniel was on the verge of marrying Tara. Their wedding had been set for mid-June. Here it was June second. The community must be in a buzz about it. Organizers and volunteers must have already sent out hundreds of invitations to Amish communities from Pennsylvania to Iowa. Surely the community by now had completed rebuilding Daniel's farmhouse, destroyed by that tornado. Daniel had been renting his land to an English farmer. After the wedding, he and his bride would certainly want to live there and raise a family.

No use even thinking about any of it. His dream of Daniel was dead. As dead as that opossum, lying on the side of the Interstate east of Rockford, he had just whizzed by.

The remainder of the way to Montana, he stopped by a few sights he'd always wanted to see: the Badlands, Mount Rushmore, Devil's Tower. Three days after leaving Maryland, he crossed the Wyoming border into Montana. He'd made it. He was driving through a state he had dreamed about visiting since he had set out on his first backpacking trip with Conrad seven years ago. Nerves fluttered inside his stomach like a flock of birds.

Nine hours later (a huge span of time, he thought, for traveling halfway through one state), he reached a place outside Kalispell, thirty miles south of Glacier National Park. A small convenience store designed to look like a log cabin grabbed his attention away from the looming Rocky Mountains and lush foothills. He reckoned he should load up on a few supplies before entering the park, where he was going to spend his first few days backpacking. There would be few services once inside the park.

The young store clerk was congenial. His familial warmth made Aiden more at ease. While the clerk tallied Aiden's items, he warned Aiden to wear layers for his trip into Glacier, for it was still cold up in the mountains.

"How did you know I was going up there?" Aiden asked.

"I can see all your gear stuffed in your car." The clerk nodded toward the large window overlooking the parking lot. "And your license plate. Maryland, huh? That's a haul."

Aiden chuckled. "Sure was. But worth the trip."

"Made snow up on the Lewis Range the other day," the clerk said. "Winter hasn't yet left us."

The clerk's manner of speaking struck Aiden as familiar, but he was unable to put his finger on it. Perhaps it was a local twang he'd heard before maybe on television.

As the clerk handed Aiden his bag of purchases, the sound of the shop's door chimes made both men glance toward the man who had just stepped in. Aiden could not believe his eyes. Mouth and eyes agape, he caught his bag in time before dropping it.

The man had a moustacheless beard and was wearing broadfall denim pants, a navy blue collarless shirt, suspenders, and a straw wide-brimmed hat.

Aiden glanced out the window. Tied to a post was a sleek horse hitched to a market wagon. Just as he'd suspected. The man was unmistakably Amish.

The Amish man, taking off his hat, grabbed for a newspaper and strolled up behind Aiden by the cashier. His beard was newly sprouted, as if he'd recently married.

"I didn't expect to see any Amish here," Aiden blurted, surprised by his own boldness. But the tall Amish man was as kind as the store clerk. He grinned at Aiden.

"Ya. We're just about everywhere these days." He chuckled. "Somewhat of a new settlement here. Only one or two in Montana as far as I know. It's been here about fifteen years. I just moved here last spring from Indiana."

Reflecting back to last summer when he had ridden in the market wagon with Daniel on the way to the horse auction, Aiden remembered Daniel telling him about a fledgling Amish settlement near Glacier National Park where he'd once backpacked.

"Is this the town of Rose Crossing?" he asked.

"Ya, sure is."

"I've heard of it. A friend of mine once told me about it." He refrained from mentioning his association with Daniel and the Amish in central Illinois. There was so much emotion attached to his experiences there, to bring it up so flippantly would be almost blasphemous.

As Aiden wished them both goodbye and turned to leave, he overheard the Amish man speak Pennsylvania German with the young store clerk. Aiden then realized that the clerk, too, was Amish. His peculiar way of speaking became clear. Walking to his car, he gazed through the store window and recognized the clerk's attire, which hadn't stood out to him until that moment. He was dressed identically to the other Amish man; his Amish straw hat hung on a hook next to a medical marijuana dispenser behind the counter.

Driving to the park, he wondered if he was ever going to be able to get away from the Amish and put Daniel solidly in his past.

An hour later, Aiden checked in with the Apgar Visitor Center. The park ranger handed him his backcountry permit, which Aiden had reserved online the day before he left Maryland. The ranger also gave him a bear-proof canister, mandatory for all backcountry use.

"You picked a good trail to hike," the military looking ranger about Aiden's age said. "It's about the only trail clear of snow. South facing most of the way. We've had a lot of snow this spring."

"I heard. You think I'll need snowshoes?"

"You'll be okay. You might hit one or two snowfields once you get above eight thousand feet, but it shouldn't be too deep."

"That's great," Aiden said. "I'm looking forward to it."

"Now be careful out there by yourself." The ranger winked. "Make sure to make lots of noise to scare away the bears and cougars."

THAT ranger was kind of cute, Aiden mused as he drove the Going-to-the-Sun Road to his trailhead. He took in all the wondrous sights along the way, feeling better about his adventure. To his left the oblong Lake McDonald, reflecting the verdant conifers and the towering mountains, most with snow still on their craggy peaks, stretched for several miles until edging against Lake McDonald Lodge. Past the lodge the road paralleled McDonald Creek. The creek gurgled with frothy white water and tea-green glacial silt that cut deep into the steely bedrock. Just before heading down his trailhead turnoff, he spotted a black bear's rump as it grew smaller through a cluster of red alder bushes.

Aiden could hardly believe he was actually here, inside Glacier National Park. He had made his dream come true—or at least partly. He was on his way, anyhow, surrounded by some of the most pristine and vast wilderness in the contiguous United States. There were no other cars parked at the Packers Roost trailhead, so he figured he would be alone on his chosen twenty-two-mile loop trail. It was still early in the season, and the bulk of the park's visitors wouldn't be filling the trails and campsites until closer to the Summer Solstice.

After strapping on his seventy-pound backpack, astutely filled with all his gear, including the bear canister the solicitous ranger had given him, he signed the register at the kiosk that had important information about the backcountry: wildlife facts, fire dangers, grizzly and cougar warnings. Consulting his topo map, he traced with his finger the route for his first day's hike. Because he knew he would be arriving at the park late his first day, he had reserved his first of three backcountry campsites only five miles from the trailhead. He wanted to make sure he still had ample daylight to set up camp. He tucked the map inside the hip pocket of his convertible hiking pants and set off for his first-time solo backpacking excursion. Curious white-tailed deer nibbling on leftover stock hay at the trailhead eyeballed him as he made his way alone into the forest.

There was a chill in the air, but soon the sun beaming through the hemlocks and firs and the healthy body heat he worked up warmed him. Nearly four years had lapsed since his last backpacking trip, but it was much like riding a bicycle. A mere few hundred yards into the trail and his muscle memory recalled every terrain he had ever traversed. The crush of earth under the weight of his sturdy hiking boots gave him a sense of verve. He inhaled, breathing in all the invigorating aromas of the forest.

He wasn't really afraid of running into bears or cougars. Glacier, he knew, had a reputation for such encounters. But even so the chances were low. He had a higher probability of drowning or falling off a cliff—or running into the handsome ranger. Still, he heeded the thoughtful ranger's advice. Over and over he crooned an old tune he remembered from grade school: *On top of spaghetti, all covered with cheese, I lost my poor meatball, when somebody sneezed....*

Within two hours he arrived at his first campsite, nestled in a small meadow surrounded by conifers. Solitude engulfed him. Hemlocks and firs and the occasional osprey yelping like a lap dog in the sky were his only eavesdroppers.

Like any good backpacker, he first set up his two-man tent (the same one he had used with Conrad), tossing in all his sleeping gear and releasing his zero-degree sleeping bag from its stuff sack so that it would regain its plumpness before bedtime. His tent erected, he cooked supper in the meal preparation area with the water he pumped from a nearby pebble-strewn stream using his state of the art micro-filter.

Dinner consisted of freeze-dried lasagna with meat sauce along with oatmeal cookies for dessert and a cup of hot green tea. He cleaned his dinnerware using biodegradable soap and stored all his food, toiletries, cookware, and garbage in the bear canister. He tucked the canister inside his backpack and rigged a urethane-coated suspension cord over a sturdy cottonwood branch and fastened it to his pack. When ready for bed, he would be able to easily hoist it up out of the reach of bears.

Before it became too dark, he collected several armfuls of dead dry white pine from the forest floor and formed a fire tepee in the designated fire pit around strips of newspaper he'd packed in. He was certain his fire tepee would have earned respect from the most ardent Scoutmaster.

Finished with his camp chores, he at last sat on a log by the fire pit and rested. As his body temperature dropped, a chill swept through him. He slipped on the woolen sweater tied around his waist. A mountain cottontail hopped into view from behind pinegrass. Noticing Aiden, it turned and scampered for a patch of alders. Aiden chuckled, then flushed like a dejected suitor, a reoccurring feeling lately. Somewhere a badger let loose a squeal so strident it made Aiden jump.

As the forest dimmed, he brought his knees to his chest and hugged himself. The first real stab of loneliness pierced him. Why, out here in the Montana backcountry, a place he was hoping to call home, did he feel so alone, so much like an intruder?

The sky, with the passing of evening twilight, turned pitch-black. Multifarious stars, more than he'd ever seen, emerged in the sky above the tree crowns. Darkness loomed everywhere. He set a match to his fire tepee, and soon orange flames leaped from the hissing wood and crackling sparks disappeared past the shadowy conifer branches.

With the waning full moon rising higher in the sky bringing out more murky shadows, the uncertainty of his life took on a new reality. If he didn't belong here, then where did he belong? For a long time he stared into the flames, his thoughts like smoldering embers. The smoke stung his eyes whenever the breeze shifted. He didn't mind. He liked it. The discomfort allowed his mind to focus on more corporeal things.

The heat on his face soon tired him. He doused the flames with his urine and hoisted his backpack up the cottonwood branch, securing the rope to an opposite tree to make sure no crafty bear could loosen it. Sighing, he climbed inside his tent for needed sleep.

NEXT morning he awoke to the sound of distant elk mooing. He ate a hasty breakfast of oatmeal, granola, and hot tea to fight off the morning chill, and quickly broke camp so he could get on the trail and get his blood pumping. With the rising sun warm on his naked calves, he hiked farther up the Livingston Range. Steam rose off the forest floor and the dew on the trees glistened as the sun lifted higher over the mountain peaks.

By late morning, he reached tree-line. Shortly after, he came to his first snowfield. He zipped on his pants legs and carefully traversed the sloping mass of snow, about fifty yards wide. The snow at times reached to his hips. With only a few stumbles, he made his way through.

Hungry after the arduous climb, he rested by a boulder for a lunch of granola bars and several handfuls of gorp and drank from the icy glacial water he had pumped from a nearby stream. He continued his climb and came to a vast alpine meadow where yellow glacier lily, lavender lupine, and pink monkey flower revealed their first shoots.

A herd of Bighorn sheep grazed upslope. They seemed unaware of the backpacker. Amazed, Aiden took several snapshots using his digital camera, already stored with more than two hundred photographs of his journey from Maryland. The sheep leisurely munched on lichen and lupine. About one hundred yards downslope, a wolverine stood tall on its hind legs and gawked at Aiden. It must've realized Aiden was human and raced off into the nearby alders before Aiden could snap a photo.

He switchbacked to the ridgeline and caught his first glimpse of the massive blue glaciers that give the park its name. He hiked alongside this showcase for the remainder of the day. By late afternoon, he made his way into his second campsite.

Alone again, he set up camp under a canopy of red cedars, snacked on more granola and gorp, strung up his backpack away from bears and other opportunistic animals. Still early, with plenty of afternoon sunlight left, he decided to take a side trail that led to what he recognized from his topo map as an old abandoned fire tower. Without his heavy seventy-pound pack weighing him down, the steady switchback climb up the side trail was easy. In thirty minutes he made it to the base of the lookout tower.

His lungs filled with fresh blood, he scampered up the rock face to the stone tower, stationed directly on the ridgeline of the Western

Continental Divide. From the tower steps he could see the thin ribbons of waterfalls twisting down from the distant mountain crags where glaciers silently and sluggishly pushed downslope, and the dozens of glacial lakes that had punctured tiny holes into the verdant alpine valleys.

As he circled the tower, snapping many pictures of the impressive three-hundred-sixty degree view, he noticed the tower had been vandalized, but nothing severe. Remnants of recent hikers were visible. A broken window where someone had tried to gain entrance into the tower disquieted him, so he headed down to the high rock overlook below the tower.

He sat on a large outcropping looking west and took in the waves of green masses of hemlocks, cedars, and aspens. The talus slope swept about fifty yards to the forest edge where the lookout trail headed toward his camp, then swept back up to the purple crags and eventually down to Mineral Creek. Chilled, he pulled on his woolen sweater.

Meadowlarks and swallows twittered flirtatiously in the pines. An osprey circled overhead against the periwinkle sky, its bark echoing through the forest. He could hear a woodpecker somewhere, its erratic drilling filling the intermittent void of sound. He stared, silent, absorbing all the raw beauty that nature had to give.

For the first time since he was a boy, he prayed.

He did not drop to his knees or fold his hands. He simply prayed. There was no forethought; the prayers just came. They flowed from him as naturally as the rhythms of the wilderness, as naturally as the run of the streams and glaciers and the wind. As naturally as his own blood flow.

He prayed for his parents; he prayed for the Schrocks and all those he knew in Maryland and Illinois; he prayed for Daniel.

He prayed for himself.

Tucked in his prayers, the world seemed to open up, inviting him in. There, sitting on that outcropping with a view of the endless span of wilderness, he experienced a oneness with nature, with the universe…

with God. All that mattered at that moment was to just live, breathe, allow the boundless mysteries of the universe to flow through him.

A rustling noise to his right made him jerk up. A mountain goat, no more than eight feet away, straddled the outcropping. The hoary goat sidled closer to Aiden. The animal seemed completely at peace with Aiden's being there, its black eyes full of tranquility. It stared at the scene with him, as if they were old friends. Aiden breathed in the air, his head light. He too felt a sense of kinship and peace, sharing a moment with the animal, as if they were the only two living creatures left on the entire planet.

Aiden stayed as long as the goat did—nearly a half hour. When the goat tired and wandered farther down the talus slope, glancing up at Aiden as if to say "farewell" before leaping nimbly off the slope and into the alpine forest, Aiden hiked back to camp.

On his way down he passed a small group of day hikers. They exchanged greetings and nodded pleasantly as they passed. They were the first people he'd seen since he'd left the visitor center at Apgar yesterday afternoon.

When he reached camp, he noticed another backpacker had claimed one of the other campsites. He was napping against his bulky pack leaning against a red cedar. Things are starting to pick up, he thought with a grin.

Aiden lowered his pack from the tree and began preparing supper, Thai chicken with rice, when the napping backpacker casually strolled up to him.

"How you been?"

Aiden turned, startled. He nearly knocked over his butane stove that sat on a flat outcropping. He widened his eyes, scrutinizing the man who stood about five yards away. The man, over six feet, with a military-style buzz cut, had dark eyes that seemed to penetrate everything. His thick lips were supported by a fiercely rigid jaw line. In his hiking pants and flannel shirt, he looked like a combination commando-lumberjack.

Aiden remembered running into such men while hiking trails back east with Conrad. Sometimes these men spent so much time out in the backcountry they forgot normal social protocol. They would come across as uncomfortably familiar and hyper-gregarious—and sometimes aggressively territorial. The last thing Aiden wanted was to stir up trouble with one of those types.

Keeping his cool, he put on his best friendly face. "I just came from the fire tower," he said, twitching a smile. Hoping to convey a subtle warning, he added, "There're some more people up there. They should be along any minute."

The man stared at Aiden with a knowing smile, one that suggested he harbored no fear of either Aiden or the group up at the tower.

All of a sudden, he threw his head back and laughed.

Aiden stiffened. Instinctively, he took a step back and scanned the ground for some kind of weapon. All was fair when it came to survival in the backcountry. Gawking at the laughing stranger, the subtle whiff of recognition slowly enveloped him, as if he had sluggishly awakened from an itchy nap. "Daniel?"

"Ach, you recognize me after all," he said, easing his laughter.

"It can't be. How… how is this happening?"

"It's happening; believe it."

"How… how did you get here?"

"Same way you did." Daniel chuckled. "On the loop trail, from the Packers Roost trailhead."

Aiden stared, wordless. Daniel was standing before him. In the middle of the Montana backcountry. He looked so different. His moustacheless beard had been completely shaved, leaving a taut jaw line, nearly three shades lighter than the rest of his face since it had been covered from the sun for so long. Gone too was his thick bowl cut. His new military cut accentuated his strong, masculine features.

"You… you look so different," Aiden said. So different, yet the closer Aiden studied him the more unmistakably he was all Daniel.

Those dark coffee-brown eyes, firm nose, protruding lips... all Daniel's. Taking a nervous step forward, Aiden noticed a faint scar on his forehead where Daniel had received the sixteen stitches from his buggy accident six months before.

"I got my beard and hair shaved while at the Denver airport," Daniel said. "I didn't want to stand out while traveling. I had time to kill and was feeling kinda rebellious. I figure none of it will grow back much in time... in time before the wedding in a few weeks." He flushed and glanced toward the ground. "But I don't care. I'll come up with some excuse."

"You... you haven't left the church?"

"Nay. I just needed to get away. To find some solace. I needed to think before getting married. I call it my bachelor party with God." He chuckled. "Being around nature always helps me think better. But I'm still with the church. Can't get married unless I am."

"What about your family?" Aiden asked, gazing unremittingly at Daniel. He stepped closer, stunned. "Do they know you're here?"

With the chatter of ground squirrels in the background, Daniel said, "Ya. They know I'm here. They come to expect it, I figure, since I ran off last time just before marrying Esther. Tara wasn't too pleased, but I told her I was going and she couldn't stop me. Elisabeth seemed to understand the most. She hugged me before I left and told me she hoped I find whatever it was I was looking for."

"I still can't believe it's really you."

Daniel chuckled. "It's really me."

"Did you know I was here?"

"Not until I got to the trailhead this morning. I recognized your car with Maryland tags. Then I saw your name in the register. Seemed too impossible that it could be you. I had to see for myself. I followed your fresh prints, saw you took the south loop at the fork. I went the opposite way hoping I'd bump into you. I figured you'd been out on the trail at least overnight. The last six miles I wasn't sure I'd see you. I started thinking I was on a wild goose chase, and that it was somebody else's car down there, some other Aiden Cermak from Maryland with a light-blue Chevy. When I reached camp here, I saw someone had set up a tent and hung up a pack. I recognized the same prints from the trailhead. I was hoping it was you. You weren't around so I figured you were up at the tower. I was beat and took a catnap, waiting for you."

Daniel smiled a smile Aiden had never seen on him before. It was so wonderfully unreserved. Fresh and open as the calypso orchids growing in clusters at the forest's edge.

Shaking his head, Daniel said, "I didn't even plan on this route. I wanted to hike through Many Glacier, but the park ranger told me it was snowed in. Got another six inches last night. He told me I wouldn't be able to get through without snowshoes. So he recommended this loop. Aiden Cermak, God has put you before my path more often than goose poop."

"Oh, that's a pretty picture." Aiden giggled.

"Ach, you know what I mean."

"God's will, maybe?"

"Ya, God's will, I figure."

They both stared at each other. The osprey barking and the wind rustling the leaves filled the silence.

The reality of Daniel's presence covered Aiden like a warm blanket. Daniel was really here, in Montana, looking at him with those penetrating eyes of his, so dark they looked like black gold. The pine needles beneath their boots were soft and real. The towering conifers, spraying their moist pine scent upon them, protecting them almost, were all real. The smell of Daniel from his rigorous hike from the trailhead that morning was as real as the sky and the earth.

"I'm sorry I never said goodbye to you or your family," Aiden said, not knowing what else to say. "Things were a little strained before I left, I guess."

"Ya, I understand. Everyone wanted to say goodbye to you, too, but Dad ruled against it. He said it wouldn't be such a good idea. The kinner still talk about you, a lot."

"I miss everyone. How are they all? Elisabeth, Mark...?"

Daniel filled Aiden in on his family. Elisabeth had been working as an assistant teacher the past spring, and most likely would be teaching full time in the fall at the district's one-room schoolhouse. Mark met an Amish girl last December in Texas during his rumspringa. He'd been back three times by bus, helping her family rebuild English homes after the gulf storms. She might be moving to Henry. Marriage seemed likely. Grace was dating a boy from the eastern district. He was nice enough, chored hard on the farm, although Daniel didn't think he was the right boy for Grace. Moriah and David were growing fast, like weeds, but at their age nothing really exciting much happens to them, and they seemed all the happier for it.

"And little Leah?" Aiden worried why Daniel had failed to mention the youngest of the Schrocks.

Daniel peered toward the pine covered floor. "Leah isn't doing too good. It's hard for her to even sit up, much less walk. The past few months she's had to be in a wheelchair most of the time."

Aiden brought his hand to his mouth. He wished there was a way he could be of some support to the Schrocks. He never did stop thinking of them as his second family, even when he had thought they had rejected him.

"She's handling it as good as she does these things," Daniel said. "Happy as a chickadee despite everything. I figure we can all learn from her."

"How are Rachel and Samuel holding up?"

A flush stretched along Daniel's hairless jaw line. "Last Christmas Mom found out she's with child. She's expecting in August."

Aiden shared Daniel's flush. "Just in time for the threshing season."

"Ach, I figure."

"What about your shop?"

Daniel went on to tell Aiden about the shop permanently closing last month; they could no longer justify keeping it open. Orders had slowed to a trickle. Others were in the same shape. The family hoped to sell the furniture Daniel crafted over the Internet, lowering overhead costs. Uncle Eldridge had an English friend who could design and run the website for them. Lots of Amish were doing it that way nowadays. It was practical and cheaper. Daniel stored his crafts in a warehouse shared by three other families.

Aiden remembered that evening they had strolled at the county park along the pond. "You're becoming more English every day," he said, using nearly the exact words Daniel had uttered then.

A perceptive glimmer appeared in Daniel's eyes. He took a step closer. Shaking his head, he nearly threw his head back and laughed again. "I remember you said you always wanted to backpack Glacier. Never expected in a million years to find you here when I flew out from Chicago yesterday."

"Why did you come, Daniel?" Aiden said. "Why did you need to get away before your wedding, like last time?"

A bald eagle flew over the crowns of the trees against the cornflower-blue sky. Out of habit, Daniel reached for where his beard used to be and pulled on his smooth chin.

"Last week, Reverend Yoder and his family were hosting church services," he said. "It's usually considered something special when one of the ministers hosts. But I didn't think so. Not that time. I didn't even join in the singing waiting for the ministers to come downstairs from their meeting. I didn't care if anyone looked at me wondering why I wasn't joining in. I didn't feel like it, or care what they thought. It was strange. I never felt so apart from everyone, even after Kyle's death.

"When Reverend Yoder came down, I tried to get him to look at me, to lock my gaze. But he wouldn't. He never does hold anyone's stare. Then I remembered he wasn't always like that. He used to stare hard at people, knowing how his piercing blues could make people feel small like a field mouse. I thought, didn't he stop looking people in the eye around the time Kyle died?

"Where I sat I could see out the window to the Yoder's barn. I could almost see Kyle hanging there from the rafter. I pictured what it must been like for Kyle just before he did it. Then your words came to me. What if you was right? What if Reverend Yoder did kill Kyle in some scuffle because of what he saw us do in the barn? What if he hung his son up in the barn like a deer kill to make it look like a suicide? I suddenly thought you was right the whole time.

"Then I saw Tara sitting on the women's side in her black bonnet I pictured us kneeling together before the bishop on our wedding day just a few weeks away. I saw her as nothing but a stranger. I didn't know her. I didn't know any of them.

"I ran from the house sick. I needed fresh air. Just ran out. Didn't care what anyone thought. That's when I knew I had to come back here. To collect my thoughts. Think things through before I got married, like last time. I needed a good few days to be alone. To make sure. I always wanted to come back to Glacier. I like it here. I wouldn't mind moving to Rose Crossing. Out here I feel closer with God. Like He talks to me more. I figure I can see His clues clearer."

"Have you seen God's clues clearer this trip?" Aiden asked, his eyebrows raised.

Daniel drifted to the base of a red cedar. The sun was setting beyond the trees and a dance of light sparkled through their powerful branches. He looked back to Aiden; his mouth opened slightly. Tugging at his chin, he looked like he wanted to say something weighty. Aiden's eyes were unmoving from him.

"When I found out about Dad asking you to leave," he said, staring beyond Aiden into the deep forest, "I got all empty inside. I figured it was for the best, but I was angry yet. You just wouldn't know how miserable I been. Having you around for sure didn't make things easy, but once you left Henry.... Well, I just didn't like life much. I have to admit, I stopped feeling things. Choring in the field, taking care of the horses, being in my woodshop, none of it mattered. I didn't even care much after the shop closed. It was all boogered."

"I know what you've been through," Aiden said, taking another step toward Daniel. His heart lifted into his throat. "I've been feeling all boogered too."

"You have?"

"Yes, of course. I don't think a day has gone by when I haven't thought of you. I've never met anyone like you, Daniel Schrock."

"I been wanting to call you since you left," Daniel said, flushing. "I carried your number around with me for a while. Then I finally just threw it away. I figure there was no point."

"I wish you had called me. I would've come to you if you needed me."

Daniel averted his eyes. "I remember the first time I realized you grabbed my heart," he said, his words deliberate, thoughtful, as if he had rolled them over in his mind many times. "We were coming back home from the horse auction. Remember? When we stopped by that country store and you fed Badger those granola bars." He blew out a quick chuckle. "I knew then you had turned my life upside down."

"I think that's when I knew I loved you too," Aiden said, unabashed about expressing his true feelings now. It seemed easier, hidden away in the Montana backcountry. His mind raced back to that time in the market wagon. Almost a year to the day. "It was right after we got home. The way you looked so pensive at the coming storm. I would've given anything to have eased your load. I still would."

They stood quiet, gazing at each other. Aiden considered all that had brought them together. All the events that had led to them standing at that exact moment face to face in Glacier National Park. Aiden had taken such a colossal risk coming all the way to Montana, to start a new life alone, that to run into Daniel, literally in the middle of the forest.... It was incomprehensible. He was now at that juncture in his mind where fears, doubts, worries ceased to exist; just unadulterated existence, where peace and matter fused, frozen in one moment.

How could he not believe in God when Daniel, so beautiful, so masculine, stood before him?

Images from their first meeting, like pictures from a slide show, popped on and off in his mind. It seemed implausible really, to be standing within steps of each other. Aiden inched closer. They were a mere arm's length apart.

"I always wanted to be a strong man," Daniel said under his breath. "To stand tall, and do what is right by God, right by my family. That's all I ever wanted, nothing more than that. Why does it come so hard?"

Under the towering conifers, Daniel looked so frail and alone. Aiden wanted to throw himself into him, to hold him. To save him. Just like that time when they had returned from the horse auction. Just like when Daniel had lain so helpless in the hospital.

Daniel looked to the ground. "I used to think everything was a test from God, a test for me to prove myself to Him, to everyone. I thought even you were a test, my biggest test yet."

"Maybe it's not a test," Aiden said. "Maybe it's God's way of trying to tell you to just take what He puts in front of you and embrace it." Aiden again wanted to fall into Daniel, to comfort him the way he'd so often dreamed.

But before Aiden could budge, Daniel stood directly in front of him, gazing down at him, his breath sour. There was a slight resistance in Daniel when Aiden rested his hands on Daniel's chest.

"It doesn't have to be so hard to do what you think is right, Daniel," Aiden whispered. "All you have to do is trust yourself. Trust me."

"No matter what I do, you'll always be there," Daniel said, hypnotic-like, "whether in my dreams or for real, either way, you'll be there. Marrying Tara, having kids, none of that will change it. You'll be hovering all around me." He looked up at the sky, then back to Aiden. "Took me a while to see it, but I figure I found what I been looking for. It's all too clear now."

Daniel's heavy breath parted the curls on top of Aiden's head. Peering down at him, Daniel said, "I can't marry Tara. I'll have to fly home and let her know. I'll have to tell her face to face, that I can't marry her. I figure I never could. After running into you out here…. If God doesn't want for you and me…. Ach, then what does He want?" He looked long at Aiden, nearly stopping Aiden's heart. "I can see the clues clear now, Aiden Cermak. Finally, I can see."

Daniel wobbled a bit on the uneven earth. This time, Aiden stood stronger, braver, and refused to let Daniel waver so easily. He had the liberty to touch him now, the right to embrace him.

He wrapped his arms around Daniel's torso, his cheek flush against his pounding chest.

Daniel reciprocated Aiden's embrace. A frisson traveled through Aiden's body. His head rose and fell with Daniel's heavy breathing. Dreamlike sleepiness enveloped him and he relished the warmth coming from Daniel's hard body and strong arms. It felt so good to be touched again.

Daniel twined Aiden's hair with his broad fingers. He gently lifted Aiden's head from his chest so that their eyes locked on each other. He was quiet a moment, staring down at him, his large hands stroking Aiden's black curls the way Aiden had so often fantasized. "Your eyes," Daniel murmured. "I forgot how golden they are, like the sunset."

They hugged again, harder, longer. As if they were trying to push through each other.

Suddenly Daniel nudged Aiden and looked away, almost stricken. "But we can't live in my world," he said toward the trees, "and we can barely live in yours."

With a soft smile, Aiden guided Daniel's smooth chin to meet his eyes again. He found his hands, and their fingers weaved together. "Then let's live in our world," Aiden said, simply.

Reaching beyond the massive trees and soaring beyond the monolithic mountains, riding on the wings of eagles, their declaration of love was tossed up to whoever cared to have it. It didn't matter. They had each other.

Daniel and Aiden, both stuck in the middle of two worlds, belonging nowhere. Yet it was in the middle where Aiden realized they had discovered each other.

A short year ago, Aiden had been lost bumping along the central Illinois country lanes, searching for the Interstate for Chicago. It seemed he'd been trying to find his way home his whole life.

Surrounded by the pines and cedars of northwestern Montana, Aiden had, at last, found his way.

Wrapped in each other's arms, Daniel and Aiden breathed life into each other, their saliva and tears flowing like nectar. They did not pause when, during their passionate kiss, they spotted the group of day hikers from the fire tower wandering into camp. They were insignificant. They were outsiders in their world.

Breaking their lip lock, Aiden looked up into Daniel's eyes, their arms snug around each other. "Would you like some supper? I bet you're hungry after your long hike."

"I for sure could use something to eat." Daniel smiled at him. His thick lips glistened with both their tears and spit.

"But first we better get your tent set up before dark, don't you think?"

Daniel eyeballed Aiden's erect tent to his right. Looking back at Aiden, his eyes lustrous, like onyx, he smiled impishly. "I don't figure we need to do that."

Aiden flushed. His heart beat wildly against Daniel's chest. Inside, his whole body simmered with love and happiness. Daniel leaned in to kiss him lightly on his lips, a kiss full of awareness and promises. Aiden locked his fingers with Daniel's, and together they walked to the flat outcropping to prepare supper, the sun beaming on them through the branches of the trees.

SHELTER SOMERSET enjoys writing about the lives of people who live off the land, whether they be the Amish, nineteenth-century pioneers, or modern-day idealists seeking to live apart from the crowd. Shelter's fascination with the rustic, aesthetic lifestyle began as a child with family camping trips into the Blue Ridge Mountains. When not back home in Illinois writing, Shelter continues to explore America's expansive backcountry and rural communities. Shelter's philosophy is best summed up by the actor John Wayne: "Courage is being scared to death but saddling up anyway."

Made in United States
Orlando, FL
22 March 2026

79559160R00134